HOLIDAY HOM...

Officer Horitz turned the monitor for his computer toward her. "We have a 3D program that allows us to discover how fast the vehicle was going that hit David, in relation to things around him."

"Oh?" Charlene thought back to exactly what she'd seen. David's head had been turned toward the flashing red dentist Santa holding a giant toothbrush.

"There were no skid marks on the street," he told her, "which means that the driver didn't stop. Duval and Crown Point Road have speed limits of forty miles an hour. According to this"—he gestured to the diagram—"David was hit at thirty to thirty-five miles per hour."

"That doesn't seem very fast," Charlene said, unable to take her eyes away from the red X on the monitor.

"It was bad luck for David," Officer Horitz agreed. "The vehicle hit him at an awkward angle and broke his neck." The policeman sighed and got to his feet. "Thanks for coming in."

And just like that, Charlene was escorted out of the station.

Bad luck? Someone on the phone or texting. Even changing a radio station—the driver would have heard or felt something, and made a decision not to stop.

At thirty miles an hour, whoever had run over David *had* to have known what they were doing as they left him on the street to die. . . .

Books by Traci Wilton

MRS. MORRIS AND THE GHOST

MRS. MORRIS AND THE WITCH

MRS. MORRIS AND THE GHOST
OF CHRISTMAS PAST

Published by Kensington Publishing Corp.

MRS. MORRIS AND THE GHOST OF CHRISTMAS PAST

Traci Wilton

KENSINGTON BOOKS
www.kensingtonbooks.com

KENSINGTON BOOKS are published by

Kensington Publishing Corp.
119 West 40th Street
New York, NY 10018

Copyright © 2020 by Patrice Wilton and Traci Hall

To the extent that the image or images on the cover of this book depict a person or persons, such person or persons are merely models, and are not intended to portray any character or characters featured in the book.

This book is a work of fiction. Names, characters, places, and incidents either are products of the author's imagination or are used fictitiously. Any resemblance to actual persons, living or dead, events, or locales is entirely coincidental.

All rights reserved. No part of this book may be reproduced in any form or by any means without the prior written consent of the Publisher, excepting brief quotes used in reviews.

All Kensington titles, imprints, and distributed lines are available at special quantity discounts for bulk purchases for sales promotion, premiums, fund-raising, and educational or institutional use.

Special book excerpts or customized printings can also be created to fit specific needs. For details, write or phone the office of the Kensington Sales Manager: Kensington Publishing Corp., 119 West 40th Street, New York, NY 10018. Attn. Sales Department. Phone: 1-800-221-2647.

Kensington and the K logo Reg. U.S. Pat. & TM Off.

First Kensington Books Mass Market Paperback Printing: October 2020
ISBN-13: 978-1-4967-2155-6
ISBN-10: 1-4967-2155-1

ISBN-13: 978-1-4967-2156-3 (ebook)
ISBN-10: 1-4967-2156-X (ebook)

10 9 8 7 6 5 4 3 2 1

Printed in the United States of America

This book is for my mother—who is nothing like Charlene's mother, thank heaven! My mom is my first reader and I couldn't love her more.
—Traci Hall

I would love to thank my husband/partner Ralph for being by my side for each and every wonderful year we've been together. He's given me strength, a belief in myself, and the will to be the best I can be. I love him with all my heart. He's been my main support through years of rejections, plenty of tears, and to celebrate each and every success. I regret all the hours and days when I've been too busy to support him, but as a team, we've done it all!
—Patrice Wilton

Acknowledgments

We would like to thank our editor, John Scognamiglio, and the production and publicity teams at Kensington, for helping us make this book the best it can be! Thanks also to our agent, Evan Marshall, who guides us with a wise hand, and thanks to Christopher Hawke at Community Authors for all you do.

Chapter One

It was dark at seven thirty, the 17th of December, when Charlene Morris entered Bella's Italian Ristorante with her parents, Brenda and Michael Woodbridge. Her frayed nerves required some serious holiday cheer, and tonight's charity auction to support the Felicity House for Children was exactly what she needed. Her mother had been with her for only two days, and it was two days too long.

David Baldwin, the manager and maître d', greeted her with a broad smile. She'd eaten at Bella's many times in the three months since she'd moved to Salem from Chicago and liked it so much that she recommended it to all of her customers at Charlene's Bed and Breakfast.

"Charlene!" David crooned, arms outstretched to give her a hug. "So nice to see you again." He had a natural charm, salt and pepper hair, black glasses, and a slight paunch in his black suit that revealed his love for pasta.

Her mother eyed David with interest, until her gaze landed on his thick gold wedding band.

From the podium, Charlene peered into the restaurant. Each of the round tables had been decorated with a candle and pine centerpiece. Baskets of auction items sparkled with red and green bows on long folding tables set up against the walls. Savory Italian spices wafted from the kitchen. Half the price of every meal purchased tonight was to be donated to Felicity House, and Bella's was packed.

"David, this place looks great. Really festive." The décor, and the cause, kindled her holiday spirit.

"It's all about the kids tonight," David said cheerfully. She'd read the big news in the local paper that he'd won the lottery last week. Would she still be at work if she'd won ten million?

Maybe—she loved her bed-and-breakfast, which had come with a resident ghost. Until three months ago, she'd never believed in such things, but Dr. Jack Strathmore was part of the reason she required some cheer. He wasn't fond of her mother—and though he'd promised to never disturb the guests, he couldn't seem to help himself around Brenda. He moved her boots just out of reach and kept hiding her reading glasses. He even put salt in the water she used for her false teeth.

His antics were mostly innocent and sweetly protective but had to stop—she couldn't call him out in front of her parents, as he was visible only to her, or she'd look like she'd lost her mind, and they'd *never* leave.

"I'm glad we reserved early," she said to David. "You have a good crowd."

A metal rack in the doorway handled the surplus of

coats for the evening. They handed theirs to an orange-haired teenager Charlene hadn't seen before—a new hire?

David flung his arm toward the ten-seat bar at the rear of the restaurant. "We have a lot of supporters here for Felicity House. Even my wife has graced us with her presence." He pointed at a petite bleached-blond woman in a gold sparkling sheath who leaned her elbow on the bar to chat with the bartender. "I'll bring her by later to introduce you, Charlene."

"I'd love to meet her."

David peered over the rims of his black glasses as he studied her mom and dad. "Are these your parents? I think I see a resemblance." He smoothed the lapels of his jacket. "No, no, this young lady must be your sister."

Her mother tittered like a Victorian maiden—all she needed was a fan. "Oh, you sly fox. I'm Brenda, *her mother*."

Her father reached out his hand. "Michael Woodbridge."

"David Baldwin, manager and part owner of this lovely establishment."

Part owner? Charlene hadn't realized he'd been so invested in Bella's. Would he buy the place now that he had millions, or sell his investment and move on?

"You must be so proud of Charlene," David said. "Her bed-and-breakfast is an outstanding piece of property."

Her father nodded, while her mother had to think about it before she said, "It is beautiful, I'll give you that, but we miss having her in Chicago."

David chose three menus and gestured at Jessica, waitressing tonight. Charlene genuinely liked the young woman, who had just become a physical therapist, from very humble beginnings.

She'd lobbed her cocoa-brown hair to a new style at her shoulders and greeted them cheerily as she took the menus from David. "Hi, Charlene. Glad you all could come tonight. Should be a fun evening." Jessica patted her red half apron. "You must be Charlene's parents—she said you'd be her dates. It's going to be super busy, so get your bids in early."

"I've put Charlene and her family by this first window," David said, pointing to his right.

"Perfect." Jessica touched David's arm. "Tori wants you."

David's expression dimmed slightly, but he kept his smile. "Enjoy your dinner. Be sure to look over the raffles and auction items—let's give these kids a holiday to remember." He moved on, wending his way through the crowded restaurant, pausing at various tables to say hello on his way to the bar.

"This way." Jessica bypassed an oval table for two at the very front of the restaurant to the next round table, which had a merry view of the Christmas lights outside the window. She could see the two-lane street, bare of snow, and the strip of businesses across the road—none open. A giant red Santa holding a toothbrush twinkled from the dental office.

Jessica handed them each a menu once they sat down, pointing out the auction items listed on a sheet of green paper bordered with holly. "You'll see that Charlene donated a stay at her bed-and-breakfast."

"She's always had a generous nature." Pride emanated from her dad as he looked at Jessica over his menu. "Charlene was in first grade when she donated her tooth fairy money to a kid in her class with leukemia. We added a check for more, of course."

"Dad, no embarrassing stories, you promised," she said with a laugh. When Jessica had approached her last month for a donation and explained about the kids at Felicity House, she'd welcomed the chance to give a weeklong stay, and in the process had gotten to know Jessica and Jessica's success story—all because of Felicity House.

"It's going to raise a lot of money," Jessica assured her. "Can I start you off with some drinks?"

"Merlot for me, please," Charlene said. "The house wine is superb. Mom, Dad?"

"Let's get a carafe for the table," her father suggested.

"I suppose," her mom conceded, and then removed her red-framed glasses to gaze at Jessica. "We'll need some bread too. *Before* the drinks?"

"Absolutely." Jessica hurried to the kitchen.

Charlene had taken the chair closest to the window so her mom couldn't complain about a draft. It also gave her the advantage of seeing everyone in the room dressed up for the event.

Kevin, the scruffy blond bartender from Brews and Broomsticks, wore a navy suit and sat hip to hip at a table with a woman Charlene hadn't met before—girl-next-door pretty, with long light brown hair. Even from across the room, Kevin looked besotted. She hoped he was on a date. Around Halloween, he'd hinted at an attraction to her, which she'd ignored, though he was cute, kind, and funny.

Charlene's husband, Jared, hadn't even been gone two years. Her heart was not quite as raw, thanks to a certain gorgeous ghost and a very much alive detective, Sam Holden of the Salem Police Department. Sam had invited her out numerous times, but she'd always declined. Her heart wasn't ready yet.

Charlene spotted Brandy and Evelyn Flint sharing a table with Theo Rowlings, and whispered to her parents, "See the auburn-haired woman near the baskets, with the silver-haired lady?"

They both turned to look.

"They own Flint Wineries and can trace their ancestry back hundreds of years in Salem, which is very important to the locals," she said. "They supply the house wine here at Bella's, as well as my label for 'Charlene's.'"

"I'd like to see the winery," her mother said. "Do they offer tours?"

"I can ask." Charlene wouldn't mind a peek behind the scenes.

Jessica dropped off a selection of breadsticks, a sliced baguette, and a dish of savory oil for dipping. "I'll be right back with your wine. One of our servers called in sick so we have Avery, from Felicity House, stepping in to help out. She's very new, so please be patient."

"Don't worry—we're not in any hurry," Charlene reassured Jessica.

Her mother picked up a thin, crisp sesame breadstick and broke it in half, not interested in any excuses. "This is hard, and it's cold."

"A breadstick *is* hard, Mother." A loud laugh came from the back and Charlene turned toward the sound.

"Tori." Jessica barely bothered to hide her dislike of David's wife as she smoothed her hair behind her ear. "She keeps the bartender's attention, which slows the drink orders—but I can get your wine myself."

Her mother perked up at the hint of drama and craned her neck to get a glimpse of Tori, who bared a lot of thigh. "Hmm. She's a hot one. Second marriage?"

Jessica shifted the empty tray from one hand to the

other. "I think for both of them. David has a son just a few years younger than me."

"No offense," her mother said, which always made Charlene cringe, "but I bet his new wife is about your age too."

Jessica's eyes rounded in surprise at Charlene's mother's bluntness. "Uh, maybe . . . let me get that wine."

After the waitress was out of earshot, Charlene said, "Mom, do you have to be so critical?" She tapped the laminated menu. "Why don't you decide what you want to eat?"

Charlene leaned back in her chair and exchanged a glance with her father. He was unaffected—having decades of practice at ignoring his wife's negativity. There had been a time when her mom hadn't been so hard. What had changed? Charlene had memories of her mother being happy. Now it seemed bitterness seeped from every pore. Charlene had escaped, but her dad? How did he handle it day and night, years on end?

"Maybe breadsticks are supposed to be hard, but these are enough to break my teeth." Brenda dropped the half-eaten stick to her bread plate.

"Dip it in your water," her dad suggested, going back to the menu.

He couldn't be serious! "Try the baguette." Charlene offered her mom the basket. "And the oil." The girl who had taken their coats rushed by and accidentally bumped the back of Charlene's seat. She was pale, skinny, and utterly out of place in a too-big apron. Avery from Felicity House, Charlene guessed. A spider tattoo was visible on the back of her neck.

Her mother pointed in the direction of the bar and David's wife. "Look at her ring. Can you believe she's flashing that gaudy thing around? I bet she bought herself some new jewelry with David's lottery money. New wealth makes a person trashy. They can't help it. They gotta buy, buy, buy just to show it off."

"And you know this how?" Charlene folded her burgundy cloth napkin across her lap before she strangled her mother with it.

"I watch the crime shows," her mom said with a huff that stretched her green plaid sweater across her ample top half, above her stilt-thin legs—her mother's figure reminded Charlene of a long-legged bird. Not a flamingo, but a crane, maybe, that had to make trouble to get anyone to notice her at all. The thought surprised Charlene, and she felt a sudden spurt of tenderness toward her mother, who, at seventy-five, wouldn't be around forever.

Her balding father's black reading glasses were poised on the edge of his long nose. He embodied the art professor he'd been for half a century as he scanned the menu.

Life had cruelly taught her that death could happen at any time.

The candles on the tables flickered when the restaurant door opened again, bringing with it a rush of cold air. Sharon Turnberry, a faux-redhead, and her husband, John, arrived, and Jessica seated them on the opposite side of the room. Charlene waved at the manager of Cod and Capers.

Another creak from the front door, another swoosh of cool air, made Charlene shiver as she turned to the podium, where David greeted a short, squat gentleman with dull gray hair and a silver mustache who wore a black trench coat and black cowboy boots. "Vincent. I saved you a table by the bar."

"You were very mysterious, telling me to be here

tonight." Vincent's demeanor was hard. "You better not waste my time."

Jessica returned with the wine. "Here you are. I made it, unscathed," she said dramatically.

"Who is that?" Charlene asked, subtly pointing at Vincent.

"Oh—Vincent Lozzi. David's business partner and our 'silent' boss." Jessica, a tray in one hand, used her free fingers to make air quotes. "We don't see him around that much, but now that David's won the lottery, you wouldn't believe the people who've oozed from the woodwork. Even one of his old college buddies, he told me."

Jessica scurried off to assist Vincent. He tossed his jacket over the chair, sat down, and plunked his elbows on the table for one. The co-owner glared at Tori, who waggled her bejeweled fingers at him. He refused to let Jessica hang up his trench coat.

Charlene pulled her gaze from *that* drama to continue her perusal of the diners—she couldn't have asked for a better seat.

A plump woman in evergreen velvet, her hair a mousy brownish-gray, smoothed in a bun with a red silk poinsettia tucked in the knot, rubbed her hands together and beamed with pride as she went up and down the length of baskets for the auction. Charlene recognized the rosy cheeks from the photo for Felicity House on the table. The director, Alice Winters.

Her mother held the green paper and pointed to the picture of Jessica. "It says here that our waitress used to live at Felicity House, before she was adopted."

"That's true, and she's also a physical therapist." Charlene admired the young woman's drive toward success.

"Why is she working here?" The question was asked in a snide tone that made Charlene twist her napkin.

"I imagine because she wants to, Brenda," her dad said. "Don't you dare ask."

Jessica arrived to take their order, and her mother thawed slightly. "I'll have the veal parmesan, with a salad."

"Wonderful choice," Jessica said, turning to Charlene. "And you?"

"Lobster ravioli. I'll also have the salad instead of soup. Dad?"

Her father collected their menus. "Chicken scaloppini and pasta fagioli. Thank you."

"I'll get these in so you can enjoy your meal by the time the auction starts!" Jessica hustled off, her hair swinging.

Charlene contemplated the barren trees out her window. "Snow sure would be pretty."

"It's in the forecast, according to the Weather Channel," her dad offered.

"If you want snow, you should live in Chicago." Her mom's mouth thinned into a red seam.

"I'm happy here, Mom," Charlene said. "Can't you be happy for me too?"

"I am! What kind of mother would I be if I wasn't happy for my own child?"

Jessica arrived with their salads and soup, saving Charlene from having to answer. "Enjoy!" The waitress circled her way to Sharon's table next.

At precisely eight o'clock, David tugged the lapels of his black suit jacket. "I'd like to introduce Alice Winters and Pamela Avita."

Pamela, the co-chair for the charity event, was the opposite of dowdy Alice, in a sleek green skirt and fitted jacket, styled black hair, and pearls.

"Now there's a woman who knows how to dress," her mom said. "Tori should take notes."

David had moved the podium so that it faced the diners, and Pamela stood behind it. She was a natural auctioneer, listing each item with a starting bid and creating excitement as she worked the crowd, the patrons generous to the cause of Felicity House. Alice would declare the winner's name, and Tori, whose gold sequined number showed off her dynamite figure as she paraded before the baskets, delivered the prizes.

They ate during the show, Jessica expertly maneuvering around the action.

Her mom raised her hand to bid on a pair of diamond earrings, which she won, but she lost the mystery box from Vintage Treasures to a woman sitting next to Brandy's table. Charlene had her eye on a cashmere scarf and gloves but was outbid by Kevin's dinner date. Her dad put in a lackluster bid on a whale tour, but was more content with his soup.

Before she knew it, all of the items had been presented and Pamela announced the auction a success. Her eyes shone brightly. "I'd like to thank everyone on behalf of Felicity House."

Alice clapped and the whole room erupted with applause—except for Vincent, who hadn't bid on a thing as he'd nursed his drink. Whiskey on the rocks?

"Check the website tomorrow for our silent auction winners—the children are so appreciative." Pamela gracefully returned to her seat with a flip of her head, exposing a large pearl in gold at her ear.

Alice rose, her cheeks as bright as the silk poinsettia in

her hair. "Thank you for hosting our event, David. I hope to do this again next year at Bella's."

Vincent Lozzi smacked his hand on the table. "We'll see about that," he groused.

Charlene's pulse raced, the show of aggression at odds in the festive atmosphere.

David clenched his hand as he glared at his partner. What was going on?

Alice whispered something to him, and David gathered himself. "I'd like to give my thanks to Jessica," he said, nodding at Jessica, "for bravely sharing her adoption story. And to all of you for your generosity tonight. We're just getting started, my friends, and I plan on doing more."

Charlene applauded, hoping that his windfall would be put to good use. With a promise to herself to help Salem's at-risk youth, she folded the green sheet with Alice's name and contact information and put it in her purse.

David, his back to a pouting Tori, gestured for the bartender. "Bring the Dom Pérignon." He faced the rapt audience. "As some of you know, we have much to celebrate."

Low laughter and hoots resounded. Ten million dollars was indeed a lot.

"Lottery winners are never happy," her mother said in a foreboding tone. "They don't know how to spend their newfound money."

"Be happy for him, Mom, will you? I wish them the very best."

The door swung open and Charlene rubbed her arms at the frigid temperature. A young man with dark brown hair and heavy brows unwrapped his scarf and scuffed his motorcycle boots along the small carpet at the entryway next to David's podium.

Tori saw him and rolled her eyes. "Kyle," she drawled. "Why am I not surprised?"

David whirled toward the young man. "Son! What are you doing here?"

"I left a message for you earlier, Dad." He waited by the oval table between Charlene and the door. "I need to talk to you."

Tori's mouth puckered like she'd downed sour apple schnapps.

David looked to Jessica. "Jess? Will you see if the kitchen can make up something for Kyle?"

"Don't bother." Kyle checked the time on his phone. "Ten on the dot. Kitchen's closed, right, Dad?"

"It'll only take a second," Jessica said. "If you aren't picky?"

"I don't want anything but a few minutes of my dad's time." Kyle helped himself to the lone chair at the table near Charlene.

Jessica disappeared into the kitchen and the scent of garlic escaped.

A clatter sounded to her right, and Charlene turned. Avery, orange hair quivering, knelt to pick up plate shards around a woman's high heel. Sauce coated the lady's shoe and Avery's apron. "I'm so sorry," Charlene heard the girl say. She dabbed at the woman's foot with a table napkin.

"Just get me some water," the woman snapped. "I'll clean it myself."

"Yes, ma'am." The girl sniffled and kept her head bowed.

Alice took a protective half step in Avery's direction.

David apologized to the woman but glared at Avery. "Finish up in here. Don't come back tomorrow," he said under his breath.

What a terrible way to speak to her—Avery was no more than a child. This was a side to David that Charlene didn't like.

Kyle, still in his motorcycle jacket, rose, sympathy on his face. He grabbed her arm, but Avery shrugged off his hand. "Don't, Kyle."

The teens were friends?

Jessica delivered Perrier and a white linen cloth to the woman with the marinara-doused stiletto, and a plate of pasta with red sauce to Kyle.

David, like a consummate actor, gazed at the jubilant faces before him in the dining room as if his son or Avery didn't exist.

"You should all have a flute of champagne." He held his glimmering glass high. "To all of you, for coming here to help Felicity House. Thank you again for your generosity tonight. Cheers!" He snagged Jessica as the young woman tried to pass him toward the kitchen.

"Wait!" He poured Jessica a flute. "Jessica has been with me since I first opened Bella's five years ago. My thanks, my friend."

Tori scoffed and twirled her diamond tennis bracelet. Her pettiness diminished her beauty, and Charlene almost felt sorry for David.

"Not only are we gathered for the auction," David raised his voice, "but I've invited some of you here to deliver extra holiday cheer." He lifted the bottle of Dom and spoke sincerely. "I have not always been the best friend, or husband, or business partner, or father"—he turned to

Kyle and then back to the group—"but I want you to know how much you all mean to me."

He drained his flute and set the glass on the table of unclaimed baskets.

Jessica, standing close to Charlene, sniffled, tears welling in her eyes.

Kyle slurped a forkful of spaghetti, his suspicious gaze on his father.

Tori's phone *dinged* and David eyed her with outrage.

"Sorry," she murmured, quickly reading the text. The light from her diamond ring flashed brightly from the candles on the centerpieces.

"Let me see your phone," he whispered angrily, reaching for it, his "friends" momentarily forgotten.

"No—it's nothing." Tori shifted on her gold heels, pressing buttons as if deleting messages.

"It better not be Zane," David said, his mustache trembling. "I warned you."

"David, please," Tori snarled. "Get on with your show, would you?"

He turned his rigid back to her and pulled a stack of envelopes from the podium.

Who is Zane? Charlene sipped her excellent champagne. This was a madhouse—she couldn't wait to tell Jack all about it.

David handed an envelope to Jessica, who smiled at him affectionately and slid it into her apron pocket.

He gave one to Brandy and Evelyn Flint, one to Vincent Lozzi—whose anger still simmered judging by the scowl on his face—and another to Alice and Pamela. With each passing check, Tori's mood deflated. She continually touched her tennis bracelet, as if to assure herself it was still there.

"Is there an envelope for me and Mom, Dad?" Kyle pushed his empty plate aside.

David winced. "Not tonight," he said. "But I haven't forgotten you, son." He went back to the podium and the bottle of champagne, slyly watching from his post.

Vincent opened his envelope and then snorted an ugly laugh. "This is nowhere near what you owe me. I thought you'd be signing it over." He got to his feet, grabbed his coat, and strode between the tables to David at the podium, hand clenched. "My lawyer will be in touch."

David didn't back down. "That amount is fair, and you know why."

Vincent glared at David and then glanced at Kyle before lowering his fist—racing out the front door on a flurry of cold air.

The others who had received envelopes opened them and peeked inside. Brandy used a butter knife to slit the envelope open. She showed the check to Evelyn with a nod and put it in her purse.

Jessica immediately grabbed a bottle of champagne and started topping off everyone's glasses. Kyle smirked from the sideline, as if he knew something about his father that nobody else did.

Charlene felt terrible for David—everybody had their hand out. But why was he doing this? "It's so ugly," Charlene said under her breath to her parents.

Her mom sipped her water sagely. "Winning the lottery isn't guaranteed good luck."

Alice, seated next to Pamela, opened her envelope, and her plump, rosy complexion turned the color of curdled milk. She showed it to Pamela, who gasped, quickly covering her mouth.

David took off his glasses and scanned the room, resting his forearm on top of the podium. "Winning the lottery has been a miracle, but my funds are not immediately accessible. I will donate more when my bounty comes in."

The majority of diners had not received an envelope, so they applauded David's intent. From Charlene's table she saw Tori, who stood next to David, whisper, "You don't owe anybody. That money is ours."

Ignoring his wife, David announced to the diners before him, "Dessert will be served—and again, I thank you all for coming. Felicity House thanks you."

The crowd cheered, but Charlene was just as eager to leave as she had been to arrive. She read the time on her phone. Ten thirty. What would Jack think? The whole check-giving thing had been awkward and in poor taste—as if David had wanted to prove a point.

David walked over to Kyle and put his hand on his son's shoulder. "I'll be sending a special Christmas card to you and your mom, okay? This was business."

"I wanted to talk to you about a call I got today, but I can see you're too busy." Kyle stood and looked his dad in the eye, his voice hoarse. "Why can't you follow through, just once?" He zipped his black leather jacket and darted out the front door. Moments later, a motorcycle roared and peeled off.

Poor Kyle!

"We need to talk, David." Tori tugged at David's arm to have a heated discussion by the kitchen door. The waitstaff brushed by them with trays of cannoli.

Charlene waved at Jessica, ready for the bill rather than dessert. Her festive joy was squashed by the greed surrounding David's lottery win.

Alice rose and stepped shakily toward the long table

with unclaimed prizes, but Pamela urged the older director to enjoy the cannoli while she loaded the SUV.

"Get Avery to help," Alice suggested, tugging the silk poinsettia from her hair.

"Good idea," Pamela said. "Save me a bite, would you?"

Jessica delivered the bill, the envelope from David peeping from her apron pocket. She hoped for Jessica's sake that David had been generous. Charlene's dad insisted on paying for dinner to do his part for the kiddos at the center.

Within moments they were ready to leave and Charlene got to her feet, searching for David. "Let me just say goodbye. . . ."

David, Tori clinging to his side like a golden leech, left his spot by the kitchen door and stalked toward Charlene and the window over her shoulder, his bushy brows arched in surprise above the frames of his glasses as he focused on the streetlamp outside. His body quaked with fear and he shook Tori off. "No!"

"What?" Tori's hand flew to her mouth. "I told Zane to stay away, I promise."

"Freddy?" David asked in confusion. "But no—it can't be." Concerned, Charlene reached for David as he swayed unsteadily, not from drink, but shock. He stared out the window—she turned, seeing nothing, then focused on David.

He wobbled, grabbing the back of her empty chair. Was he having a heart attack? Her lobster ravioli flipped in her stomach as she recalled what she knew of CPR.

"Doug is supposed to be dead!" David's shaking finger touched his bottom lip in sheer terror, and then he lunged away from her and raced out the front door of Bella's restaurant.

She swiveled toward Tori. "Who is Doug?" It all happened so fast—the next thing she knew, Charlene heard a sickening thump. Slowly, slowly, she glanced outside the window, to where David's body sprawled across the center line of the road, his glasses shining beneath the streetlamp. Nobody else was there.

CHAPTER TWO

Charlene gasped, her hands to her chest as she tried to make sense of what she saw through the restaurant window. David splayed, his torso twisted, in the center of the street. His head was turned at an awkward angle toward the Christmas Santa with the toothbrush flashing on the other side of the road.

Sharon's husband ran out—Charlene couldn't move.

Charlene's parents wore identical expressions of disbelief. "My God! David . . . !" She raised her voice. "Someone call nine-one-one."

Several people already had their phones out. Her friend Kevin left his date at the table and reached her side. "An ambulance is on its way. What happened?"

"I have no idea." Her breath was tight in her chest.

Tori had dissolved into a golden puddle at the table

Kyle had used, sobbing hysterically while Jessica tried to calm her down.

Her mom and dad leaned against each other in support, and Charlene thought of Sam.

"Excuse me." She stepped aside to dig her phone from her purse, looking out the window as John hovered near David, and hit the first name on her speed dial. Detective Sam Holden's deep tones sounded on a recorded voice mail message, but he didn't pick up.

"It's Charlene." She shivered, the phone cool against her ear. "I'm at Bella's Italian Ristorante. David Baldwin might have been hit by a car. He ran outside, and now he's lying on the pavement." Her voice hitched. Her parents conversed softly with Kevin. His companion had joined them, eyes glazed with shock. "Can you come quickly?"

She ended the message and joined the four crowded together. "Kevin, he isn't moving. Do you think he's de—?" Charlene choked on the last word. *Please, don't let it be true.* David was supposed to be the lucky winner, and now he was either badly injured or . . . worse. Charlene peeked out the window. Others had followed John, but they all stood around David.

Why wasn't anyone giving him mouth-to-mouth?

"I don't know," Kevin said. "Charlene, this is Amy Fadar. Amy, Charlene. You stay inside and I'll go see." He rushed out.

Alice Winters jumped to her feet, wiped cannoli cream from her mouth with a napkin, and grabbed her jacket. "We'll need to divert traffic."

"I'll help," Sharon said, following the plump, take-charge director.

Luckily, there weren't many cars this time of night. Charlene stayed with her folks; her mom had barely stopped trembling.

Brandy, Theo, and Evelyn whispered amongst themselves at their table, but the wailing of the ambulance halted all conversation. Not many dinner guests remained; most had flocked outside to see the horror show. Jessica peered out the window closest to Charlene while murmuring to Tori, who had her head buried in her arms.

Tori wailed harder, her fists pounding the table. Charlene placed her hand on the woman's heaving back. "Be strong," Charlene whispered. "We don't know anything yet. He might be okay."

The young woman stumbled to her gold heels and pushed past Charlene, running out the door to the ambulance as they loaded David to a stretcher. "David, David," she screamed, and then threw herself onto his body.

Charlene watched from the doorway as the medics pried the grieving wife off of him, but then allowed her inside the ambulance to ride to the hospital. His glasses were no longer on the road.

Her mother stepped beside her and put an arm around her back. "Charlene, my dear. Let's go." Her words were brittle and her face as white as her hair.

"Sure, Mom. We can't do anything here." Charlene pulled her car keys from her purse and handed them to her dad. "Help Mom to the car, okay? I'll be with you in a minute."

As they walked away, Charlene found Jessica sitting by herself at a back table, a check in her hands. She was crying silently, big tears rolling down her cheeks. She looked up at Charlene. "He's a good man. What if he doesn't survive? It's not fair. This should be the beginning of a wonderful new life."

Charlene slid into the chair beside her and squeezed her shoulder. "I'm sorry, Jessica—what an awful end to a wonderful event. I sure hope that David will be okay."

Jessica swiped her eyes. "Me too." She waved the check. "He kept promising to give me a substantial raise, but, well, that didn't work out." Her shrug conveyed she didn't hold a grudge. "He gave me two thousand dollars for my student loans, which might not be much, but it helps and he didn't have to."

Charlene handed her a napkin for her tears.

"He was doling out checks—but no one appeared very grateful. What did they expect from him? And now he's being rushed to the hospital, and might not live. . . ." Jessica's voice broke on a sob.

"It's shocking and terribly sad. If I can help in any way, give me a call, or just stop by." Jessica sometimes took the back way from Bella's to Dr. Matt's, which was Crown Point Road.

"Sure . . ." Sniff. "I will." Jessica pocketed the check in her apron.

"Is there someone you can call? Maybe the other owner?" Charlene didn't feel right leaving Jessica with this mess. Pamela Avita had cleared all the baskets for Felicity House, the empty tables forlorn. Charlene searched for Avery, the young girl who'd dropped the plate, but she was gone.

"Vincent." Jessica tucked her hair behind her ear. "Good idea. He'll know what to do. His number is in the back office—I'm pretty sure he lives in Boston." She slowly rose from her seat and glanced around in confusion, as if she didn't know where to begin. "I guess I can clean up while I wait?"

"Yeah, and then go home and rest. I'm sure the police will want statements from everyone tomorrow."

"Right." Trancelike, Jessica gathered dishes on a tray, making her way toward the office.

Charlene next examined the restaurant for Brandy, but she and her party had slipped out without saying goodbye. What a night. She headed for the door, just as Sam returned her call.

"Charlene. I heard." His rich voice rumbled across the phone line.

The back of the ambulance sped away with red flashing lights. People were making their way to their cars, shaking their heads, muttering to one another. Why had David run out of the restaurant?

She sucked in her bottom lip, refusing to break down. How many tragedies did this make? In the months since she'd arrived in town, she'd helped solve three murders. Not that David was dead—but still, he'd been hit and left in the road. Her brain wanted to connect it to his lottery win, but that might not be the case. Who was Freddy? Or Doug?

"I'd like to speak with you, Sam." Charlene would never forget the startled expression on David's face. What had upset him? He'd been disoriented, frightened, and had nearly stumbled on his way out. "Are you on your way here?"

"No. Sorry, I can't make it tonight, but Officer Horitz is there, or should be." He sighed. "Go home, Charlene. Get some rest. I'll come by in the morning. Are your mom and dad okay?"

"Shaken, but I'll get them settled at home. I feel so bad for David." As she spoke, she exited the restaurant and stopped near the spot where David had lain. Police cars with bright blue and red lights blocked the area, and cones with yellow tape surrounded the space. How could someone hit him and drive off? Perhaps someone who'd been right here celebrating with them, someone who'd had a few drinks too many? A chill ran up her spine.

"We'll get a hotline set up for anyone who might have seen anything. There should be plenty of witnesses. We'll find the person who did this. You were at an auction, right? For Felicity House?"

"Yes, that's correct. But everyone was inside. The party was just winding down." She couldn't get the image of David out of her mind. Had he seen someone outside, an old enemy maybe? Had that person heard about his lottery win and shown up to threaten him? "Sam. David bolted to the street, frightened—and confused. There's more to this, I know it."

"Charlene?"

She hated that tone in his voice. "Yes, Sam. Just hear me out. I know what I saw."

"Did you *see* the make and model of the car?"

"No, my back was turned." That didn't sound helpful, so she rushed ahead. "David seemed very generous to his guests tonight, but . . ."

"But what?"

She released a breath. "I have a hunch that he has more enemies than he does friends."

Silence greeted this remark.

"Are you still there?"

"I'm here. But, please, Charlene, don't start making

assumptions. Let's just stick to the facts, okay? And leave it to the authorities. Believe it or not, we actually know what we're doing."

"But I . . ."

"What? Can't help yourself?" His voice was gruff. "Try, Charlene. Try. Go take care of your guests and leave the police work to us."

Charlene took that as her cue to leave. Head down, and muffled from the cold, she headed toward her Pilot SUV, where her parents waited. As she slipped behind the wheel she noticed that her dad had warmed the Pilot up so at least they were cozy. Her mom was in the passenger seat and her dad in the back. "Sorry, I just got a call from Sam. I told him what happened."

"Who's Sam?" asked her father.

"Her boyfriend," her mother responded, buckling up. "The detective. When are we going to meet him, Charlene? Thought he'd have shown up by now." She glanced at her husband behind her. "Probably frightened of us, right, Michael?"

His balding head gleamed in the dark car. "It's been a long time since we scared off any boyfriends. You like this fella Sam?"

Charlene backed carefully out of the parking spot and drove around the rear of the strip mall to avoid the police cones blocking the direct route, then answered her dad's question. "I just moved here a few months ago. We've eaten a couple of meals together, but we've never been on a date. No kissy-kissy, so just forget about it. We're *friends*. That's all."

"You always were good at keeping secrets." Her mom faced the window and the barren trees that lined the road.

"Seriously, what's that supposed to mean?"

"Don't mind her any, Charlene, my girl. Your mother's had a broom stuck up her skirt ever since you left Chicago. I told her it was good for you. Move to where you could start over. Get your mind off Jared. But does she pay attention to me?" He scoffed and waved his hand. "No sirree. Blames me for everything. If I'd been a better dad, you might have stayed. If I'd invited you to live with us, you might not be here right now. On and on it goes."

Charlene bit back a smile. "Dad, you're the best father a girl could hope for, and, Mom, I know you mean well, and that you miss me—I miss you, too, but I've been so busy getting the place together and building my business that I don't have much time to call, or have a boyfriend. I'm just starting to get to know people here."

Her mother gave her a sharp look. "I saw you talking to that good-looking Kevin. He was with that younger girl, so I wouldn't get my hopes up there."

"Brenda, hush now. Don't make Charlene feel bad. What a rough night. Darn good pasta fagioli, though. Wouldn't mind trying that again."

"Oh, all you think about is your stomach," her mom complained. "That poor man! His wife might be turning on the waterworks now, but boy oh boy, she'll be spending his money so fast she'll be broke in no time."

"Mom, stop it—we don't know how David is faring yet, and I think Tori was actually grieving." Had Tori's extreme reaction been shock, or guilt? David, while enamored, had also been suspicious. "We don't know what their marriage was like."

"I don't know," her dad murmured. "A guy named Zane was texting her, and David's face turned red. Like yours does, Brenda, when you see me talking to the pretty women at church."

"Ha! As if any pretty woman would give you the time of day." Her chest heaved in her red winter coat.

Charlene drove around the curve, never more glad to see her house looming ahead. When Charlene had wanted to hire a service to put up the Christmas lights outdoors, her handyman, Will, wouldn't hear of it. He and his son-in-law had outlined the entire three-floor home in blinking clear lights. The beautiful oak trees and evergreens were well lit, too, and half a dozen gorgeous crystal deer with gold glitter antlers, heads held high, graced the front lawn. It was a masterpiece.

The only reason she could afford this place was because it was haunted. It had been unknown to her at the time or she'd never have purchased it, but now she was glad she had.

Dr. Jack Strathmore had been murdered in this house and his spirit had been trapped. Lonely, he'd roamed the corridors for years, scaring off any resident who had lived there—before her, nobody had been able to see him. They only knew that doors opened and shut, TVs turned on and off at will, and sometimes haunted music would play from the grand piano that had once been in the parlor. The piano was gone, but Jack remained.

"Here we are, folks." Charlene turned her Pilot down the flagstone drive. "Home sweet home." She parked and they walked up the porch steps and into the foyer. The lights were on timers, so she never had to worry about a dark house. The heat was set at 72°F, but she still felt a chill. Was it Jack waiting for her? She glanced around, looking down the hall to the living room, where Jack liked to sit near the fire, but it was shadowed. The grand staircase leading up to the second and third floor had no ghostly presence, but she had a good idea where he might be. The wine cellar in the basement.

"Mom, Dad? Should I put on the fire? Would you like some coffee or something to drink?"

"Nothing for me, dear," her mother said. "All this drama tonight has made me tired." She shrugged out of her coat, folding it over her arm. "It's past our bedtime. I'm going to turn in, if you don't mind." Her hand was on the railing—decorated festively for the holidays with green garland and red bows—and she waited on the first step. "Coming, Michael, or do you have pretty women to call?"

He chuckled. "None as pretty as you, my dear. Turn the blanket down, I'll be right up. Just want to get us a couple bottles of water. Maybe some cookies? That Minnie is a wonderful cook. You did well hiring her."

"Yes, I got lucky." Charlene walked with her dad to get him his favorite shortbread cookies. They were moist and crumbled easily, so she put them on a fancy dish. "There you go. Good night. I love you both."

She waited until they were upstairs and out of sight, then ran down the steps to the wine cellar in hopes of finding Jack. The basement was divided in sections, the smallest part stored the water tank, the heater, and all the essential things that kept the house running. Before he'd died, Jack had designed a wooden wine cellar built up against the stone in the far corner. A long table in dark walnut, the height of a high top, with four chairs around it took up the center.

"Hey," she said, catching her breath at the sight of him. Jack Strathmore would forever be forty-seven; tall, slim but broad-shouldered, with a face that was hard to find fault with. He had the bluest turquoise eyes and the longest lashes she'd ever seen on a man. His nose was elegant, over a full, sensual mouth, and he had thick sable hair, only lightly graying around the temples. He was movie-star good looking and put George Clooney to shame.

Was she attracted to him? Of course not! He was a ghost! There were moments when she could see right through his body to the wall behind. It had been disconcerting in the beginning, but not so much anymore.

"How was your evening?" His question was delivered in an educated tone—he'd gone to Harvard. "Did you enjoy the auction?"

She poured herself a glass of an expensive Sonoma Valley merlot and sipped before answering. "I am so thankful that you waited for me tonight."

"Why? What's wrong?" He leaned toward her and searched her face. "Are you upset?"

"Remember David Baldwin, from Bella's?"

"Yes—the guy who won the lottery last week. Shauna and I would go to the restaurant once in a while. It wasn't fancy enough for her, but I enjoyed the food. Good pasta fagioli."

She raised her glass. "My father agrees with you."

"He's a charming man. Your mother, however... well, let's say your dad is a saint."

Charlene covered her mouth, but a surprised laugh escaped. "You always make me feel better, and yet I shouldn't! Poor David was celebrating his bright future and a few hours later, he gets run over."

Jack immediately reached out as if to touch her but stopped short. "Why didn't you start with that? Is he all right?"

"I don't know. I don't think so. He wasn't moving when they loaded him into the ambulance."

"What happened?"

"The auction was over, and David had ordered champagne to celebrate his lottery win—which was awkward, but that's another story—and then afterward he glowered out the window, with his wife clinging to him, which was also odd. Then, he got weird."

"Weird how?"

"Like he was scared. He shouted something, then rushed outside, and bam—got hit, hard enough that his glasses fell off. Whoever it was, they didn't stop." Restless, Charlene paced the small space.

"He wasn't moving? That's not good." Jack ran a pale finger over his square jaw. "So, what do you think spooked him?"

"That's the big question, isn't it?" Stopping beside him, Charlene swirled her glass of wine and took another sip. "His wife, Tori, is much younger than him and didn't seem very nice. She was real flashy, you know? Wearing a gold slinky dress, waving her jewelry all over the place. And David picked tonight to hand out checks."

"To everyone?"

"No, just select people. Every time he did, her mouth got tighter and tighter, until I feared her lips might crack. She was really upset that he was throwing his money around."

Jack's eyes brightened. "Upset enough to have someone run over him?"

Charlene returned to the table with alarm. "Oh, I don't think that." She thought back to the night. "But Tori was getting texts from a guy named Zane. What if she'd had an affair and David knew about it? Maybe he saw Zane outside the window?"

"You said he shouted before he ran out—what did he say?"

Charlene leaned against her stool rather than sit. "Two other names—Freddy and Doug."

"Who are they?" Jack's tone was incredulous.

"I don't know, and I didn't meet anyone at the auction with those names. Tonight David struck me as someone who might have more enemies than friends. You know the type. Acts like he's everyone's best buddy. A big talker, a little loud, but I liked him. So does Jessica, who was waitressing tonight. I know you remember her? She's a physical therapist with Dr. Matt, at your old building. He gave her a check too."

"Long dark brown hair—you made her tea when she came for a donation to Felicity House. Why did she get a check?"

"She told me it was for student loans. That was pretty generous of him, I think. But I got a feeling he wasn't so generous with others. His son turned up, uninvited. Kyle. He didn't get a check, which ticked him off. He stormed off on his motorcycle before all this happened. He might not even know his dad is in the hospital . . ." Her voice faltered.

"If it's serious, the police will inform him," Jack said consolingly.

Her shoulders drooped. "It was an awful night. Awkward, with the passing out of checks. Tori's resentment was obvious even to me, and I didn't know her."

"Did the ex-wife make an appearance?"

"No, she wasn't on the invitation list either." She held

up her empty glass. "He rushed out so quick that he must not have checked for traffic."

"You look exhausted. You have blue circles under your eyes."

"Attractive, huh?"

"You always look good to me." His intense gaze told her more than words that he meant what he said. "Go to bed. Get some rest. We'll talk again tomorrow."

"I will. Thank you, Jack."

"Anytime. I'm not going anywhere."

"Yes, lucky for me, not so much for you."

"I honestly don't mind. I get to hang around the beautiful wine cellar. What could be more pleasant for someone who enjoyed his wine so much?"

"Being able to drink it?" Charlene made sure to add a smile to her quip.

"Touché!" His short burst of laughter followed her up the stairs. When she reached the top, she blew him a kiss and turned off the light.

CHAPTER THREE

Sunday morning, a week from Christmas, Charlene topped off her parents' coffee from a black carafe as they ate bagels and fruit in the dining room. Her silver Persian cat, Silva, sat on the windowsill, her fluffy tail flicking back and forth.

Charlene had just poured her second cup of the day when Minnie arrived, her car keys jingling. Setting down her mug, Charlene strolled from the dining room to the foyer. "Morning, Minnie!"

Minnie shifted the bags of groceries in her arms, and Charlene stepped forward to assist before one fell.

"How are you? It's all over the news," Minnie said, her gray curls bobbing over her brow. "Poor man!"

Charlene had kept her television on in her suite all morning. According to Channel 7, David had never regained consciousness, before passing away with his wife at his side. "It's so sad," she agreed, leading the way down the hall to the open kitchen.

"Weren't you at Bella's last night?" Minnie set the cloth grocery bags on the counter. "For the auction?"

"Yes, with my parents."

"Well, they've set up a hotline, so hopefully whoever did this will come forward." Minnie reached into a bag and pulled out the ingredients for homemade chili and cornbread.

As the housekeeper at Charlene's Bed and Breakfast, Minnie had free reign of the menu and no one had ever been disappointed. Her husband, Will, did the yardwork outside.

Jack appeared with a puff of cold air that made Minnie shiver. Unable to see him, she rubbed her plump arms and went about her business, unloading the second bag. The cloth sack was filled with a variety of cheese and crackers for Charlene's cocktail hours.

The Garcia family was due to arrive this evening after seven and planned to stay for the whole week. The Chilsons, parents of Nikki from the veterinarian's office, had booked the room overlooking the great oak tree. They would fly in from San Diego on Friday, the day before Christmas Eve. Her parents' room was at the end, with a view of the side lawn and front road. The three smaller rooms were vacant and ready for a last-minute guest.

Charlene retrieved a bag of onions and brought them to the butler's pantry. Christmas was meant to be a joyous time, but she knew it wouldn't be for Tori, or Kyle, or Jessica, who'd be mourning for David.

The doorbell rang and Jack manifested himself by the side window, telling her, "It's your detective."

Jack had a jealous streak, which she found, at times, both annoying and endearing.

"Be nice," she mumbled, then opened the door.

Sam Holden stood on her front porch, in jeans and boots and a thick winter jacket, his brown eyes warm as whiskey. Dark brown hair styled short, and a full mustache of the same color that hid a sensuous mouth.

"Morning, Charlene," he said. He patted his jacket pocket, where he kept his notebook and pen. "Is now a good time to talk?"

She opened the door wide and welcomed him in. "Of course."

Jack had been a doctor when he'd been alive, a handsome, classy man—the exact opposite of ruggedly gorgeous Sam.

The detective kissed her cheek in greeting, while Jack glowered over Sam's shoulder—it was all Charlene could do to keep a straight face.

She closed the front door and Sam put a hand on her forearm to ask, "Have you heard? David Baldwin died?"

"Yes, it's been all over the news," she said. "I can't believe it—I suppose I was hoping, since they'd taken him in the ambulance, that he'd be all right."

Sam faced her in the foyer, out of earshot of her parents. "He wasn't breathing when they arrived on the scene, but the paramedics managed to get a pulse—they just couldn't keep him alive."

Charlene wrapped her arms across her chest, her warm sweater no barrier against the sad news. "I feel so bad for his family, his son—but mostly for David." He could have done so much good with his newfound wealth.

"I'd like to talk to you about what you saw last night." Sam cupped her shoulder, commiserating.

"Not the accident itself."

"Right." He brought his hand to his side. "You said on the phone David acted oddly?"

Charlene, aware of Jack behind her, stayed a few inches from Sam when she'd been tempted to move slightly closer. "I thought he might be having a stroke or something, and then he ran outside. I turned to talk to Tori, and the next thing I knew, I heard an awful sound and David was on the road." She stuck her hands in her sweater pockets. "Mom and Dad might have more to offer—we're just having breakfast. Can I interest you in a cup of coffee?"

"Always," Sam said.

They entered the dining room, and Charlene introduced her parents to Sam. Jack had followed them in, taking a ghostly seat next to her mother, at the opposite side of the table from Charlene and Sam.

Her mom shrugged her sweater closer to her body. "Brr. I think this old house has drafts."

Her dad shook the detective's hand. "Nice to meet you. Call me Michael. This is Brenda." He gestured to his wife.

"Finally!" Her mom preened under Sam's hello. "We've heard so much about you—all of it good."

Charlene tamped down the impulse to bang her head against the table. She'd warned Sam what her mother was like, so she hoped he didn't take anything Mom said personally.

Sam shook her hand and sat down as Charlene poured him a cup of coffee. Minnie darted into the dining room, exchanging the black carafe for a silver one. "Is everyone okay? I've got cinnamon rolls in the oven, if you're still hungry in about ten minutes."

Her dad's eyes lit up.

"Hi, Minnie," Sam said. "I'm fine, thank you."

Charlene nodded at her housekeeper. "Thanks!"

"Where are you from, Sam?" her mother asked. "Is that a New York accent I hear?"

"It is," he said. "But I consider Salem my home."

"Charlene loves it here," her father said.

"Coming from Chicago"—Sam winked at Charlene—"our winter shouldn't scare her away." He smiled at her, his expression challenging. He unbuttoned his coat but didn't take it off. Could he feel the cold emanating from Jack?

"Quite the opposite. I'd like some snow for Christmas, if that's not too much to ask." Charlene added a splash of coffee to her cup to warm it.

"How are you folks holding up after the accident last night?" Sam searched their faces with concern.

Her mom straightened her red-framed glasses and pursed her mouth. "Well, it was a shame, I don't mind saying. One minute David's pouring champagne, and the next minute he's dashing out the door, calling some man's name."

"Zane," her father said. "David seemed perturbed at his pretty, young wife over some guy named Zane."

Sam arched a brow in her direction for explanation.

"It's true that David was upset about Zane, but just before he ran out, he was yelling Freddy, and then Doug. He seemed shocked." Like he'd seen a ghost—not that Sam would appreciate that comparison.

Her mother reached for the handle on her mug, but Jack had rotated it so that it was on the other side. She scowled, and turned it back.

"Do you know any of the three?" Sam nudged his cup aside.

Charlene shrugged and sipped her coffee. "Sorry, but no. They weren't dinner guests, that I'm aware of."

Sam brought out his notepad and pen. "Who was there, that you do remember?"

A list-maker herself, Charlene visualized the room, starting from the back. "Tori, who flirted with the bartender, Brandy, Evelyn, Theo, Kevin, Amy—I forgot her last name, but Kevin can tell you—oh, the people from Felicity House, who ran the auction, uh, Alice and Pamela, Sharon and her husband, John."

"Sharon?" Sam repeated in a deep voice.

"Turnberry. Her husband was the first one to run out and check on David, after . . ."

"Who else?"

"David's son," her mom chimed in. "Kyle. And Jessica, the waitress who lucked out at Felicity House, and another girl who dropped a plate. She had one of those things in her nose—you know?"

"A nose ring?" Sam asked.

"Is that what it's called? Rings are for fingers and earrings for ears, not cheeks and eyebrows." Her mother took off her glasses and frowned. "What is the world coming to?"

Nobody answered. Charlene snapped her fingers, getting on with the list. "Avery from Felicity House . . . and

Vincent Lozzi—David's business partner. From what I gathered, they disagreed on the amount of the check. They almost got into a fistfight, but then Vincent left."

"Still mad?" Sam asked with interest.

"Definitely." She wadded her paper napkin, wondering if Vincent had returned to the restaurant after Jessica called him for help.

Sam made a note—what was he writing? She wanted to be helpful and give him useful information, not gossip or speculation.

She crossed her ankles beneath her chair and leaned forward, resting her elbows on the table. "Sam, there had to be another dozen people there that I don't know, but Jessica might, or Alice, from the auction. It's why we were all there." To help the kids.

Jack said, "Remind him about the checks, and David wanting to be Santa."

Charlene nodded without acknowledging Jack and told Sam, "It was like David had a Santa wish—he was handing out envelopes with checks for certain people. Not for his son, though—which Kyle thought was unfair."

"Oh?" Sam's head stayed down as he added more, then flipped to a fresh page.

"Yeah, it was awkward because not everybody got one—and some didn't seem pleased by the amount they'd received." She exchanged a look with Jack, still seated next to her mother. Not just playing Santa, but making a point. Now they'd never know what it was. "Vincent for sure, and Alice, the director from Felicity house. Whatever had happened there really rocked her world, in a bad way."

Sam glanced across the table at her. "Did you get an envelope?"

"No, I was there to donate for the charity." She thought for a sec. "Jessica got one too. She seemed happy, though. Two thousand, I think it was."

"The wine ladies got one," her mom said.

Her dad cleared his throat. "The son, Kyle, asked if he was getting a check, and his dad said something about business but that he'd take care of family later. The kid didn't seem to believe it. He left early, too, in a huff."

Sam scanned his notepad. "Kyle, that's David's son from his first marriage, right?"

Charlene cupped her hands around her coffee mug. Kyle had said he'd wanted to talk to his dad, but his dad hadn't had time. She'd seen for herself the dismissive way David had treated Kyle, as well as Avery. Being a neglectful father wasn't illegal, unfortunately.

Her mom squinted at the place Jack sat and shivered, then gave a dramatic sigh. "On my true crime shows, it's usually the wife who wants the husband dead."

"Lucky guy," her dad observed. "Peace at last."

Her mom tossed a bagel crumb at him. "Hush."

Jack's laughter could only be heard by her and Silva, who jumped off the windowsill to sit by Jack's chair. The cat tried to leap into Jack's lap, and Jack disappeared with a frizzle of energy that Charlene was surprised nobody else could see or feel.

Silva, back arched, hissed and raced from the dining room.

Charlene hid her amusement from their antics the best she could by sipping her coffee.

"Anything else?" Sam asked. "Did you see the scene at all, before the ambulance arrived? Broken glass, or a piece of plastic?"

She recalled the bare road, the streetlamp. "David's

glasses had been knocked off his face, but I don't remember them in the street on our way out."

"Let me see if he had them at the hospital." Another quick scribble was added to the paper. "Forensics might need to talk to you. You have my number if you remember something." Sam closed his notebook and tucked it back in his jacket pocket. His casual pose, his arm on the armrest, let her know he was done with his interview. "I got word that I'll need to be in New York all day on Friday for a court case."

Disappointment welled. "Oh no! Will you be back for Christmas Eve? I'm making a prime rib."

Sam smiled and finished his joe. "I'll do my best. Crime seems to pick up around the holidays . . . but this is an old case that requires my testimony to put the bad guy away."

"I understand." His dedication was one of the things she admired most about Sam.

Charlene's mom gave him a pointed look. "What about David's killer? It's a horrible thing driving off like that. They were probably drunk."

Sam rose to his full height, well over six feet, and nodded at her mother. "We can't speculate, ma'am. Drunk or not, it's a felony hit-and-run. We'll find the person responsible."

"You inquire into the wife, now," her mom said, as if she'd gone to the police academy or something. Charlene sucked in a breath, but her dad handled it.

"Brenda, Tori was with us the whole time!" Her dad smoothed a hand over his mostly bald head. "This is serious."

Her mom's chin jutted out stubbornly. "Michael Woodbridge, I will have you know that I am a very good judge of character. And that woman is no better than she has to be. Flashing her diamonds around." Her mom wagged her finger at Sam. "Just see. Maybe she hired someone."

She hated to give her mother credence, but she couldn't get David's angst out of her mind. "You might want to ask Tori about Zane," Charlene suggested. "David seemed pretty upset about something between them last night. A text, I think."

"I've given up asking how you know things," Sam declared. He touched his jacket pocket and the notebook as if to assure her he was on it. "I will review everybody on this list."

"Thanks, Sam." Charlene escorted him to the foyer, leaving her mom glowering at her dad in the dining room.

"Your mom is a character," Sam said when they paused by the closed front door. "I'm glad you warned me."

Charlene gestured behind her and laughed. "That was nothing. She was on her best behavior."

"I have the feeling that if I don't hurry up and catch the killer, I won't be invited for Christmas Eve." His brown eyes flashed with humor.

"It's still my house, Sam. You're invited. I'd love for you to come."

He chuckled. "What are you doing for the rest of the day?"

"Taking my folks down to the wharf. They like to window-shop and buy souvenirs. Mom collects coffee mugs on her travels."

Sam tipped her chin up. "Have fun, Charlene. The time will pass before you know it."

She could have gotten lost in his compelling gaze, but

she pulled herself free and opened the door, walking with Sam out to the white porch. Bless him, but that man was made for jeans—since he had his back to her as he took the steps, she looked her fill and then waved as he drove off. Only ten days left until her parents went back to Chicago. Ten days of nagging from her mom and sweetness from her dad. She'd focus on the good.

Chapter Four

Charlene's mom snagged the front seat of the Pilot, so her dad took the back, and they headed into town to see the holiday lights at Pickering Wharf. Sunny but chilly, they'd dressed for the weather to enjoy walking around while she pointed out places of interest. Charlene was delighted to show her parents more of Salem, wanting them to like it as much as she did.

"We can have lunch at Cod and Capers," she told her folks. "It's on the wharf and has a wonderful view. Sharon Turnberry is the manager there. You both met her last night. The redhead . . . her husband was the one who ran out after David?"

"I remember." Her mother shifted in her seat so she could include them both in the conversation. "A tall lady, midforties I'd guess, but it's hard to say with all the plastic surgery people do these days. Her hair was dyed. Nobody but Lucille Ball, or maybe Carol Burnett, had that color of hair."

"You forgot Prince Harry," her father said dryly. "He's a redhead too. Doubt he gets his hair colored."

"Don't be ridiculous, Michael. He was born with it, and everyone wondered where it came from. Charles didn't have it, and Diana was a mousy brown until she got highlights. You know how these things go."

"No, I don't," he said to his wife. "Why don't you tell us?"

"Okay, you two. No more snarking at each other. Let's enjoy this beautiful day." They were passing Bella's when Charlene spotted some cars in the parking lot. Police tape still secured the area where the crime had been committed.

"They're open." Her mind swirled and she thought about stopping. "How can that be?"

"It's probably just police business," her father said. "I can't imagine they're serving lunch today. I've been thinking about that wonderful soup ever since my cinnamon roll this morning. What was that? A few hours ago?"

"You want to stop, Dad? We can have your soup and then go to the wharf for the afternoon."

"Whatever you want is fine by me." He shot the restaurant a longing glance.

"I wonder if they've caught the hit-and-run driver yet." Her mother rubbed her hands together. "I can't resist a good mystery. Let's make a quick stop and see if there's any new information. Then we can go shopping and see the sights."

"All right." Charlene switched plans and pulled into the parking lot, avoiding the area taped off. As she climbed out of the SUV, she couldn't help but feel a tightness in her chest. David had been maybe ten years older than Jared when he'd been killed by a drunk driver.

The restaurant was at the end of a row of businesses, and the only food establishment. A green and white awning drew the customers' attention, and today's specials were listed on a blackboard. Next to Bella's was a fabric store, and there was a dry cleaners at the far side.

Jessica greeted them when they entered. "You're back so soon?" Her voice quivered. Her smeared mascara indicated that she was a wreck and probably should have stayed home.

"We came for the soup," her dad said.

Jessica tried to smile, but tears slid down her cheek. Charlene gave the pitiful young woman a quick hug.

Why had David given Jessica that check? Jessica had said herself that he didn't have to, but he wanted to help her with her student loans. Why would he give her money and not his own son?

Jessica showed them to a table far away from the window, with a Sorrento mural painted on the wall behind. She handed them each a menu. "It's been awful around here. Everyone's in shock, calling and asking questions. They can't believe David is gone. Me either."

"I'm so sorry, for you, for everybody," Charlene said gently. "Especially his family. They must be hurting so much."

"Good thing he gave out all those checks last night." Brenda nudged the menu on the table. "Had it happened going in, nobody would have got a thing."

Michael shook his head, giving his wife an incredulous look. "Don't you have any empathy in your heart?"

"Course I do. I feel sorry for David. He didn't live long enough to spend his cash, and now his wife will be up to no good while he's churning in his grave."

Jessica took a step back, bumping into the chair behind her. Her face had paled, her mouth trembled.

"Mother. That's quite enough." Charlene held out a hand toward Jessica. "Excuse her, she doesn't mean half the things she says."

"I just speak the truth." Her mom had the good grace to lower her eyes. "I don't mean to be hurtful."

"I'll bring you some water while you decide on your order." Jessica hurried off.

"Now see what you've done? I swear you have Tourette's," her father grated out the words. "Probably get extra salt in my soup because of you, woman."

"I think I'll have the clam chowder." Brenda ignored her husband's comment. "What about you, Charlene?"

She wasn't really hungry. "The Caesar salad with blackened shrimp."

Jessica dropped off their iced waters with lemon and picked up their menus. There were only two other occupied tables and both of them had been served. "Have you decided?" she asked in a tight voice.

They gave her their order, and Charlene excused herself from the table. "I'll just be a moment. I'd like to wash my hands."

Instead of using the ladies' room, she cornered Jessica when she came out of the kitchen. "I want to apologize for my mother. She takes some getting used to. I tried for about forty years, then moved here from Chicago." Charlene rolled her eyes. "Dad ignores her most of the time."

Jessica crossed her arms. "Well, she had a point, unfortunately. I just can't make sense of it. I spent half the night trying to understand why David hurried out of here like that. What was he saying? Shouting names I've never heard of. He looked confused, stumbling. Do you think he had a stroke?"

"That occurred to me. I'm sure the medical examiner will determine the cause of death. Of course, he died from his injuries, but what happened before that? It was such odd behavior. I heard something about a person named Zane?"

"Yeah, Zane works at the gym with Tori. You know she's a fitness instructor, right? Well, he's a body builder and does weight training."

"Do you think . . ." She left the sentence open-ended but alluded to an affair.

"I don't know anything for sure." Jessica looked around to see if anyone was within earshot and lowered her voice. "David told me that he and Tori were having problems recently. They were discussing divorce last summer. Then, of course, he wins the lottery and Tori is all smiles again."

Charlene had seen more sour expressions than smiles but let it drop. "What was with all the checks that were passed out? Did David owe everyone money?"

"He didn't owe me that—it was a gift. I don't know about the others." Jessica stuck her hand in her pocket, regarding the diners to see if she was needed.

"I'm glad David did what he could. Hey, how is that new girl, from last night? Poor thing must be traumatized."

"Avery's tough—she has to be. But yeah . . . last night was rough—David told her not to come back. He'd given her a try, despite her lack of experience, as a favor to me."

"Does she live at Felicity House?"

"At the teen house. No parents to speak of. As I said, she's had it tough. I like her, though—she reminds me of me. Only with piercings and tattoos."

Charlene laughed softly.

"Thanks for caring, Charlene." Jessica stepped aside as one of the diners headed toward the restroom. They stood in the narrow hallway between the kitchen and the manager's office. "Let me check on your order."

Charlene was about to return to her table when she heard Vincent yelling at someone in his office. She stayed to listen.

"I'll fold up this restaurant before I sink another cent into it," she heard him say.

She didn't hear a reply and figured he might be on the phone. Just then the door opened, and a red-faced Vincent with a big cigar in his hand stormed into the hall to survey the nearly empty restaurant.

He seemed surprised to see her standing outside the door. A young man in a white chef's jacket ducked past her on his way to the kitchen.

"Last warning, Dalton," Vincent called after the chef's retreating back. His eyes narrowed on her. "Did you want something?" Vincent breathed heavily.

"No, I'm sorry. I was about to visit the ladies' room." She took a step back. "You might not remember me. I was here with my parents last night. Charlene Morris. I own the bed-and-breakfast down the road."

"Yes. Yes, of course." Vincent tugged a hand through his graying hair. "David couldn't have died at a worse possible time." The cigar shook between his fingers. "We were in the middle of negotiations. He didn't want his share of the restaurant any longer."

"That makes sense I guess, since he won the lottery; he probably planned on traveling or something."

"You have no idea what's going on. Nobody does! I gave David a start here, loaned him the money for his half, and this is how he pays me back?" His voice grew louder, making heads turn. "I've got my lawyer on it right now."

She met his gaze as they were about the same height, glimpsing sorrow beneath the anger. "I'm sorry for your loss. For the whole family—I met his son briefly last night. Will they be all right?"

"I don't know what David's intentions were toward Kyle, but if that scrawny yoga instructor has anything to do with it, he won't get a cent. His poor wife too. Ex-wife, I should say. Linda's a damn fine woman."

"It must be a terrible shock to both of them. I'd like to pay my condolences to her and her son."

"Yeah? Kyle lives with his mom, right across town. That kid's nothing but trouble, but Linda dotes on him like he's the second coming."

"What kind of trouble?" she asked pleasantly, hoping to prolong the conversation.

He didn't need much poking, his emotions had no filter.

"Petty stuff, mostly, but it's not entirely his fault. They both got shafted when David took up with the town tramp. I hope he left something to them in the will, and that it's someplace safe so Tori can't dispose of it."

"You think she'd do that?" Charlene softened her voice and looked down the hall to make sure no one was around. "She wasn't very likable last night. I could see she resented giving any of the money away."

"That's putting it mildly." Vincent chewed on his cigar. "I wouldn't put anything past her. Now, if you'll excuse me, I've got an appointment in town—had to pay my lawyer extra to meet on a Sunday." He brushed past her, and Charlene rejoined her table.

"Well, I got quite a bit of information in the past few minutes." She slid into her seat. "Eat up, and I'll tell you all about it on the ride to the wharf."

Jessica had dropped off their lunch while she'd been talking to Vincent, so she dug into her salad while her father wolfed down his favorite soup. Her mother complained that the clam chowder was too salty and didn't have enough clams.

Charlene's dad told her to "clam up."

As they were leaving, she asked Jessica for Linda and Kyle's last name and their address, if she knew it, so she could send a sympathy card. The waitress returned with the information written on Bella's stationery. Charlene's father insisted on paying the bill, adding a generous tip for Jessica.

The three of them put on their winter coats and traipsed out to the Pilot. Her mother nabbed the front seat, leaving Dad in the back again. This was a new game her mom was playing—or maybe Charlene hadn't noticed before. She shared what she'd learned on the short drive to the wharf.

"What I don't understand is who killed David," her mother said. "I've got my thinking cap on and decided it can't be the floozy. We saw her all night. But I like the secret lover for this. What's his name? Zane? Such a lame name—you think he made it up?"

"Mom, you watch too much crime TV." She sounded like a detective in a noir cop show, Charlene mused.

"Hit-and-run accidents happen all the time," her father pointed out. "Doesn't mean someone was out to kill David. It could've been an unfortunate accident."

The route to the wharf took them past the station, and Charlene glanced at the building, wondering how much of this Sam knew. A large American flag waved in the breeze. "That's the police station."

Charlene noticed a motorcycle with KYLE on the license vanity plate parked in front. In a city with fewer than 45,000 people, chances were good that the bike belonged to David's son. She pointed it out to her parents. "I wonder if Sam brought Kyle in for questioning."

"Probably. If his ex-wife didn't do it, or the lover, then it had to be his son." Her mother spoke with authority. "It's always a family member, everyone knows that."

"Brenda, don't you ever get tired of knowing everything?"

Charlene drove on by. It was true that Kyle had left in a fit of anger. But could he have had something to do with his father's death? Vincent had said the boy was nothing but trouble, but patricide was more than "trouble." She wished she could talk to Sam about this, but he'd drawn a clear line in the sand, and they weren't on the same side of it. He couldn't discuss the cases with her and wanted her to stop poking around and interfering in police business. So far, that hadn't worked out.

This past Halloween, she'd been kidnapped by a couple of boys for asking too many questions about a young woman's death. And before that . . . well, she'd been having a house party when a killer had entered from an unlocked window. A knife had been held to Minnie's throat.

She gulped, shutting down the reminders that Sam was probably right. Twice she'd been in harm's way—but it hadn't been her fault. Death had happened around her, same as David's tragic accident. The irony that she'd moved from Chicago to escape the quicksand of Jared's passing was not lost on her.

She parked at the pier, lucking out with a spot near Vintage Treasures antique shop. The town of Salem was festively decorated, from the large fir tree in the square to each individual store window: lights, ornaments, poinsettias, and evergreens. Streetlamps were wrapped in garlands, and restaurants had their awnings out. It was an old and beautiful city, a far cry from the bustle of Chicago, but Charlene loved this seaside town and wanted her parents to be happy for her. She had found her forever home, whether they liked it or not.

Chapter Five

Charlene and her parents strolled a few blocks, admiring all of the beautiful holiday displays in the windows. Her mom had purchased mugs for her bridge group back home, and her dad carried the bag. The briny smell of the wharf competed with the scent of dark roast from the coffee shop on the corner.

They crossed the street to the bookstore, which was directly across the road from Vintage Treasures. Archie Higgins had decorated the front picture window with an antique Santa doll, and wooden elves worked on miniature toys in Santa's workshop amid fake snow. Salem's streets, however, remained bare.

"I want to see what kind of books they've got," her dad said, opening the door to Bartholomew's Bookstore. "I might do some reading on the history around here."

"You're welcome to read the books I have on the

bookshelf by the stairs, Dad." She'd collected some wonderful true Salem tales.

He murmured something agreeable, and her mom followed him in.

Her phone *dinged* and she read a text from Kevin.

Don't forget the Winter Solstice party at Kass's on the 21st! Amy and I hope you can come. We'll be burning a yule log on the beach afterward.

It hadn't taken Charlene long to realize that Salem, famous for its witches, had a large Wiccan population. Kevin had given her a lot of information about modern witches and had told her that while they practiced witchcraft and spells, they were normal people doing everyday things: shop owners, history professors, people you bumped into every day. She'd also learned that they celebrated the seasons and had their own calendar for holidays. Winter Solstice, or Yuletide, welcomed the rebirth of God on the longest night of the year, and practitioners gave thanks and made merry, by lighting a fire to usher in the light.

Charlene reread the text, noticing his phrasing, "Amy and I." Did that mean Kevin was serious about her? If so, Charlene really wanted to meet her. She texted back, **That's still three days away and my parents are here—can I let you know?**

No problem. Any word on what happened to David?

Charlene drew in a breath and shuffled her feet as a cold wind snuck down the back of her jacket. **Just that he died from the hit-and-run. It's a felony.** She thought of Kyle, who'd left angrily, with good reason, and was now at the police station. Was there a chance that the accident was no accident? **Have a great day—and it was nice to meet Amy.**

She peeked into the bookstore, the bell above the door ringing. Her parents were on opposite ends of the shop, each engrossed.

With a wave to the clerk, she ducked back out and retrieved the phone number and address for Linda Farris, Kyle's mom, that Jessica had given her.

Should she call and offer her condolences? The woman must be at her wits' end. Charlene thought of how David hadn't even noticed his son was gone last night, and how hurt Kyle had been at being excluded.

But did that mean he'd come back and run his father over with his motorcycle?

The bike had been loud; she'd noticed it when Kyle had first arrived at Bella's restaurant last night. It was loud enough to be heard over the clamor of the party.

She hadn't heard that roar before David had been hit, and she didn't want to believe that Kyle could be capable of taking his own father's life.

David might not have been a saint, but she'd found him outgoing and even charming—a hard worker. But as she'd observed, that didn't translate into being a good father or husband. Had he cheated on Linda with Tori?

Since moving to Salem, her Midwestern sensibilities had collided with reality. Real life was actually very messy, with human beings not behaving at their best. Every day people had affairs, or cheated, or lied, and they all had justifications, as if that made them right.

It made her realize that the life she'd shared with Jared had truly been special. Perhaps she'd been naïve, but she cherished the memories. Maybe that was why she struggled with letting him go.

Charlene blew out a breath of frosty air and took off her mitten to tap in the numbers on her phone's keyboard.

She'd just leave a message, sharing her condolences. Surely Linda would be busy—maybe even at the station with Kyle.

The phone rang and to her surprise, a woman answered in clipped tones. "I'm not interested in talking to the press." The call ended without Charlene having a chance to introduce herself.

Why on earth would Linda be hounded by the press?

Her gaze drifted toward the direction of the police station, where she imagined Kyle might be. Had Sam arrested him for running over David? *No! No. No.*

Her mom exited the bookstore with a scowl, informing Charlene, "Your dad is dabbling in witchcraft. No good can come of that. What is Father Benedict going to say?"

Her dad followed, grinning like he'd scored an extra dessert.

"What did you find, Dad?"

In addition to the mugs he'd been carrying, he now had a heavy green and red paper bag. He lifted it to show Charlene—the top book was about Salem's history in witchcraft and spells for the modern practitioner.

Her mom mumbled her disapproval and hurried down the sidewalk.

Because her mother wasn't waiting for them, he also showed her the book underneath. The latest Dan Brown, his favorite author.

They shared a smile. So far as rebellions went, she had to give her dad credit. "You can leave that with me at the bed-and-breakfast when you go home, if you want," she said. "My guests might be interested in it. Unless you're planning some midnight mojo? Winter Solstice is in a few days, and I've been invited to a party if you want to come."

"The clerk inside was telling me all about it—mistletoe, yule logs, wine and food, candles—he said that Christians incorporated the ancient celebration to get the pagans to convert. You should have seen your mother's ears turn red! Sounds smart to me. And what's wrong with giving thanks before a fire? I plan on doing that when we get back to your house."

One of his favorite places was the love seat before the fire, a blanket over his lap and Silva at his side.

"Mom doesn't do change," Charlene said as they kept in sync down the sidewalk. "And spending the holiday here has her well out of her comfort zone."

"You can't grow unless you stretch your wings a little, and while I might be in my seventies, I have plenty yet to see." They reached the Pilot, where her mom waited with her arms crossed, her toe tapping.

"That's the best attitude, Dad." She couldn't imagine her parents actually *gone*.

"What are you two whispering about?" her mom snapped.

"We aren't whispering anything, Mom." Charlene pressed on her key fob and unlocked the doors. "Let's go home and have some hot chocolate. Did you buy a book too?"

Her mother relaxed her shoulders after buckling her seat belt. "I found a book by Ann Rule that I haven't read before."

The Pilot was parked so it faced Vintage Treasures. "I don't know how you can read those true crime books and still sleep at night." Charlene laughed as she turned on the engine. Archie waved at her from his window, looking a little like Santa himself, his half-glasses on the bridge of his nose, red suspenders holding up his slacks beneath a round belly.

She lifted her hand to him and pulled onto the road, gesturing to the shop. "That's the place I got my telescope for the widow's walk."

"You've done a beautiful job decorating your business," her mom said.

Charlene waited for a jab, but nothing came. She accepted the rare compliment without strings and turned on the radio for Christmas music.

The three of them sang along the whole way home.

She helped her dad with their packages, and they entered the house. The spicy scent of chili wafted toward them. Minnie was amazing, plain and simple.

Out of nowhere, Jack appeared on her left in a flash of blue light, and she gasped in surprise. It had been a while since he'd startled her like that.

"Ja—" Charlene bit her tongue and set her parents' packages on the bottom step of the stairs. "Just make yourselves at home," she managed, avoiding looking at Jack, though it was difficult because her handsome roommate flickered in and out of clarity, as if he was very upset or excited about something.

"Charlene," Jack said urgently, "I was watching television and . . ."

She wanted to hear what he had to say, but he had to wait until she could meet him in her suite, so she raised her hand to Jack as she faced her parents. "I'm going to change my boots for slippers. You two could do the same? I'll meet you in the living room."

"What about that chili?" Her dad rubbed his hands together as he stepped toward the kitchen, and her suite. "Is Minnie here? Can I get a bowl?"

"Just hang on a sec, okay, Dad? Minnie left already—I can help you."

"Charlene," Jack said. "You have to listen to me. Your detective was on the television."

She tuned out Jack to focus on her dad, who was insisting he could serve himself without making a mess of her kitchen.

"It's not that, Dad." She could feel Jack's tension like a cold tsunami and it wasn't pleasant.

"Charlene." Her mom entered the fray with a raised tone that meant business. "We don't require anybody waiting on us." She bypassed the stairs and her packages for the kitchen. "If your dad wants some chili, I can get it for him."

What she wanted was privacy to speak with Jack, and her mom might overhear her if she and her dad didn't go upstairs.

Jack brushed his hand across her back and her body broke out in shivers, making her teeth chatter. They were going to have a serious discussion later about boundaries, she thought.

"It's for the guests," she said quickly. "We have to make sure they have something when they arrive."

Her parents backed up a step with understanding. "Ohhhh," her mom said.

Now she felt bad for making up an excuse—she just needed a minute! "We can all have a bowl, as long as we make sure that there is plenty for the Garcias."

"I'm sorry, Charlene," her dad said. "I forgot that this is a business. It's so cozy, I think of it as your home. We don't want to be any trouble."

"It is my home, and you are welcome. Just give me ten minutes, okay?"

Her mom picked up one bag and took a step. Her father chose the heavier bag of books and climbed after her.

She waited until they were out of earshot before going to the pot on the stove that had been left on simmer. There was more than enough.

The clock on the stove blinked four p.m., which gave Charlene three hours before the Garcias showed up.

"Plenty of time to get everyone situated. Okay, Jack—tell me, what are you saying about Sam?"

"He was being interviewed by a reporter, that cute one from Channel 7?"

"Jack, hurry," she said, eyeing the hall to the stairs. Her parents could be back any second. She understood that he was trapped in the house; his favorite thing to do while she was gone was to watch the news or Netflix medical documentaries. She didn't point out that his ghostly hands probably wouldn't save lives in the real world, but he loved learning.

"Sam asked for drivers crossing Crown Point Road and Duval from ten to midnight to call the hotline. He has a team of officers going over camera footage at the intersection, and he'd like to rule out possible suspects."

Jack's energy waned in and out, allowing her to see the sink behind him, right *through* him. She brought her gaze to his face.

"That sounds smart to me." Crown Point Road led up to her house, and Duval was the other cross street by Bella's. She lifted the lid on the pot and stirred the chili with a wooden spoon. "What else did he say?"

"Nothing." Jack lifted his shoulder smugly as if his news had been worth almost giving his presence away.

Exasperated, she set the spoon down harder than she

meant to on the stove. "Nothing new, so please, no more games!"

"Charlene, don't be mad." Jack faded to a gray tone, like a sepia photo. It required energy for him to manifest for her.

"Let me take care of my parents and my guests. I'll talk to you later." She regretted her abrupt tone.

Offended, he said, "Sorry to bother you." Jack disappeared in a cold snap of air.

"Jack!"

But he was gone. She quickly ladled out two generous bowls of chili, cut squares of cornbread, and got the dish of butter from the pantry. She loaded everything on a tray for the dining room and met her mother and father coming down the stairs. "Here you are—Minnie must have made a double batch."

"Why are you making dinner for people? You can't make money feeding everybody," her mom said.

Charlene exhaled and counted to ten. "It isn't something advertised—that's just the full breakfast on the weekends, but I want to make people feel welcome, and food is part of that. I offer an afternoon coffee or tea, with cookies or scones. Sometimes we have cocktails or dessert, depending."

"I like it," her dad said, going into the dining room. "And it isn't that different from when you entertain, Brenda. Remember when we were first married and didn't have two cents to rub together? Somehow you still made amazing meals. Good food doesn't have to cost a lot, and I'm sure our Charlene knows what she's doing."

Her mom sat at the foot of the dining table. She'd switched her red framed glasses for green. "Will you tell us if you need help, Charlene?"

She imagined the strings that would entail, and to herself said, hell no, but she smiled gamely. "Sure. But I don't, so don't worry."

"I do worry—I think we need to call in someone to check the insulation on this place—your heating bill must be atrocious. I am constantly feeling a draft."

Charlene realized that her mom was *feeling* Jack; no amount of extra insulation would help with that. "I am fine."

"Join us?" her dad asked. He'd taken the chair to her mother's right.

Charlene hid her impatience. "Let me get a bowl." She hurried back to the kitchen and dished out a tiny bit of delicious chili. She couldn't see Jack, or sense him either, but wanted to apologize.

"Jack?" she whispered.

"Charlene! Will you bring another piece of cornbread? Mine is too crumbly. Cut it toward the edge, not the center," her mother called from the dining room.

Ugh. Charlene grabbed the pan and the knife, along with her own chili, and went to keep her parents company.

Her mom insisted on doing the dishes afterward, and Charlene let her just so she could catch a break and check her business e-mail and phone. No messages. Jack was also absent.

At five, she was going to suggest settling down for a movie when a knock rattled the front door. Giggles sounded from the porch.

She'd been working at the kitchen table and now closed her laptop to answer. Her parents hovered by the stairs. "Go wait in the living room, okay? No helping with the luggage or offering to show them around. You're also guests, got it?"

Her dad's shoulders slumped.

Her mom sniffed and shot her chin high, slinking into the living room. "Fine. We'll stay out of the way. You don't have to tell *us* twice."

"Mom—it's not personal," she whispered. A louder knock pounded.

She opened the door and put on her most welcoming smile. "Hi! You must be Andy and Teresa? I'm Charlene."

"Sorry we're early, is that okay? We got a head start driving from New York—and I'd allotted more time for potty breaks," Andy said. The pair were in their thirties: Andy, dark haired to Teresa's blond, and the girls each had a golden mix that seemed a blend of both parents.

"Come in! I'm glad your travels were uneventful," she said.

"I'm Teresa." The woman shouldered her purse, a little girl on either side of her body. "And this"—she nudged the daughter on her left forward—"is Emily."

"I'm seven," Emily said with a serious expression in her round brown eyes.

"I'm Maddie!" The other little girl grinned—the opposite of her sister.

"Maddie's five," Teresa said. "Our little chatterbox."

"Mom," Maddie giggled. "I am not."

"Are too," Emily whispered, glancing at Charlene from a fall of golden bangs.

The family shuffled into the foyer. Andy gestured to his car, parked next to Charlene's in the wide driveway. She had a garage to the right of the house, but she hadn't put her Pilot away for the night yet. "Is that all right?"

"That's fine. Did you want to get your luggage now? Or I can show you around and you can bring it in later." She'd given them the center suite, spacious enough for a family.

"Let's get the girls settled first," Andy said.

As they went to the stairs leading up, Charlene noticed her parents watching avidly from the love seat in the living room. No doubt her mother would have pointers for her later.

"I hope you all like chili—I've got some on the stove, if you're hungry—with cornbread."

"I like cookies better," Maddie said.

"You're in luck." Charlene reached the landing and turned left to the middle door. "Minnie makes the best cookies in Salem."

After the family settled in, she offered them bowls of chili, a platter of cornbread, and then a dish of cookies. Her parents were resting in their room, tired from the long night before. Charlene kept the Garcias company, offering advice as to what they should see and do. "I know it's dark, but the Pedestrian Mall and harbor shops will still be open until nine."

Andy and Teresa thanked her, bundled their girls up, and herded them out the door. "We'll let them run off some energy," Andy said as they left.

Charlene speed-walked from the foyer to her suite, closed the door, and breathed a sigh of relief. "Jack?"

Nothing.

How long could he give her the *very* cold shoulder?

Switching the television on to lure Jack out, Charlene sat at her narrow desk and reached for her ivory notepad. Sam had been so specific about times. David had been hit before eleven, she was fairly sure. She'd looked at her watch at ten thirty.

Doodling circles was like meditation for her and she edged the notepad in swirls.

Would Sam cross off the people at the restaurant? Nobody had left the party at that time. Vincent and Kyle had gone earlier. She doodled skid marks and wondered if there were any on the road, but she hadn't heard anyone slamming on the brakes, or a squeal of tires. Just a thump, and then . . .

She put the pad aside and logged on to some popular social media sites, curious about Kyle. She'd felt sorry for him that night, a tough kid on the outside, just wanting to talk to his dad. He wasn't very active, but in his photos, he was always drinking (underage) and partying.

What about Tori—was she really a homewrecker? Ah—there was more on her, since her move to Salem from Boston and her marriage to David.

Thirty years old. Most of her pictures were taken at the gym. Very fit.

So, what about David's first wife? Linda Farris had been so defensive on the phone earlier, not giving Charlene a chance to even say hi. Google offered two sites of information, but Linda hadn't posted anything in years. Her picture showed a tired blonde with a wary smile. She worked at Salem Hospital and had been there for five years.

Noises sounded from down the hall, outside her room—time to stop snooping into poor David's life. "Jack?" Nothing. How long could he hold a grudge, anyway?

Children's laughter echoed down the hall to her room. Charlene closed her laptop and left her suite.

As she headed to the living room and the sound of voices, she straightened a figurine on the bookshelf, admired her silver shell planter in the foyer. In the living room, her dad sat on the velvet armchair with Silva on his lap; Maddie and Emily listened as her dad shared a story.

The family scene brought her to a halt. She was overcome with sorrow for what might have been. If she and Jared had only had children, these might be her daughters, listening to their grandfather so raptly.

She'd want them to have blond curls, like Jared, she thought, her nose stinging. Or maybe Jared's dimples. God, she missed him. She sucked in a deep breath to keep her emotions in check, and cleared her throat before entering the living room as if nothing was wrong.

"Hey, guys." She heard the hoarseness in her voice. "Can I get you anything?"

Her dad looked up at her tone. "I am very content, Charlene," he said. "Aren't you, girls?"

"This is the best place ever," Maddie enthused as she pet the cat. "Can we take Silva home?"

"You can't do that," Emily argued. "Silva belongs to Charlene. Right?"

Oddly enough, she'd never wanted a cat, but she couldn't imagine her life without Silva. "Right." She quickly shared the story of how Silva had hitchhiked from Chicago on her moving van.

Her dad burst out laughing. "Guess she really wanted to be with you, honey."

"Why did you call her honey?" Maddie stood on her tiptoes to lean closer to Charlene's dad.

He settled back in the chair. "She's my daughter."

Maddie and Emily scrutinized Charlene to see if this was true.

"He's right," she confirmed, drawn forward into their sphere.

"Do you have kids? Like us?" Maddie asked.

The bitter sorrow, always just beneath the surface, stung her throat. "I don't. I wish I did." She touched her heart-shaped gold and diamond earrings, Jared's last gift to her. If only . . . but "if only" wouldn't change things, and the past needed to stay in the past.

Her dad caressed her hand in understanding. *When would the pain go away?*

Silva's ears perked as Jack manifested before the fireplace. Something in Charlene eased at his ghostly presence. She turned her back to her dad and the girls, and mouthed, "I'm sorry."

"Apology accepted," Jack said aloud since nobody could hear him but her. "Any chance you can meet me later for a glass of wine? You look like you need to unwind."

She put her hand over her heart with a grateful nod—Jack knew just how to make her feel as if things would be okay, and she'd learned that sometimes it had to be enough.

Chapter Six

Charlene woke up early on Monday morning, feeling refreshed from a good night's sleep. After Jared's death, sleep became a distant memory. Now in her new home she was getting six or seven hours of uninterrupted rest. It was a blessing.

She took her shower and made her bed, still chuckling over Jack's story about Maddie and Emily from the night before. "They saw your father, asleep in the chair, and snuck up behind him with Silva, brushing his nose with the cat's tail." Jack had reenacted her father's surprise—Dad had jumped awake, but seeing the two girls and the cat, he'd waggled a finger at them—they feared they might be in trouble until he couldn't hide his smile, and they'd all laughed.

Charlene had dressed for shopping later in jeans and a red sweater, her long hair down past her shoulders. Entering her sitting room, she was surprised to see Jack in the armchair by the window. "Good morning. Have you been here long?"

"I have little concept of time when I'm not with you, but since you have clocks everywhere, I know it's been thirty minutes." He grinned up at her and tapped his fingers silently against his denim-clad leg. "So, guess what two angels tiptoed down the stairs last night, looking for presents under the tree?"

She eyed the closed door from her suite to the kitchen. "What are you talking about?"

"Maddie and Emily, of course. Only kids we have in the house, right?"

"Right—and they *are* sweet."

"It must have been around midnight—I was sitting by the fire when the girls tippy-toed down the stairs to count the presents under the Christmas tree. They'd been looking to see if any of the presents were for them."

Cute! "Ah—were they disappointed?"

"A little, but Emily said it wasn't Christmas yet, so Santa still had time to deliver their gifts."

"Thanks for telling me, Jack. I'll put presents for them on my list of things to buy today when I go shopping. I was planning to hang stockings."

"It's beginning to feel a lot like Christmas," Jack sang, "everywhere you go . . ."

She held up her hand to interrupt him. "You're right—I have to go. Want the television on?"

"I can do it." He snapped his fingers and on came Channel 7. *Loud.*

"Jack . . ." She cringed and gestured to the door. All she needed was her mother stepping in.

"Fine." He turned the TV back off and disappeared.

Charlene shook her head. Jack could be a darling, but overly sensitive too. One thing for sure, he rarely allowed her to get the last word.

She left her suite, glad that she and Minnie had devised a plan for a substantial breakfast since they had more people over the holiday. The Garcia children were already downstairs, as was her father.

"Good morning," she called. Her dad and Emily sat at the kitchen table while Minnie made breakfast. Silva batted at a toy that Emily had on a string, and Maddie colored on a piece of paper, a cup of hot chocolate cooling before her.

They greeted her with various hellos and smiles. Her dad said, "And good morning to you, Charlene. You look chipper today."

"I feel good," she replied. Amazing what sleep could do. She patted Maddie on the head in passing. "How about you, little munchkin? Did you sleep well?"

Maddie nodded. "Yes, I like the fluffy bed. Feels like a big pillow."

"That's what I like to hear," she said. Charlene kept her knowledge of her and her sister sneaking out of bed to spy presents between her and Jack. "Are your parents up?"

"Yup." Maddie stirred a marshmallow in her cup and attempted to chop it with her spoon. "They're in the room, making plans for us. We might go see some witches."

"That sounds like fun, doesn't it?" Charlene had left brochures in their room giving them information on all the tours and museums. It might be Christmas, but witches and ghosts never went out of style in Salem.

"What's that?" Maddie pointed to a quiche that Minnie had pulled from the oven. "It looks like pie. I like pie."

"Why, that's a cheese and mushroom quiche, and the other has ham and tomato," Minnie told her. "We also have a tray of blueberry muffins, or chocolate chip. Does that sound good to you?"

"Uh . . . chocolate chip?" Maddie rubbed her tummy. "Yes, ma'am."

"You don't have to ma'am me, I'm just Minnie. That's good enough."

"Minnie—like Minnie Mouse?" The little girl laughed, her brown eyes wide.

"Well, I'm too big for a mouse"—Minnie wiggled her nose—"but yes, we have the same name."

Happy listening to the banter in her kitchen, Charlene cut up fresh fruit—juicy slices of honeydew, cantaloupe, and watermelon—to put on a large, oval tray. They always kept a basket filled with red apples, mandarin oranges, and bananas for the guests to help themselves.

Maddie peeled a mandarin orange in between sharing her thoughts with everyone. Charlene couldn't help but be charmed by her.

"Did you do one of the tours last night?" Charlene asked.

"Nah, we just walked around down at the harbor. There were some shops there. See my bracelet? Do you like it?" Maddie put her little arm out and Charlene admired the beaded bracelet with a black cat charm.

"Very much. What did your sister get?" Emily wasn't paying attention to them—too focused on Silva.

"She got one with a witch on a broom." Maddie giggled and covered her mouth. "It's spooky."

"Are you scared of witches?" Charlene asked, washing her hands after finishing with the fruit.

"Yes!" She made a face. "They're scary."

"I used to think so, too, but in Salem we have people that call themselves witches who aren't scary at all. Kass, a friend of mine, runs a tea shop. She sometimes gives visitors—like you—ghost tours." Charlene took a sip of her hickory roast coffee.

"Does she wear a black hat and have long, crooked fingernails?"

"Hmm, I'm sure she doesn't. Kass is very tall and slim, pretty too, and likes to wear black clothes."

"That's weird," Maddie declared.

Minnie laughed. "Salem has a lot of weird. Isn't that right, Charlene?"

"Sure does."

Her house phone rang and she took the cordless receiver into the living room for quiet. "Charlene's Bed and Breakfast."

"Charlene Morris?"

"Speaking."

"This is Officer Horitz. I was wondering if you could come to the station today. We have some questions regarding David Baldwin's accident that Detective Holden said you might be able to help with."

"Of course—any particular time?"

"At your convenience, but today would help."

"I'll be there." She hung up, wondering what it could be about. Sam had suggested she could help? How unusual! Charlene went back to the kitchen, and her mother joined them all soon after, dressed for the day in a tunic top and leggings.

"I smell coffee." Her mom sniffed. "Morning, everyone." She spotted the two large quiches fresh from the oven. "Oh, we're having quiche for breakfast? I had my heart set on a nice omelet."

"Then you can make it, Mom." Charlene forced a smile. "We try to keep things simple around here."

Minnie made a clucking sound. "I'd be happy to whip you up an omelet if you like, Brenda. Michael, would you prefer that as well?"

Her dad pulled his attention from Emily and the cat. "Don't go to any trouble for me, Minnie." He stood and put a hand on his wife's shoulder. "I haven't had quiche in a while."

Her mom smoothed a strand of short white hair behind her ear with a sniff.

Minnie handed him a quiche on a trivet. "Would you be a dear and take this to the dining room for me? We're ready to start serving as soon as Andy and Teresa appear."

"We're right here," Andy called from the bottom stair.

"Help yourself to coffee," Charlene said, "then let's gather at the dining table."

Teresa collected her older daughter from beneath the kitchen table. Silva was draped over her chest and shoulder, carried like a baby. "The whiskers tickle me." Emily's nose scrunched. "I want a cat when we get home."

"No cats," her mother said. "We have Charlie, our Schnauzer, and that spoiled dog is enough to care for. Especially since I'm the one who has to walk him . . . and feed him and groom him."

"Put down the cat," Andy told his daughter. "Let's go wash our hands. Hurry now."

Teresa led Maddie from the kitchen, and Charlene picked up the platter of fruit, handing it to her mom. "I don't want Minnie making any special-order breakfasts or everyone will want one. There's plenty of food."

Her mother made a huffing noise but marched off to the dining room, her shoulders back, chin high.

"That woman will be the death of me," her dad murmured when he returned for the other quiche.

Minnie bit her lip as she followed Charlene's dad back to the dining room with a basket of bread.

"And me," Jack whispered, watching the antics from the doorway. Devilishly handsome as always, he wore a long-sleeved navy T-shirt that was different from the sweater he'd worn earlier. He turned to face her, and she sputtered. It was one of those touristy shirts that they sold everywhere in Salem. The slogan read: GHOSTS DO IT BETTER.

Where could he have gotten that? She shook her head, wanting him to find someplace to hide, but he just laughed and folded his arms, looking like a hunky ghost centerfold.

"You like my shirt?" he asked, blue eyes twinkling.

He loved to make her laugh when she had people around, but she was getting good at ignoring him. Being rude was better than appearing crazy.

She refilled her coffee mug and breezed by him, saying in a very low voice, "Go play with Silva. Do something, but not in the dining room. Mom gets cold with you around. Got it?"

"Did you say something?" Minnie asked as she returned to get a pitcher of juice.

"Oh, you know me." Charlene lifted her mug. "Always talking to myself. Bad habit."

She hurried to the dining room and her chair at the head of the table. "Help yourself. The quiche is already sliced. Teresa, want to start us off?"

Everyone dug right in. Minnie made sure the coffee

cups were full and that the girls had enough juice. Another successful breakfast at "Charlene's," she thought with pride.

After the breakfast dishes were put away, the Garcia family went upstairs to dress for their outings. They had a full schedule ahead of them, including a trip to the Witch House to see a reenactment of the witch trial and The House of the Seven Gables.

When they came downstairs, Charlene told them about the oldest candy store in the country, Ye Olde Pepper Companie. "It's across the street from Seven Gables, and their chocolates and candy make excellent gifts."

"We'll be sure to visit after our tour," Andy said.

Once they left, Charlene helped Minnie clean up and then put on a holiday movie for her mother to watch, as her father had already taken his favorite chair near the fireplace. He was engrossed in his Dan Brown novel, with Silva purring loudly from her perch on his lap. She hadn't told them about going to the station in case it was something Sam wanted under wraps.

Jack cornered Charlene when she headed for her rooms to get her purse. "Don't blame you for wanting out," he said conspiratorially. "But don't leave me alone with your mother too long, or I might do more than hide her false teeth."

"Jack!"

"Just kidding! I wouldn't harm a hair on her head." Jack peered into the living room. "Besides, your dad is a real hoot. He manages your mother like a pro."

"Years of practice."

His beautiful blue eyes warmed as he gave her a long look. "You don't resemble her a bit, thank heavens for that."

She laughed. "If I did, you'd have scared me off by now. But we make pretty good roommates, don't we?"

"Agreed. You're a wonderful companion, intelligent, amusing, a pleasure to be around."

"And you are a darling. A darling *ghost*," she said, putting on her boots. "So, before I go shopping, I'm stopping at the station to help with the investigation."

"Isn't that your *darling* Sam's job?" Even Jack's smirk was handsome.

"Of course it is, but he told the officers that I could help with something. How intriguing is that?" She was dying to know what.

"Very. I can't wait to find out." The outline of his navy-blue tee began to dim, as did his jeans and hair, and he slowly faded away with a sad expression. Jack had limitations, and exerting energy as he had been lately zapped his strength. That's what happened when you were a ghost.

She left her suite and walked down the hall to the coat tree and her black down coat, when a loud knock sounded on the door. Opening it by the second rap, Charlene was surprised to see Jessica standing there.

"Hey, Jessica. How are you holding up? Want to come in?"

Jessica shook her head and stayed on the porch, bundled up in a gray coat. "I'm on my way to Dr. Matt's for my shift." She pulled a tissue from the jacket pocket that she wore over blue scrubs, and dabbed her eyes.

"What, hon?"

"I . . . I . . . went to the bank this morning. You know . . . to cash my check."

"Yes?" Charlene touched her arm. "You're really shaken up. How about a cup of tea?"

"No, I have to get to work. I just wanted you to know."

"Know what?"

"They wouldn't cash the check. Not just mine." Jessica's big brown eyes welled. "Nobody's."

"Why in the world not?" The answer suddenly dawned on her as she remembered how resentful Tori had been about David giving out money. "Are you telling me . . ."

"Yes, Tori closed the account the moment the bank opened. Nobody had a chance to deposit or cash their checks."

"Can she do that?" Charlene frowned. What about the children's charity?

"Apparently, it's totally legit, because she's his wife." Jessica's red-rimmed eyes spilled over. "I called Vincent. He's furious and threatened to sue the estate. David died still owning his share of the restaurant, which will now go to Tori. They were haggling over the price—Vincent figured it should be gifted to him, I heard."

Charlene remembered how angry Vincent had appeared when he'd opened his envelope.

Jessica released a big sigh. "Everything's a mess. Why did David have to die? This leaves folks in a bad way and right at Christmastime too. Now the only one who'll benefit is Tori, and maybe her boyfriend, Zane." Her mouth trembled. "I put in a call to Alice—she sounded ready to blow a fuse."

"It's terrible that Tori won't honor his wishes," Charlene murmured. She hadn't been impressed by Tori, but to run off with the money and leave everyone empty-handed was unconscionable!

Jessica's voice hitched. "She lives by the bank, so I drove by. That money-grabbing witch is leaving town. There's a moving pod in front of her house. David had told me in confidence that he'd called a lawyer, who had recommended that he and Tori go underground for a while. It's why he wanted to give the money he owed everyone the night of the auction. Now she can do anything she likes. Spend it on gold nipple studs for Zane if she wants." She wiped her eyes with the soaked tissue. "I can't believe it."

"I'm so sorry too. It isn't right."

Jessica pulled herself together. "I have to get to Dr. Matt's, but I'll be in touch—there's a remembrance at Unity Church tomorrow afternoon. See you there?"

"I'll check my schedule."

"I've got to go. Sorry to be the bearer of bad news, Charlene, but I wanted you to know. I feel so bad for the kids at Felicity House. What can we do?"

The children! They had the money from the actual auction prizes that Tori couldn't snatch, but was it enough? "I'll do my best to make it tomorrow—and, Jessica, if you think of anybody that might have had a grudge against David, would you let me know?"

"Sure. That list just keeps growing, doesn't it? You never really know somebody. Argh—I'm going to be late!"

Jessica left, and Charlene returned to the living room to tell her parents what had just happened.

"What really cooks my goose is the fact that the children might not get what they need for Christmas." Charlene paced before the fireplace in angry strides. "It's enough to break my heart. I'm going to pay Felicity House a visit this morning"—after the police station—"and see what I can do. Maybe get each kid something?" She'd buy gifts herself if necessary.

"You've got a kind heart," her father said.

"You're not made of money," her mom countered. "Do you have a big enough wallet to be so generous?"

"I'll do what I can. If I asked around and everyone pitched in a little something . . . Kevin would, and Sharon. If enough businesses open their tills, we could buy presents. It wouldn't take much. Twenty, thirty dollars. It's peanuts, really."

Her mom looked doubtful.

Charlene hated that her mother might be right, but she would think of something. Christmas was only days away. "Would you like me to pick you up anything while I'm out?"

"No, dear, you run along and enjoy your shopping," her mother surprised her by saying. "You work hard here, I can see. I didn't understand why you gave up your career in marketing, but you're good at this business too. I just never thought about you waiting on people, but what do I know?"

"Not a blasted thing," her dad opined.

Charlene wasn't sure if she'd just been paid a compliment or highly insulted by her mother. Either way, she didn't really care. She loved her bed-and-breakfast, her new friends and her life here, and her mother's opinion didn't matter.

"I just wish you'd let us help," said her mother.

"If you really want to, then if I'm not back by four, would you mind peeling the potatoes for tonight's dinner? Minnie is making us a pot roast."

"Don't mind a bit—I've been peeling potatoes most of my life."

Charlene put on her coat. "Thanks. I have my cell phone

if you need to get hold of me. Otherwise, I should be back by five at the latest. There's leftover chili for lunch."

"I couldn't eat another thing," her father said. "Maybe one of those cookies, or a brownie or two."

"You'll get fat," her mother said. "Bald and fat."

"Better than skinny and mean," he answered back.

On that note, Charlene rushed out the door.

Chapter Seven

Charlene left the bed-and-breakfast determined to help the kids at Felicity House—Tori might be greedy and self-serving, but to deny this center for children the money promised was unforgivable.

Officer Horitz's request hadn't sounded urgent, so Charlene decided to go to Felicity House first. She drove by a large double lot and parked in front of a wood-framed, single-story farmhouse that might have been built a century or more ago, painted brown with ivory trim, the door a cherry red.

There was a small brick schoolhouse to the left, complete with playground, and to the right and back of the lot, a two-story clapboard house, big enough for at least a dozen bedrooms. The property was fenced in, with high barbed wire, to keep people out or the kids safely in, she wasn't sure.

A little sign over the red door on the farmhouse read: OFFICE.

Charlene climbed the steps to a narrow porch, not sure what to expect. With a knock, she went inside—pleasantly surprised by the enormous fresh Christmas tree, decorated with handmade ornaments and prettily wrapped presents underneath.

Comfortable but worn sofas and chairs had been grouped together around a desk with two computers. A large sixty-inch TV took up one corner, and in the other were bookshelves that held hundreds of books. She smiled at the row of *Harry Potter* paperbacks, having read them all herself.

Eight young children were seated on the floor around a fourteen- or fifteen-year-old girl who was reading to them. They looked up with shy glances at Charlene. She waved. "Good morning. I'd like to see Alice Winters?"

A little girl with an adorable smile waved back, her teeth like white pearls in her brown face. "Mrs. Winters is in her office," she said, pointing down the hallway. "I'm Tamil. I'm six and a half."

"Nice to meet you, Tamil. That's a pretty name."

"What's yours?" Her hair was in thick braids tied with red and green ribbons, her personality precocious.

Charlene was immediately captivated. "My name's Charlene."

"That's pretty too. Would you like to adopt me?"

What?

"Tamil!" The older girl hushed her. "You can't ask everyone that. It's not polite."

"Yes, I can!" Tamil stood up and stomped her feet. "I can too. People come here to adopt us, right?"

"It doesn't work that way," the older girl said with a

surly expression. "I've been around for four years and I'm still here."

Why hadn't she and Jared adopted a houseful of children? All the time they'd spent trying to conceive had taken a heavy toll, until she'd felt she had nothing more to give. Then, she'd buried herself in her job and poured all her love into Jared.

Now it was too late.

She felt the weight of the children's stares. "I'm here on business." *Not to adopt.*

"Sit by me, Tamil," the older girl said. "Let me finish this chapter."

Tears smarted her eyes, and Charlene brushed them away as she stepped down the hall, past the kitchen to a door marked MRS. WINTERS. She gave two firm raps on the wood.

"Come in." Charlene entered and Alice stood from behind her desk, almost as round as she was tall. The red Christmas sweater with a dancing reindeer and her red pants were not slimming.

"Hi—I don't know if you remember me from the auction the other night? I'm Charlene Morris."

"I do, I do. You donated a week's stay at your bed-and-breakfast." The two women shook hands. "How can I help you?"

Charlene gave the cozy office a quick scan, noting the framed pictures on the walls of the director shaking hands with the mayor and other dignitaries. There were awards and certificates, and a photo of Alice Winters graduating with her PhD, another of her and Pamela Avita surrounded by kids.

"I'm here to see what I can do to help. Jessica dropped by this morning and told me that Tori had closed David's checking account, and that you won't be getting the money promised to you."

"Jessica is a sweetheart." Alice gestured for Charlene to take a seat. "She makes us very proud."

"I like her too." Charlene sat in a hard-backed wooden chair that demanded good posture. "Now, I can't replace the money from David, but I'd like to solicit support from some of the other business owners in town. I can make some phone calls."

"Yes, we thought of that, too, but so many have already been generous. If *you* do it instead of us it looks a lot less like begging," she said with a twinkle in her eye. "Not that I'm above it—I'd do anything for Felicity House and the kids."

It was obvious to Charlene that the business-savvy director not only cared deeply for the children, but it was her life's work.

"I have a degree in marketing and advertising, so maybe I could help you plan something global for next year?" Tamil and the other kids made a compelling argument for adoption, and if she could find a way to help them into forever homes? Her heart swelled at the chance to act. "I've had success in the past with crowdfunding."

Alice positively beamed as she considered this new option for bringing in money. "I can hardly refuse."

Pamela Avita walked in, so tailored she could have been on a magazine cover for executive working women. Slim black pants, high-heeled black boots, and a white blouse under an ornate red wool jacket—accessorized with chunky gold at her throat and ears, her chin-length black hair framed her youthful face. Her painted lipstick and nails matched the red of her jacket. All in sharp contrast to the plump, ugly-sweater-wearing director. But what a team they made!

Alice greeted Pamela with a relieved smile. "Pam, I'm so glad you're here. Charlene wants to help us drum up cash from our local businesses, before Christmas, as well as devise a long-term plan for global fund-raising for next year."

Pam looked slightly dazed, glancing from one face to the other. Then her shoulders dropped and she gave a sigh of relief. She shook Charlene's hand. "I can't wait to hear what you have in mind. I was praying desperately that someone could save this place."

Charlene's marketing brain imagined Tamil's sweet plea for a family going worldwide.

Pamela smoothed her jacket over her slim hips, her fingers trembling. "First, I want to thank you for your contribution to the auction. Your week's stay brought in over two thousand dollars." She took the seat opposite Alice.

"Pamela, why don't you tell Charlene what our plans were for the hundred thousand that had been promised us? Though the check David gave was only for ten." Alice spoke like they'd make the best of it, no matter what.

Charlene hid her surprise. David had pledged the center a hundred thousand dollars and didn't deliver? What a blow!

"And now we don't even have that." Pamela folded her hands in her lap, her painted mouth tight. "We'd planned to build a new wing that would shelter another twenty children under thirteen. We're overcrowded right now. Thank heavens the teen house has separate funding." Her fingers fluttered in the air before returning to their position. "Nobody wants to adopt an older child." Pamela and Alice exchanged sad looks.

Charlene thought of Avery. "Do the teenagers get training so when they turn eighteen, they have skills to support themselves?"

"To a certain degree," Alice said. "But it's pretty basic—I'd love for them to be offered scholarships to trade schools. Our teens, boys and girls, helped build the new schoolhouse, under the direction of one of my old wards who now owns a construction company."

Charlene considered that triumph full of talking points when it came time to put together her campaign. "That's great. What about computer skills, or maybe accounting?"

"We suggest those things," Pamela said, "but they would all rather be famous chefs or musicians. Maybe an athlete." She gripped her hands so tightly that Charlene could see the whites of her knuckles. "We hate to squash dreams. . . ."

"But we must be realistic," Alice said.

Sparked by the idea of on-the-job training, Charlene cleared her throat and hoped she wasn't making a big mistake. "I could use some help at the bed-and-breakfast. Weekends, maybe? I felt bad for Avery the night of the auction. When she dropped that plate, it was clearly an accident, and she was mortified."

Alice straightened. "Avery Shriver is a hard worker. It was her first night in that environment, and I thought I could help if needed, but—if you give her a chance, you won't be sorry."

"Let's have a trial period to see how we get along. I would pay her minimum wage?" Charlene wasn't sure that Avery would even want the position.

Alice nodded so hard her brownish gray hair came loose from its clip to fall over her eye. "She's sixteen and healthy as a horse."

"Would you like us to call her in? She's doing a school project while helping with the younger kids, since they're on holiday break," Pamela said.

"They're off until after the first of the year, so if you need help over Christmas, I bet she'd love it." Alice smiled. "You know the old saying, busy hands are happy hands."

"Indeed, I do." Charlene considered her schedule as she stood. "We could do four hours per day, starting this Wednesday." She had the remembrance tomorrow. "Why don't we try this for three days to see if she likes it? It'll give her a little cash before Christmas. We'll discuss it the following week and see about making it permanent on the weekends."

"Lucky girl." Pamela also got to her feet. "I'll go get her right now."

"Thank you so much—could you have her meet me outside, by my car?" That way Avery wouldn't be on the spot if she wasn't interested. "Alice, it was a pleasure speaking with you today. I look forward to what we can accomplish next year."

Alice walked her to the door. "Thank you for everything, Charlene."

"I'll get back to you after I've spoken to the local businesses—by Christmas Eve."

"I appreciate that." Alice tugged the red reindeer sweater over her broad hips. "Somehow we manage to make it through another day."

Charlene waited inside the warmth of her Pilot, and within minutes Avery ran out from behind the office, without a jacket, orange hair spiked. Charlene rolled down the window.

"Mrs. Avita said you wanted to see me?"

"Yes—would you like to start work for me at my bed-and-breakfast on Wednesday? Four hours a day for three days while we train you, and then if you don't like it, no hard feelings."

Avery shuffled her feet from the cold and shrugged. "Yeah, I guess."

Not the best reception, but Charlene didn't let that deter her. "I'll see you Wednesday at nine thirty, then. Casual clothes are fine."

"That's all I got," Avery said. "See ya." The skinny, long-legged girl darted out of sight.

Charlene hoped she wasn't making a big mistake.

She reversed out of the parking spot to the street and drove to the police station. Would Sam be in? Should she ask to see him? No, he'd passed her name to Officer Horitz.

Charlene couldn't deny being curious as she entered the station and signed in at the front desk. "I'm here to see Officer Horitz."

"One moment," the young male officer said, turning to buzz him. "Charlene Morris to see you." He gestured to a row of plastic seats. "You can wait there."

Officer Horitz didn't keep her waiting. Medium height, short dark blond hair, brown eyes, and clean-shaven, she vaguely recognized him, though they hadn't been introduced. He wore a navy-blue police uniform.

"Mrs. Morris, thank you. Come with me?"

"Call me Charlene, please." She followed him down the hall, past Sam's office, which was dark. A dart of disappointment stung.

"This way." Officer Horitz shared an office with three other desks, all vacant. "Have a seat. Detective Holden said that you'd seen David Baldwin's glasses on the road the night of the accident, yet they weren't with David's things at the hospital, which means someone picked them up." He shook his head as if whoever had touched evidence had made a big mistake. "I was hoping you could tell me where they were on the street."

"Sure." They each sat before his desk in black office chairs.

"Were they broken?"

She recalled the black frames, the streetlamp flickering off the intact lenses. "No."

He turned the monitor for his computer toward her. "We have a 3D program that allows us to discover how fast the vehicle was going that hit David, in relation to things around him."

"Oh?" Charlene thought back to exactly what she'd seen. David's head had been turned toward the flashing red dentist Santa holding a giant toothbrush.

"Time of the accident was ten forty-five. We know it wasn't fast, as his shoes were still on. This coincides with your confirmation that the lenses in his glasses weren't broken."

Her stomach clenched and she interlaced her fingers to hide her distress. This was normal procedure for the police but out of her wheelhouse. "How can I help?"

He handed her a rubber pointer and brought up a diagram of the accident. "David's body was here." Officer Horitz used a mouse to highlight the outline of a man's silhouette. There was the road, Bella's parking lot, Bella's, the intersection, and the strip of businesses across the way.

"There was a streetlamp," Charlene said. "I saw the glint of the glasses beneath it."

"Show me where?"

She tapped with the rubber stick on the screen.

"Good. And where were the glasses?"

She tapped again, and Officer Horitz made a red *X*.

"Five feet?" He hummed and typed into his keyboard.

Charlene said nothing as the officer added numbers to a file he had already. Curiosity got the better of her. "What does this mean?"

"There were no skid marks on the street," he told her, "which means that the driver didn't stop. Duval and Crown Point Road have speed limits of forty miles an hour. According to this"—he gestured to the diagram—"David was hit at thirty to thirty-five miles per hour."

"That doesn't seem very fast," Charlene said, unable to take her eyes away from the red *X* on the monitor.

"It was bad luck for David," Officer Horitz agreed. "The vehicle hit him at an awkward angle and broke his neck." The policeman sighed and got to his feet. "Thanks for coming in."

And just like that, Charlene was escorted out of the station.

Bad luck? Someone on the phone or texting. Even changing a radio station—the driver would have heard or felt something and made a decision not to stop.

At thirty miles an hour, whoever had run over David *had* to have known what they were doing as they left him on the street to die.

Chapter Eight

Tuesday morning, Charlene woke up with a feeling of dread. The remembrance service for David was being held in a few hours and she'd agreed to meet Jessica. Another man laid to rest, years before his time.

The taste of death was bitter. It was only six and the house was quiet. She slipped into a pair of jeans and a thick navy sweater, grabbed a cup of coffee from the kitchen, then put on a jacket and went outside to the deck to watch the sunrise. She hoped Jack would find her there, and just as the sun was peeking through the clouds in a dazzling range of color, she saw him, outlined in a halo of fiery orange. A ghost of a man trapped in his home.

"I felt your sadness," he said, taking a seat beside her on the steps leading to the back garden and tall oak tree.

The branches were bare, and the tree looked forlorn—an echo of her sorrow.

"Jack." He was astute to her moods and had known she needed him. "I'm glad you came."

She eyed him with appreciation. Handsome in jeans, boots, and a bulky black jacket, dressed like herself. His head was bare, his sable hair lush and curling around his ears. She knew he didn't suffer from the cold, or the wind, or anything. One of the pluses about being a ghost, she supposed, but was it really?

"Why are you sitting out here in the cold? Hiding from your mother?"

Charlene chuckled. "I was hoping you'd find me." She wished she could lean against him, to share his strength, but knew she couldn't. "It's David's remembrance service today, and I told Jessica I'd go."

"You don't want to?"

"Oh, Jack." He'd been gone last night and she had so much to tell him. "Tori closed the account at the bank, first thing yesterday morning. Every check David handed out bounced. No one received a dime. Worst thing is that Felicity House won't get an addition to host more children, which is what they'd planned to do with the hundred thousand dollars David had promised them."

Jack whistled. "Tori is a selfish woman and will undoubtedly get what's coming to her one day."

Charlene certainly hoped so. "David had shorted the promised money with a check for only ten grand—and now they won't even get that."

Jack scratched his jaw. "What are we going to do about it?"

We? She liked that. "I don't know. I can't let the kids go without this Christmas. It's just not right."

"Agreed. Let's enjoy this glorious sunrise and meditate on it. I'm sure something brilliant will come to mind."

She lifted her face toward the lightening sky. "You weren't always such an optimist." He'd been temperamental when they'd first met.

He gave her a fond smile. "I've changed. When you're facing eternity twenty-four/seven, you have to believe that the best is yet to come."

"Hmm. I like that."

They sat in silence for some time, at peace with one another. "So, what are you going to do about Tori and Felicity House? I doubt you're going to stand by and see the kids suffer."

"You must be a psychic as well as a ghost," she joked. "I've hired a girl from Felicity House to help around here—I can start with one, right? And I'm going to ask business owners to open their pockets and give a little more so that the children will all have presents. I told Alice Winters that I'll help out with advertising and focus on each child, so hopefully they'll find good homes."

He rubbed his hands together without a sound. "That's very generous, Charlene, and very much in keeping with the Christmas spirit. What did you do at the police station?"

"They have a program that can tell how fast a car was driving that hit somebody, by things around it—his glasses, for example. It was pretty amazing." It had taken hours of shopping for just the right stockings to compartmentalize the stark reality of another death. It did not get easier.

"Was Sam there?"

"No." She stood and stared down at Jack. His smooth skin had no five o'clock shadow and resembled a marble texture. "I guess I should go inside and get started. . . ."

"Tonight? Wine cellar?"

"Deal." She entered through her bedroom door and tossed her jacket on the armchair. When she went into the kitchen, the Garcia family was helping themselves to the fruit and muffins, the children sitting at the kitchen table.

"Good morning," she said. "I was on the back porch watching the sunrise."

"Wasn't it beautiful?" Teresa added a packet of sugar to her black tea. "We caught a glimpse of it from our window."

"Hope you don't mind us helping ourselves," Andy said.

"Not at all. That's what the food is here for. What are your plans for the day?"

"We're thinking of Plymouth Rock." Teresa polished an apple on her sweater. "Decided to get an early start."

"Great idea. Enjoy your day." She refreshed her coffee and then went into her room to shower. When she was done getting ready, the Garcias had left and her mom and dad were seated at the kitchen table.

"Morning." She kissed their cheeks. "Did you see the family off?"

"We did. They asked us to join them, but it didn't give us enough time," her mother said, taking a bite of her blueberry muffin. "We might like to do that later. Think you could take us there? It would be nice if you could join us."

"I'm sure I could get away after Christmas and before you leave. Does that work?"

"Perfectly," her father said. "You going somewhere this morning? You're all dressed up."

Black pants, black sweater, a looped red scarf around

her neck. "The remembrance service for David. Do you want to come, or can I drop you off in town?"

"No, we're not in a rush," her dad said. "We might just enjoy the quiet today. Maybe go for a walk after lunch."

"Okay. Suit yourselves. I'll see you this afternoon."

"Have a good day, dear," her mother said.

Charlene grabbed her jacket and boots, and headed out the door. Once the Pilot was warmed up, she slid it into gear and backed out of the driveway. The road she lived on was strictly residential, with large properties. She had yet to meet a neighbor.

She turned the radio on and drove to Fourth Street. Not in the mood for holiday music, she switched the dial to a talk show. Some guy was saying that hit-and-run accidents were up sixty percent around the US, adding that drivers were likely to be young males with prior histories of driving under the influence. She suddenly thought of Kyle. That description fit him to a T.

It also reminded her of Jared, who'd lost his life at the hands of a drunk driver.

Charlene spotted the church, but the small parking lot was full. After driving around the block, she found a parking spot a few blocks away. When she entered, she searched for friendly faces, Jessica's in particular.

Around a hundred people were seated in the assorted pews and chairs. Others stood talking in the back or along the sides. A few clustered near the lectern, reading about David's life and perusing photos.

Charlene spotted Brandy speaking with Sharon from Cod and Capers. Kevin was there as well, but she didn't see his friend Amy. Across from them and a few rows back sat Jessica with some friends. There were no seats available next to them, so she'd have to find one on her own.

At the front of the church was a large picture of David as a younger man, in his thirties, and very handsome. Only a few feet from the picture was Tori, in the first row of chairs, dabbing her eyes with a black handkerchief. Her diamonds sparkled on the outside of her black gloves, even from way in the back. Did the woman have no shame?

The ladies from Felicity House were there as well. They sat in the third row, next to Kyle, and a blond woman Charlene recognized from her online search as Linda Farris, Kyle's mom.

The ceremony was about to begin, and Charlene took a seat in the back row.

She noticed Vincent seated behind Sharon and Kevin, sitting with a man in his fifties holding a red and black football jersey, his eyes red-rimmed, his cheeks gaunt. She wondered which one was Zane. Tori had ladies around her, but no male companion, and Charlene had no idea what the gym instructor looked like.

Jessica turned and caught Charlene's eyes. She gave her a sad smile, then stood up, making her way past her friends' knees to the aisle. She gestured for Charlene to join her outside and walked out the door. Charlene followed.

What did Jessica want to tell her that was so important it couldn't wait until the ceremony was over? They took the steps of the church to the path leading to the sidewalk. Jessica was dressed in black slacks, a black blouse and jacket, her eyes red, her brown hair twisted in a clip.

"Jessica, I'm so sorry," Charlene said when they reached the sidewalk. "It's obvious that you really cared about David."

"I did." Jessica rubbed her hands together and shuffled her feet. "It's cold, so I'll keep this quick. With the whole canceled check fiasco, I forgot to tell you what I'd overheard from Vincent."

Charlene braced herself.

"Vincent was more a silent partner at the restaurant, leaving David to be the hands-on manager," Jessica said. "After his lottery win, David wanted out, but Vincent wasn't happy with the offer David made."

"I noticed that Vincent was angry, and he left early." Could he have come back to run David over?

"Vincent's got a short fuse. I heard him yelling at one of the chefs," Jessica said. "Dalton, a friend of Kyle's, David's son."

Charlene warmed her hands in her pockets. "I saw Kyle that night. He was pretty upset about his dad not giving him a check."

"I know. I like Kyle and feel bad for him and his mother, which makes this even harder." Jessica hesitated. "Vincent told Dalton that he'd heard his conversation with Kyle. Apparently, Kyle had said some awful things about his father."

"Like?"

Jessica glanced around and lowered her voice. "Like, Kyle wished his dad was dead."

Charlene put her hand on Jessica's shoulder. "Was this before or after David had died?"

With a look of distress, Jessica admitted, "Before. I cornered Dalton after overhearing that conversation and asked just to make sure. Dalton doesn't want any trouble and doesn't want to go to the police, but yeah, that's what Kyle said."

"I think he might have to, Jessica. David's dead, and his son said he wanted to do it." Cold seeped beneath her jacket.

"Not in those words. He was just angry and said that he wished he was dead, which is very different. Kids say stuff like that, but it doesn't mean anything. Right?" She sniffed. "I *know* him, and he wouldn't hurt a fly." Jessica took a Kleenex from her pocket and wiped her eyes. "Anyway, I know you and one of the detectives are friendly, so I thought you could speak up for Kyle. He's really a decent guy and has kept himself clean for the past year. No arrests—that I know about."

"Let's hope it was just him blowing off steam to his friend." Charlene lifted Jessica's chin with a gentle finger. "And where did you hear that I was friends with a certain detective?"

Jessica blushed. "I don't know . . . around. Are you?"

She took a step back. How had she and Sam become part of the gossip mill? "I am, but I don't know Kyle, so I may not be able to help him."

Jessica's shoulders dropped, and her expression closed.

Charlene put her hand on Jessica's elbow. "You inspired me after we talked yesterday, and I went to Felicity House. I'm going to spend the next few days fund-raising like crazy. While I was there, I talked to Avery. I'll give her a try while she's on school break for some extra help at the bed-and-breakfast."

Jessica grinned, all forgiven. "That's great news. I think you'll like her. She's a little rough around the edges, but deep down I think she's all right. Funny too."

"I'll pick her up tomorrow morning."

Jessica shivered and rubbed her arms. "Let me say one

thing in David's defense. He held the annual Felicity House auction for the last four years at my urging."

"I know how important Felicity House is to you." Jessica had shared over tea that day at Charlene's house when she'd collected the week's stay donation that Alice, who had been a home aide back then, had helped Jessica find her forever home.

"David would want them to have that money. Yes, he talked a big game but underneath it, he really cared."

"Did you know that the check he made out was for ten thousand? Not the hundred thousand he'd promised? Alice told me yesterday."

"No!" Jessica put a hand to her heart. "Tori was probably behind that. He'd mentioned that night of the auction that he hadn't had access to all of his funds or something."

Charlene recalled how Tori had acted as if each check David had handed out was food from her mouth. "Did you tell the police that they planned on leaving the next morning?"

Jessica scrunched her nose. "I think so. Why would that matter now?"

"I'm not sure. But what if Zane, the guy Tori was fooling around with, didn't want to be left behind?"

"You mean, maybe Tori told him the secret plan to leave Salem?" She paled. "And so what? Zane ran David over? God, Charlene—that's awful. But it makes more sense than Kyle doing it, I guarantee that." Jessica's poor lips had a blue tinge.

She didn't share what she'd learned at the police station, but because of how slowly the vehicle had been going, with no attempt to stop, it made her think that whoever'd hit David had known, and chosen to leave him there. Worse, she couldn't discount the possibility that it had been deliberate.

"Come on, let's go in before you freeze to—" Charlene stopped, not wanting to joke about death. "You'll have to point Zane out to me—I don't know what he looks like."

"Tori's dressed him up as her security guard—but she's not fooling anybody. Look for a big-shouldered blond in a shiny new suit, and that's your man." They reached the top stair. "Poor David."

"Poor David," Charlene sighed, and followed her into the warm church, taking a lone seat in the back as Jessica joined her friends.

An hour later, the service ended, and the minister directed everyone to have refreshments at the hall next door.

Charlene decided to go and have a cup of coffee, maybe talk to Linda Farris and offer her condolences in person, since the woman had hung up on her. She entered the old community hall, with cheap fold-up chairs and long tables scattered against the walls. The place was nearly as crowded as the church with people clustered together. It was also unbearably hot, so she unzipped her black coat to get some air.

Her black sweater and scarf were suffocating in this dry, little room with too many people. Fanning her face, she made her way to a table and selected a bottle of water instead of hot coffee, then took up a position next to a wall. Across the room she could see a punch bowl and a long line gathering around it. Brandy, Sharon, and Kevin, minus Amy, all joined her, each carrying a cup or mug.

Tori flashed more diamonds than tears as she commandeered the table closest to the window overlooking a side garden, barren for the winter. A tall, broad-shouldered, and muscular blond man, in a suit so new it gleamed, stood with his arms crossed between her and the guests who wanted to speak with her. That had to be Zane.

He wore a shiny watch that Charlene guessed wouldn't be silver, but platinum, and probably a Rolex. Tori sipped from a coffee mug after the man poured something from a flask into it, and dabbed at her eyes with a tissue, not removing her black velvet gloves. A diamond pendant the size of a quarter was snug at the hollow of her throat. Matching earrings sparkled.

"The girl is going to get robbed on the way to the car," Brandy murmured. "Money sure can't buy class."

Sharon and Kevin chuckled, spellbound by the spectacle of people lining up to speak with the young, rich widow. All of them had their hands clasped in front of them, heads bowed, wearing the same sad expression.

Kevin nodded toward them. "They look like a cult. Or hired mourners."

Charlene lightly smacked his arm. "Kevin, do you really think she'd stoop to that?"

Sharon pointed her coffee cup at the bodyguard. "Check out the muscles on that guy. Even his chin looks chiseled."

"Hmm," Charlene observed. "Jessica told me that he's her friend from the gym. You know the guy David was so jealous of? Rumor has it, he's her lover. Would Tori cheat on her older husband with a huge hunk of bronze?"

Brandy snorted. "*I* might even be tempted."

"Give the guy shades and he could be a character in *Men in Black*." Kevin finished his coffee and tossed the empty cup in a trash bin. "Who's the other guy?"

Charlene shifted to see where he was pointing. It was

the man with the football jersey, who looked as if he'd been crying. He'd bypassed the line of people waiting to speak with Tori, the jersey outstretched toward her. Definitely the odd man out.

Tori put her hand in the air and made a gasping noise.

Zane flexed his muscles before stepping in front of Tori.

"Wow. Watch those muscles ripple," Brandy whispered, then sighed with pleasure. "Oh, please do it again!"

Charlene snickered, surprised the stitching on the suit held firm.

"What's the guy doing?" Kevin stepped around the group to get a better view.

The emotional wreck of a man was no match for Zane. The body builder was like a cement-block building with no way around. Vincent took the man by the arm and steered him toward a platter of sandwiches.

Brandy's amusement glittered from her green eyes. "For ten million dollars the wifey should try to act a little more sorry, don't you think? At least hide the man she was having an affair with instead of flaunting him in public." The owner of the winery tapped her black heel against the linoleum floor.

Kevin shrugged. "She obviously doesn't care, and why should she? David's gone, and she's got the money. Anybody want some punch? I brought a flask from the bar."

"None for me. I need to head off soon." Charlene's parents were waiting for her back home. "Where's your friend Amy?"

"She had family obligations today . . . do you like her, Charlene?"

"She seems really sweet. I'll try to make the beach thing tomorrow."

Brandy's auburn brow swooped up. "Kevin, you invited straitlaced Charlene to a Winter Solstice celebration?"

"Hey! I think it sounds fun, but I have guests." Straitlaced? If only Brandy knew the truth, but her haunted bed-and-breakfast was her secret to keep.

"We're all going," Brandy said. "Mom and I, and my girls. They're home for yule. We have much to give thanks for, and we hope to make this next year the most profitable yet for the winery."

"Your wine is delicious—I have no doubt that you'll succeed."

"Cheers to that," Sharon said, lifting her cup of pink punch. "I'll take that hit from your flask, Kevin. This is like sugar water."

Charlene elbowed Brandy. "Uh-oh—looks like Pamela and Alice want to speak with Tori." Tori blanched an awful shade of pasty white as she saw them and called for Zane, who quickly escorted her out the nearest door.

Smart thinking, she thought. A remembrance where the widow needed an escape route.

"I heard," Sharon said, with a glimpse at Brandy, "that Tori closed the account with all of David's money so that none of his checks cleared. That can't be right, is it?"

"Jessica told me that too," Charlene shared.

"You are a sponge for gossip," Brandy declared.

"It isn't gossip if it is true," Charlene said. "I know *you* received an envelope."

"It was payment for his wine order, which I'd given at a discount for the auction, in addition to the back three months' pay he owed. I deposited it the night of the auction, with my phone app for my bank. Lucky I did."

"Yes, good thing." Kevin ruffled his shaggy blond hair. "That sure takes moxie—why on earth would Tori be at this service after making so many enemies?" He looked to the exit, as if expecting Tori to hustle back in and explain herself. Pamela and Alice shook the door, but it didn't budge. Had Zane locked it? Or was he holding it firm?

"She has to," Sharon said. "Otherwise she'd appear very suspicious to the police."

"My mother has already solved the case. The wife did it. Everyone knows that." Charlene smiled. "She reads a lot of mysteries, and it's no longer the butler but the spouse."

"You are always in the know, Charlene." Brandy sipped from her coffee mug. "What have you found out so far? Besides the affair and the checks."

Charlene tried not to take offense at Brandy's blunt observation. What else did she know? That Tori and David were going to skip town and disappear, that David had called out a man's name before running out of the restaurant. And that Kyle had told a friend that he'd wished his dad was dead. Most important, she believed the "accident" to have been very personal.

She was saved from answering Brandy by Kyle and the blond woman joining them.

"I'm Linda Farris, David's ex—how did you all know David?" Linda wore an off-the-rack black skirt and jacket with a black blouse and black flats. Her mouth was etched with lines of grief. "Are you friends of his or of that twit he married?"

Brandy chuckled. "David's, I assure you. I've never met the twit."

Charlene offered her hand. "Charlene Morris. I'm so sorry for your loss." She turned to Kyle, who continued to glare, but this close, Charlene wondered if his anger was covering up guilt. Or sorrow. Or both?

"Kyle," she said. "I was there the other night, at the restaurant. You were sitting toward the front."

The young man wore black jeans and a black polo shirt, his hair hanging limp around his face. He looked uncomfortable, but what kid wouldn't be around all these strangers who might or might not know the father he'd lost.

"I remember."

Linda zeroed in on her son with an expression of hurt. "I told you not to go there, Kyle. It was a bad idea."

Kyle lowered his head. "Yeah, I know. You were right."

Linda put her arm around his shoulder. "I'm sorry, sweetie. That explains why—well, I just thought you'd been working late when you didn't get home until eleven." She turned toward Charlene and the others, her emotions rushing across her face. "David said he'd leave Kyle something, but now what's going to happen? If that bitch has her way, we'll be lucky to get invited to the funeral."

Kyle moved out from under her arm, his mouth twisted bitterly. "He wins the damn lottery, ten million bucks, and he's married to that slut! It's not fair."

"We will manage," Linda said quietly, her hand on her son's cheek. "Don't hate him. Not now."

Charlene couldn't miss the maternal love in Linda's eyes.

"I have a right to be pissed." Kyle tossed his hair back. "You do too."

Charlene silently agreed that they each a reason to be angry at David.

Vincent and the man with the football jersey sauntered over, and Linda made room for them. "Hey, Vincent."

Were the two friends, or more? Charlene remembered how well Vincent had spoken of Linda. He'd respected her but had nothing good to say about the son.

Vincent gave Kyle a hug that the young man barely tolerated. He pulled free. "Dalton told me you were checking up on me." He glared down at his shoes. "I didn't mean anything by it, and you should know that."

"What?" Linda asked, looking from her son to Vincent.

"Later, Mom," Kyle said. "It ain't nothing."

Vincent nodded gruffly. "I had to check."

Linda crossed her arms. "Tell me!"

"We'll explain later." Vincent gestured to the man with the jersey. "I got someone I want you to meet. A long-lost friend of David's."

Linda turned to the man with a polite smile that you'd give a stranger. "Hi, I'm Linda. Thank you for coming."

"Name's Freddy Ferguson." He offered his hand. "I'm an old college teammate of David's. We played football together. This was David's."

Charlene thought that explained the jersey—wait—Freddy. Wasn't that one of the names that David had called out that night? Freddy, then Doug. When had he arrived in Salem?

Linda paled beneath her heavy blush, her lips back as if struck. "You were no friend of David's," she hissed, stepping in front of Kyle with her palms up toward Freddy. "You ruined his chances at a scholarship in that car accident. He never forgave you, and I don't blame him."

Vincent, horrified, dragged his gaze from Linda to Freddy. "Is that true?"

"It was an accident." Tears gathered thickly on Freddy's lashes. Charlene smelled beer on the man's breath and noticed his shirt was buttoned up wrong.

"Bull-loney," Linda said, her tone sharp. "You were jealous of him taking over as quarterback, and don't deny it. Why are you here? He can't forgive you now—he's dead. You'll have to live with your sins of the past."

Freddy lifted the red and black jersey. "David invited me to have dinner with him, but I . . . I couldn't make it. Now I'll never be able to tell him . . ." The man broke down, but Vincent, Linda, and Kyle stepped back rather than offer comfort.

Was Freddy outside the restaurant that night? David must have seen him, Charlene realized, and that's why he ran out. Had he been so emotional that he hadn't seen the oncoming car?

"Did Dad invite *you* to dinner at Bella's?" Kyle asked in a tight voice.

"Yeah, but something came up," Freddy said with a sniff. "I saw that he'd won the lottery in the news, and I was so happy for him, I just wanted him to know that."

"Did you call him, or did he call you?" Linda demanded. "Let me take a big guess. You called him."

Freddy didn't deny it. "I lost track of him after . . . and then, you'd left New York."

Linda tapped her toe. "No use hanging around. He's dead now, and you won't get a cent."

"I just wanted to see him." Freddy kept glancing over his shoulder like he had a nervous tic.

"Was that my dad's?" Kyle pointed to the jersey.

"Yeah, David was my best friend." Freddy lifted the jersey, which had some sort of animal on the shoulder. "You want it?"

Kyle accepted the gift before turning away to hide his eyes.

A shout sounded from the area where Tori had held court. Zane hadn't found an exit after all, but had barricaded Tori in the hallway, holding people back from her.

Tori, chin high, shuffled from the space to her table by the punch bowl.

"There she is! The thief herself!" Pamela said in a too-loud voice. "Thinking you can sneak away after closing the account. How could you, Tori?"

Alice, round as a ball of yarn in her black calf-length dress and sensible black pumps, said, "Think of the children, Tori. David promised to help. Surely you can see fit to at least put that check through? It would be a drop in the bucket for you. Please? One ounce of kindness, that's all we ask."

"You can all contact my lawyer." Tori thrust her chin forward. "I don't owe you a thing. I will choose my donations, not you. And not David."

Alice broke into tears. "I pity you. You, you have no heart."

"Well, I don't!" Pamela, red-faced, lunged for the ring on Tori's finger, trying to slide it off the velvet glove. "Give it to me. Give it to me, you heartless . . ."

"Stop right there," Zane yelled.

Pamela froze. Tori pulled back, her hand landing in the punch bowl, splashing Zane, who brushed his wet, sticky suit with dismay.

"Zane!" Tori screamed. "Get me out of here! Now!"

Pamela drew herself up and raced to the one and only entrance to the hall, throwing her hands wide to block the door. "We would appreciate it if you would reconsider, on behalf of Felicity House," she said with as much dignity as she could muster.

"Can't blame the woman for trying," Brandy said with a smirk. "That big diamond at her throat has to be worth a quarter million. I know my jewelry."

Zane picked Pamela up by the black-suited waist and

set her aside. "We are leaving." He tucked Tori close to his meaty body.

The seething widow shot them all the finger when she was safely on the other side of the door, then slammed it shut.

Charlene couldn't believe what she'd just witnessed, and the entire room held a moment of stunned silence before falling into chaos.

"If this is what the remembrance is like, I can't wait for the funeral. Christmas Eve, is it?" Brandy eyed her mostly full coffee mug with a frown. "I'll bring Mother, some popcorn, and wine."

"Mothers!" Charlene quickly said her goodbyes to Brandy, Sharon, and Kevin. "Mine has been left alone in my house for far too long." She'd probably reorganized her spices alphabetically or, worse, by size. "If I don't see you all before Christmas, have a wonderful holiday, okay?"

She looked for Jessica to tell her goodbye, but the girl was gone. Charlene walked the few blocks to where her Pilot was parked, got inside, and placed a call to Sam.

Chapter Nine

Charlene sat in her parked Pilot, her thumb hovering over Sam's name in her contacts list. She didn't have time to click on it to call him before her own cell phone rang. His name flashed on her screen. "Sam. Just the man I was about to call."

"Nice to hear. Officer Horitz told me you'd come by yesterday and helped pin down the speed of the vehicle that hit David. I know you're busy, with your parents and all, so thank you."

"I was glad to help—it's the first time you've ever actually wanted it, do you realize that?"

"Charlene . . ." he warned. "How are *you* doing?"

She went along with the subject change. "Surviving. Do mothers get worse over time, or do daughters get pickier?"

"Not sure how I should answer that, so I plead the Fifth." His chuckle made her smile.

"You'll never guess where I am, or where I'm leaving, since I'm actually in the car ready to head home." She talked to Sam via Bluetooth, hands free, as she started the car and drove toward her house.

"Don't keep me in suspense—I hate guessing games."

"At the remembrance ceremony for David Baldwin at Unity Church on Fourth. It was a zoo."

"Dare I ask?" His deep voice rumbled through her speakers. She loved listening to him talk—when he wasn't angry with her. She better tread carefully or he would be soon.

"If you don't, then I won't tell you and you're gonna want to hear this."

He sighed. "Okay. Shoot."

"Where do I start?" Just the facts. "Jessica told me that one of the chefs at Bella's is friends with Kyle and before the night of the auction, Kyle said that he wished his old man was dead. Now, before you take that as a confession, Jessica also said that Kyle wouldn't hurt a fly." She decided not to share the "gossip" in Salem about her and Sam being *friends*. "But!" Charlene paused for dramatic effect. "Did you know that most hit-and-run drivers are young men, usually under the influence?"

"And where did you hear that?"

"On the radio."

Sam inhaled loudly, then exhaled, and she imagined him at his desk, smoothing his mustache as he liked to do when he was searching for patience. "I've had Kyle in for questioning. He says he didn't drink that night—did you see him drink?"

She thought back—he'd wolfed a plate of spaghetti and had a glass of water. "Uh, no. Isn't he underage?"

"Since when has that stopped a determined teen? He says he went right home from the restaurant, and his mom corroborates that—but moms are protective, so he's not off my list just yet."

Charlene recalled how Linda had stepped between Freddy and her son, unafraid of the taller man whom she'd viewed as a threat. It was possible.

"That segues into this next incident, actually. David had invited an old friend from his past, Freddy something, who he knew in his college football days, to come to dinner that night, but Freddy said he couldn't make it. Remember how strange David was, yelling someone's name, running out of the restaurant? The name he said was Freddy—what if Freddy showed up but didn't come in? And Doug. I told you that, right?"

"Yes, it's in my notes."

"David's ex-wife, Linda, dislikes Freddy intensely. She made a bit of a scene when Vincent introduced him, not wanting him near Kyle."

"*Where* were you?"

"At the reception hall across from the church," she explained. "Tori was reigning supreme for a while, until things got out of hand."

"Freddy *Ferguson* is probably who you are talking about—and I've already checked him out. Tori tossed his name in when I was questioning her about that night. He said he wasn't there."

Rather than turn right on Crown Point, Charlene took a left, toward Bella's. "And?"

"He did time in jail for vehicular manslaughter after drinking and driving in college. He's been clean for the last twenty years as far as I can tell. But thanks for the heads-up."

Manslaughter meant someone had died. She didn't like Sam's smug tone, so she spoke up. "His driving record might be clean, but the man certainly wasn't sober. I was standing next to Linda and smelled beer on his breath."

"Good to know. Anything else of interest?" the detective asked.

"Well, two ladies from Felicity House got into a scrape with Tori, demanding that she make good on their check. One of them tried to relieve Tori of her huge diamond ring she wore, over her velvet glove." Charlene stopped at a four-way intersection and checked for traffic before continuing. "At one point it looked like Pamela was trying to tear it off—poor Alice was in tears, saying Tori had no heart."

"Sounds like a lot of drama to me," Sam drawled.

"It was! Zane had to physically remove Pamela from the doorway—she was trying to hold them hostage. Brandy Flint joked that she'd bring refreshments to the Christmas Eve service."

"How was the widow?"

"Fine. Sam, I know that the car was going no more than thirty-five miles an hour, which makes the accident seem . . . not so accidental. Whoever hit him had to have known they'd done it and deliberately left the scene." It wasn't a stretch to consider who might have wanted David dead.

He sucked in a breath. "I'll have a word with Officer Horitz."

"He didn't tell me anything that I couldn't figure out on my own." If she'd Googled it. "And I helped."

"I don't want you involved more than what you already are."

Charlene squeezed the steering wheel in frustration. "I was with Tori that night, and her grief seemed genuine. I don't feel like Tori wanted David dead."

"Thank you for sharing, but police work is more than feelings."

Charlene had heard that old line more than once. "Well, did you know that she and David had planned on doing a disappearing act? Their lawyer had suggested going into seclusion until the hoopla around the lottery died down."

She heard Sam tap something, and pictured him sitting at his desk, reading his notes. "Jessica mentioned that. Good kid."

Charlene adjusted the temperature on the dash to keep warm as she drove to Bella's. "I confirmed that Tori was having an affair with Zane Villander, from her gym."

"Hmm. She's being tight-lipped about that. So?"

"Today she'd dressed her lover up as a bodyguard, to protect her against all of the angry people she'd disappointed by blocking their checks. If I was her, I would have stayed home and missed the service."

"She'd have looked guilty," Sam said.

"That's what Sharon Turnberry thought too!" She drove past Bella's on the road where David had died, but the cones had been removed, and traffic was back to normal. Forensics must have come to their conclusions, but of course she couldn't ask *Detective* Sam anything. Thank goodness Officer Horitz hadn't been so tight-lipped.

"Sam, did anybody come forward about driving on Duval and Crown that night?" She couldn't imagine how tedious it would be, looking at grainy video on that intersection.

"We've got it whittled down to half of the vehicles identified—but that doesn't mean we'll find the right car. They could have taken the back road. Police work is a process of elimination."

"I know you don't want to hear what I think, but my opinion, low as it may be, is that Zane has the most to gain by David's death. He wouldn't like to see his lady love and her millionaire husband riding off into the sunset."

Sam burst out laughing. "What an image! You continue to amaze—and enchant me. Go home, Charlene, and drive carefully. We're supposed to get about four inches of snow later today. Say hello to your parents and enjoy them while they're here. A few days from now they'll be gone, and I bet you'll miss them."

That didn't sound like a smart bet to her. "I'm on my way. I sure hope to see you for Christmas Eve."

"Only thing keeping me away would be a crime or two."

"Well, if my mother keeps criticizing every little thing, I might have another one for you." Before he could get the last word in, she said, "Bye, Sam," and hung up with a smile.

She really didn't want to go home. Charlene drummed her thumb along the steering wheel and parked at Bella's. She got out and studied the place where she'd seen David's glasses on the road. The 3D program the police department used made deduction a science.

Charlene returned to her car. Kyle had wanted to talk to David—about what? Had he come back that night, maybe in someone else's vehicle?

She had Linda Farris's address, where Kyle still lived with his mother. How long would it take to get there? He'd worked that night and then come to the restaurant, right at ten. Had food, left in a huff by ten thirty. David had been hit at ten forty-five.

She dug through her purse and found the note from Jessica, then plugged the address into her GPS.

With traffic, she should arrive in twenty-three minutes. Charlene put her Pilot in gear and followed the directions. Twenty-two minutes later, she pulled up in front of a brick ranch house on the opposite side of town, the GPS announcing that she'd arrived at her destination.

It was an older neighborhood that hadn't seen the benefit of gentrification yet, like the area where Jack's practice had been located when he'd been alive.

Not poverty stricken—that was a few miles west—but worn. Salem celebrated their history and antiques, their ties to the past, but this poor neighborhood just seemed tired. Overgrown oak trees, bare of their leaves, lined the uneven sidewalks of a road hardly wide enough for two lanes of traffic to pass, and yet, cars were parked along the street, the wheels half on the curb.

Two vehicles passing each other would be a tight fit. Charlene wedged onto an open curb.

Kyle's motorcycle was parked horizontally on the driveway, leaving enough room for a small car, though there wasn't one yet. Was Linda still at the reception? Had Kyle ridden with her to the church?

Linda's house and garage had the look of 1950s construction and took up all the space of her lot. A narrow strip of grass was the only thing separating her from her neighbors on either side. The front yard was not fenced, the lawn the brown grass of winter.

The front picture window's beige curtains had been drawn back to reveal a Christmas tree, unplugged, which probably meant that nobody was home.

A pink nose appeared at the window, followed by a canine face—an indeterminate mix of fur with a wagging tail and robust bark.

Charlene searched her rearview to make sure nobody was around. She didn't want Kyle to be guilty and didn't think he was, but that didn't make it the truth. What would she say if Linda answered the door? She'd already given her condolences. Charlene decided to leave a message on the screen door, asking Linda to call her—she could simply offer her sympathies, maybe let her know that David had promised Kyle a special card, and during that conversation, find out about Kyle.

Taking her business card from her wallet, she scrawled the note and got out of her car. The dog's barks picked up speed but didn't seem vicious—just friendly.

She opened the screen door, which squeaked loudly, and winced—then stifled a scream when the front door opened.

Kyle stood there in jeans and a bulky sweatshirt—he had obviously driven himself to the service and had returned home. "What are you doing here?"

Charlene slowed her frantically beating heart and waved her business card. "I was hoping to talk with your mom," she said.

"About?"

She was left scrambling. Could she get him to talk? "I saw your motorcycle down at the police station the other day. . . ."

"And I saw *you* gossiping with Jessica."

Busted. Now what? "Jessica was very upset about your

dad's death, as am I." She leaned against the open screen door. The dog, a medium-size mutt, stuck his nose between Kyle's legs to sniff Charlene's pants.

Kyle scowled and she could tell that he was warring with his good manners and his desire to slam the door in her face. "Jessica's cool."

"Yeah—bringing you pasta from the kitchen. You'd said that you just wanted to talk to your dad?"

"It don't matter now." Kyle patted the dog's head. "Dad's dead." He quickly blinked and made to shut the door.

"Wait—I heard about what you said to Dalton?"

He straightened and glared at her. "I didn't run my dad over. Geez. What kind of jerk do you think I am? We didn't get along, but I wouldn't have done anything to hurt my dad."

"I believe you." Charlene *did* believe him, having just timed his route. "Your dad winning the lottery must have been exciting."

"I only saw him a couple times since his win. He bought me some new clothes. An Apple computer. Nothing major. I sorta thought . . ."

She couldn't stop herself from touching his arm in sympathy. "I heard him say he was going to send you a special card?"

"I didn't get it." His eyes welled. "Now, I won't ever know what he wanted to tell me. It's too late."

She liked that Kyle was more about the message than the money. Taking another stab in the dark, she asked, "Is Vincent your stepdad?"

Kyle rocked back. "No, Mom's boyfriend. That would be awful if they got married—he already pokes into my life." It seemed that once he'd decided to share, he was on a roll. "He had no business listening in to my conversation with Dalton and then making a big deal about it. Jessica used to hang out once in a while, but now she probably thinks I'm a loser—*he's* the loser."

"I'm sorry to bring it up." She also gave the dog's ears a scratch. "Your mom seems nice, though."

"Yeah, Dad really screwed her over, leaving her for Tori and then winning the damn lottery." He smacked his hand against the door and the dog barked, darting into the shadows of the house before returning. "Hey, sorry to be rude, but . . ." Kyle trailed off, since she had no reason to be at the house.

"No—thanks for talking with me. I really liked your dad. He was kind to me every time I came to the restaurant, and to the kids at Felicity House. He cared. And I could see that he cared about you too."

Kyle shuffled his sneakered feet and she noticed the hint of red peeking beneath the sweatshirt—was that the jersey from Freddy? "Thanks. Want me to give my mom your card?"

Charlene had no choice but to follow through, so she handed it over and wished him a Merry Christmas.

She got back into her Pilot, going over what she'd learned. On impulse, she went through a drive-through coffee shop and ordered a box of coffee and pastries for the station. She'd surprise Sam with an afternoon treat for him and his team as a way to smooth things over from their earlier conversation. Why couldn't he see that she could help him?

Parking in front of the station, Charlene got out and balanced her purse and the goodies, entering the front door with a smile for the woman at the receptionist desk. "Hi! I don't think we've met before, but I'm Charlene

Morris. Is Sam in?" She shook her head. "Detective Holden, sorry."

"I'm Danya," the young woman said. "This is only my first day. Let me buzz him."

Charlene stepped back, the coffee scent filling the small lobby. She set the box of pastries on the seat at her left. Within moments, she heard the muffled tread of Sam's boots on the runner of the hall.

"Charlene?" He came into view with a broad smile visible beneath his groomed sable mustache. "What a surprise!"

"I brought goodies for your break room," she said, gesturing to the box and lifting coffee in her right hand. "'Tis the season."

Sam peeked into the pastry box and then picked it up. "That cranberry scone has my name on it."

"You deserve first pick." Charlene followed him into a break room the size of two offices, with a sink, stove, fridge, and microwave. Lockers lined one wall, and a long counter took the other. Five chatting officers ate their lunch at a huge table in the center. Two others had their eyes glued to the TV, watching a college game.

She recognized two of them, but they were discussing something quite animatedly and she didn't want to interrupt. No sign of Officer Horitz, and she hoped he hadn't gotten reprimanded.

"Pastries. Fresh coffee. Merry Christmas from Charlene Morris," Sam said, then snagged his scone and wrapped it in a napkin to take back to his desk.

A chorus of thank-yous sounded from the officers before they returned to what they were doing.

"Want one?" Sam asked.

"No, thanks." She stayed at his heels down the hall and they went into his office.

He sat at his desk, and she took her customary chair.

"So, what brings you by that required a bribe?"

She burst out laughing. "I thought I was being so sly!"

He steepled his hands. "Out with it—I'm in a good mood."

She quickly told him about the timing of driving from Bella's to the Farris home, and how long Kyle had been there. "He wasn't drinking. And his mother said he was home at eleven. So, he can be crossed off your list in pen. He didn't do it."

Sam blew out a breath, ruffling his mustache. "I'll take that into consideration. You timed it?" He chuckled. "I am not encouraging you by any means, but I like your logic. I have my reasons for him remaining a person of interest that I can't share with you."

Charlene sighed. "In that case, I'll get going—did you know that Vincent is Linda's boyfriend?"

"Nothing wrong with that. It's been three years since the divorce. People move on in their lives. It's healthy." He pinned her with his gaze. "What are you doing tonight?"

She knew exactly what he was referring to—her healing from Jared's death and being ready to date again. She quickly got up from her chair and shouldered her purse. "Working, Sam. Enjoy your scone."

Chapter Ten

The sky had darkened considerably in the twenty minutes she'd been with Sam, and Charlene wouldn't have been surprised if it had started to snow when she drove home. The air had that certain bite to it, but she was disappointed.

Charlene opened the door and was greeted by the sound of voices singing Christmas carols. She paused in the threshold of the living room. Emily, with her hair pulled back in a high ponytail and green ribbon, stood next to her dad, and sweet Maddie was on the other side. Was that her mother, smiling and singing, hands clapping along with the little girls?

Silva, the traitor, was curled up on her father's lap. The cat lifted her head when Charlene walked in, then snuggled under his arm. Dismissing her.

Charlene felt a twinge of loss at not having Jared beside her to enjoy this Hallmark-esque scene.

Her mother caught her eyes and Charlene gave her a thumbs-up, but not wanting to interrupt, she turned away and headed for her suite of rooms to mourn her husband privately. Jack was waiting for her. He turned when he heard her enter, with a welcoming smile on his face. His blue eyes locked on hers, seeing everything at once.

"You had a bad day?"

"Yes." She tilted her head. "Is it that obvious?"

Charlene sat on the love seat, he in the armchair. She turned the TV on low in case her mother came in.

"Tell me about it?" His blue eyes rested on her, giving her strength to shake off her emotional exhaustion.

She entertained him about the Felicity House ladies and the fight for the ring over the punch bowl. "It was appalling, it really was," she said with a laugh. "But it's deplorable that Tori wants to keep it all to herself and not honor her husband's wishes. It's a worthy charity, Jack!"

"Sounds like she'll be donating to her boyfriend and her jewelry box."

Charlene agreed. "I swear Zane was wearing a new Rolex. The kids get nothing, and he's wearing an expensive watch. It's just not right."

"You'd think she'd be more discreet." Jack's image was solid tonight, which meant he was focused and strong, almost—but not quite—real.

"She doesn't seem to care what others think. She flaunts it and makes a spectacle of herself."

He cupped his hands over the armrests. "I imagine the charity could get a decent lawyer and try to sue the estate, but with her money Tori would hire an entire legal team, so what's the point?"

"You're right, Jack. I don't have a hundred thousand to give them, but I'd like to do something. Even if it's as simple as making sure each child gets a new present this Christmas."

"You'd have made a wonderful mother, Charlene. I'm sorry you didn't get the chance."

"Me too." She rubbed her chest and blinked back tears.

Jack's compassionate gaze offered solace, the only way he could. "You get to fill this house up with families and hear children's laughter and their little feet running up and down the stairs."

Her heart warmed at that. "Neither of us are alone anymore." Was it any wonder she was torn between Jack and Sam?

"Avery will start in the morning—I hope that she'll work out. Just four hours a day for now—we'll set up a schedule for the rest of the year if we all get along."

"Good idea."

They both turned to the television as the news gave the number for the hit-and-run hotline. "It's just so sad, Jack. I am sure that David knew whoever ran him over."

"The police will find the driver." He levitated the remote control to make her smile. "Oh, by the way, your mother was busy organizing your spices this afternoon. You sure you don't want me to levitate her bed?"

"I knew it!" She laughed, imagining her mother waking up in mid-air. "No, there's only five more days until Christmas. I can deal with her for a while more, and so can you."

"Will you go to the service on Christmas Eve for David?" Jack asked.

"No—I'll be right here, with my family and guests." She got up to leave. This was only her second Christmas without Jared. Would the ache ever get easier to bear? "That said, I've been out most of the day. I'd better go see what they're getting into."

"I miss our wine nights," Jack said, shimmering and handsome as he also rose to his full six feet plus. "When I can tease you out of your blue moods."

"I miss that too." Hopefully things would calm down a little once her parents returned to Chicago—and when Sam caught David's killer. She'd had enough of death for a while.

Charlene passed through the kitchen, seeing the note from Minnie on the corkboard. The pork loin just needed to be warmed in the oven, her housekeeper said, adding a smiley face.

Charlene peered into the fridge with a chuckle. Minnie would never let them go hungry. There were still leftover potatoes from the mountain her mother had made yesterday. She turned on the oven to preheat and set the pan on the counter.

When she returned to the living room, she asked Andy and Teresa if they'd like to stay in and have dinner.

Andy glanced at Teresa. "We figured Bambolina's for pizza; it's got great reviews on TripAdvisor."

"We were out most of the day, hon." She looked at her daughters and then Charlene. "We took the kids to Plymouth Rock and as much as we enjoyed it, it was a tiring trip. I wouldn't mind staying in tonight. How about you, kids? Pizza out, or 'Charlene's' in?"

"I'm tired, Mommy," little Maddie said, rubbing her eyes.

"Me too." Emily yawned. "I'm not very hungry."

"Well, that's settled," Andy said. "If you really don't mind, you have guests for dinner. Please don't go to any extra trouble. We had a big lunch."

"No problem at all. I think I even saw a loaf of sourdough bread. Does half an hour sound good to you all?"

"It's perfect," Teresa said.

"Can I help you, dear?" her mother asked.

"That would be nice, Mom. Thanks."

After dinner, the Garcia family turned in early, and Charlene sat in the living room with her parents. She shared her day, and they laughed about the fight over the ring and the punch bowl, although they all knew it wasn't amusing.

"When will you see Sam again?" her mom asked.

"I never know, Mom. He works all hours, but I'm sure he'll tell us when he finds out who ran over David. I hope it's resolved before Christmas Eve so he can be with us."

She would like to have him here. It was better for her sanity than spending too much time keeping her resident ghost company.

The following morning, Charlene peeked out the window. Snow! It had snowed during the night. Fluffy white snow covered the earth like a heavy layer of whipped cream. Mounds and mounds of it.

Maybe the Garcia girls could make a snowman. What fun! She'd love to join them, but unfortunately, she had too much to do.

Her dreams last night had rehashed the awful service, and when she'd woken up, the director's anger at Tori, along with her heartfelt plea for the children, stayed with Charlene. She'd promised to help Felicity House with a long-term goal in mind, and she intended to keep that promise.

It was only six a.m. and the house was quiet, so she dressed in her sweats and went into her sitting room. She opened her laptop and sat at the desk. It didn't take her long to find a treasure of information on Felicity House. The website had numerous pictures of holiday parties in the past. Alice and Pamela were a little younger then, more optimistic looking. In one photo they wore matching smiles, their hands entwined, lifted in victory at reaching a goal in their fund-raiser. Alice had never married, while Pamela had a husband of twenty years and two children.

How hard would it be to begin a campaign? Within minutes she'd created a GoFundMe page for Felicity House on the bed-and-breakfast website, just to get things started. She sat back in her chair, her mind filtering information.

She'd been blessed with a wonderful marriage and knew that happiness mattered most. But happiness came with trust, loyalty, kindness, and also forgiveness. David hadn't had that with Tori, which made her wonder about his relationship with Linda—had he given up something solid for Tori's youth and flash?

Linda hadn't remarried. Her job as a nurse meant she could take care of herself and Kyle, but it wasn't opulent. Why hadn't David kept up his alimony checks to make his ex-wife's life easier? He'd seemed like a kind man, and Jessica thought well of him, but he hadn't been a good father or fair to his ex. Neither of them had a kind word, which was even more sad because now there would be no forgiveness.

Suddenly a dazzling Jack appeared with a mesmerizing blue light, brushing imaginary snowflakes from his thick sweater and shaking his hair as if it had snow in it—which it didn't. His illusion could only go so far.

Grinning, she turned up the volume on her TV. "Wow! Have you been playing in the snow?"

"I did! Isn't it awesome?" His cheeks glowed. "It's a Christmas wonderland, Charlene, you should see it. What are you doing?"

"Doing a little work for Felicity House. We have Avery coming today—I'm going to pick her up at nine thirty. Since I offered to drum up donations, I started a GoFundMe page for them."

"I wish I could help." Jack gave himself a last shake.

"Me too—I'd put you to work on the phones." She tied the belt on her cardigan sweater. "When I have time to make the calls it's either too early, and businesses aren't open yet, or too late in the evening. Christmas is only four days away."

"I know how you love your lists. What have you got so far?"

It was nice that he knew her so well. She picked up her ivory tablet of paper and her black pen. "These are the places I've called already, but I'm not having very good luck." She'd pulled up Salem businesses in the online directory and started at *A*, working down to *C*. "Most places have already given for the year, but I have two solid leads for next year's budget."

She flipped the tablet to the next page and accidentally dropped it to the floor. Jack floated it up to her and she laughed, then stopped when she realized it had fallen open to her doodles on David's friends. Or not friends. Enemies?

"What are you thinking in that beautiful mind?"

"Living in Salem has turned me into a suspicious person, Jack."

He materialized behind her desk chair and read her notes. "Ah. Does that say Zane?"

She nodded. "He had the most to lose by Tori going off with David. Not only his lover, but now that she's wealthy, her money."

"You've crossed out Kyle's name."

"He couldn't have driven all the way home, which according to Linda, he did, and killed David, who was hit at quarter to eleven. The timing isn't right."

"Unless they were both in on it."

She tapped her black pen against her lower lip. "I would love to talk to Linda about her and Vincent. He has a temper, I've seen it. Kyle doesn't like him and neither does Jessica."

Jack considered this. "How long have she and Vincent been together? I remember you saying that Bella's has been in business about five years. Though business partners, I imagine he and David started out as friends."

Charlene thought back. "David would have been married to Linda when Bella's opened. Then Tori comes along, and wham. End of marriage. If Linda doesn't call me today, then I'll call her—she had plenty of reason to be angry with David." She wondered if Linda had been home all night herself.

"I agree." Jack took another peek at her list. "Vincent? Maybe David didn't like his ex-wife and his business partner being together?"

"David left Linda for Tori—he shouldn't get a say." Charlene arched her brow at Jack.

"There is no explaining human emotion." He ruffled

her hair with a cold burst of energy and she squealed. "I'm not arguing, by the way."

"I'd like to know where Vincent went that night after leaving Bella's. I'm going to stop by the restaurant to ask Vincent to donate just a little bit more for Felicity House and see what I can find out." She traced her finger down the list. "Jessica said Vincent thought that David should have gifted him the restaurant since he'd just won ten million."

Jack paced behind her love seat. "Sounds like bad blood there, and maybe not just about Linda."

"You're right." She recalled Vincent's reaction to the envelope he'd received. "Whatever he expected to get from David to end their business relationship didn't happen. But David was adamant that it was plenty." There were just so many unanswered questions. "Like Freddy Ferguson."

"What?" Jack leaned against the love seat. "I don't follow."

"Sorry." For all his supernatural ability, Jack wasn't actually a mind reader. "Freddy said that David invited him to dinner, but that something came up—yet he was so emotional about not getting the chance to speak with David that I don't believe Freddy would have missed the dinner date." The more she thought about it, the more she believed that David had seen him—or someone—and ran outside.

A knock sounded on her door and Jack vanished as the handle twisted. "Hey, hon," her dad called. "You up?"

She closed her laptop and answered the door. "Morning, Dad!" Charlene brushed by him to the kitchen. "I was just watching the news."

"They still haven't caught whoever ran over that guy," her dad said. "Damn shame."

"I know, right?" She filled the coffeemaker to the twelve-cup level and turned it on to brew. "This will just take a sec. Did you sleep okay?"

"That mattress is like sleeping on a cloud. Your mom's in the shower, but she'll be right down. How about you?"

Charlene didn't share her jumbled dreams. "Just fine." She pulled sliced fruit from the fridge and set the platter, along with Minnie's leftover muffins and loaves, on the counter for her guests.

The coffee finished with a beep, and her dad helped himself to two cups. "I'll just bring this up to your mom," he told her.

How thoughtful. Like happiness, it was a key component to a good marriage.

When he returned, she joined him at the kitchen table to enjoy their coffee and talk. Having her dad to herself for a few moments was a rare treat, and she wanted to ask him about matters of the heart. "Dad, I think it's great how long you and Mom have been together."

"Over fifty years."

She broke off a piece of banana loaf. "I want to ask you something. It's personal, and I hope my question doesn't offend you."

"What is it, Charlene? You can ask me anything." He placed his mug on the table, brown eyes full of concern.

Her stomach jumped and she glanced around to make sure they were alone. She shouldn't ask, but she needed to know. They'd been married so long, but all they did was argue. "Dad"—she put a hand over his and lowered her voice—"are you truly happy with Mom?"

"Of course!" The lines around his mouth crinkled in a smile. "She isn't easy at times, but I wouldn't trade her for the world. She loves me back just as much. We might tease and snipe at each other, but we mean no harm."

"I'm glad, Dad. I just thought . . ." She'd feared he'd been trapped in misery.

"I'm happy, Charlene. Especially now that I've seen how well you're doing here. You're healing and this is just what you needed. I won't worry . . . so much."

"You don't have to worry about me at all. I just don't want either of you to be miserable."

"What are you talking about, child?" Her mom clomped into the kitchen in plaid slippers with thick soles. "Your dad's made me miserable for years, but I just ignore it and go on my happy way. Don't I, dear?" She refilled her coffee, topped off her dad's and Charlene's, then fixed a plate of food for herself before she joined them. "If you started dating that hunky detective, you might be married this time next year. He's a charmer, isn't he?"

"I'm not ready to start dating yet, Mom. Maybe in the summer." Her shoulders hiked at the pressure her mother applied.

"Time is not on your side, my dear girl. You're getting older every day."

"Most people do, Mom." But it wasn't a certainty, she knew that. "The lucky ones at least."

Her dad's eyes twinkled over his mug.

The Garcia family traipsed downstairs and the conversation thankfully ended. Charlene helped serve them and finished another cup of coffee. When breakfast was done, she put away the fruit and loaded the dishwasher. Ten after nine. "It's time to pick up Avery."

"I'd love to see Felicity House for myself." Brenda glanced at her husband. "You coming or staying?"

He peered at his wife, smiled slyly, and winked at Charlene. "I've had enough of your yakking. Think I'll sit next to the fire and read a good book. Keep Silva company, she's nicer than you."

"My claws are not as sharp, nor are my teeth." Walking past her husband, she dropped a kiss on his balding head. "I'll get into something warm."

"Boots, Mom!" Charlene called after her, and her mother paused by the butler's pantry. "Did you see the snow? They said on the news this morning that we had six inches! Isn't that wonderful?"

"Not if you're shoveling it," her dad remarked.

"Nope, Will, Minnie's husband, will do that. I'll give him a call and see when he can come over."

"We haven't met this Will yet." Her mom headed for the steps. "If he's as handy as you say, I might get him to replace your dad."

Her dad snorted. "That'll be the day."

Her mother laughed and plodded upstairs. Charlene smiled, too, accepting that their bickering was disguised affection.

Two minutes later, the Garcia children flew down the stairs, gloved hands on the golden oak bannister. The girls were both dressed in pink snow suits, boots, gloves, and wool caps. "We're going outside. Dad's coming later," Emily said.

"I'm so 'cited." Maddie grinned. "We're going to build a snowman!"

"You want to help?" Emily asked Charlene.

"I wish I could, but I have some errands to run this morning."

"Oh, okay." She gave Charlene a crestfallen expression, complete with pouty lip. "Do you have anything for a snowman? Like a carrot or buttons or something?"

"Sure!" Where was that box of buttons she kept?

"I've got a scarf you can use," her dad said, getting to his feet.

"We have a bag of carrots in the pantry." Charlene thought the box might be in her emergency sewing kit. She had one, even though she didn't sew. "I'll get some buttons for the eyes. Dad, what can we use for the mouth?"

"I know," Maddie said. "We can use Mom's lipstick."

"You can't use lipstick on snow, Maddie." Emily rolled her eyes.

"Yes, you can." Maddie folded her arms in front of her. "Can't we, Charlene?"

"Let me see what I can find. Don't go past the yard, okay?"

"We wouldn't do that," Emily said. "We'd be in *big* trouble."

"Yes, you would," Andy said, trekking down the stairs. "Here, use this ball cap for a hat. Smoking is bad for you, so no pipe." He smiled at Charlene and her father. "Good morning! Teresa's making arrangements for a sleigh ride."

Michael rocked back on his heels. "I remember when Charlene used to get so excited about snow days, but now my girl's all grown up." He sauntered toward the living room and rubbed his hands together. "Looks like I'm going to have the place to myself."

The girls headed for the door. "Come help us, Daddy. We're going to make the biggest snowman!" Maddie jumped up and down, her cheeks flushed. "And we'll make angels too. Which should we do first?"

"Make an angel," Andy suggested. "I'll grab a cup of

coffee and be right out. Maybe we can get your mom to give us a hand too."

"That'll be a frosty Friday," Teresa said from the center of the staircase. Dressed for warmth in jeans, boots, and a red wool pullover sweater, she added, "No angels until later. We have a sleigh ride booked for eleven this morning, so I don't want you getting soaked." They darted outside with squeals of protest.

Teresa and Andy walked into the kitchen, and Charlene followed to get her purse from the counter. Andy poured coffees for him and his wife, while Teresa asked, "What are you up to, Charlene?"

"I'm going to pick up my new part-time employee." Her phoned *dinged* a text, and she was reminded about the bonfire later. "Hey, today is Winter Solstice, and Salem will have a lot of celebrations downtown, and a fire on the beach tonight." She was still on the fence about going.

Her mom yelled from the foyer, "I'm ready, Charlene!"

"That's my cue!" She shook her head, grabbed her purse, keys, and coat, and ushered her mother out the door.

CHAPTER ELEVEN

Charlene loved the crisp smell of freshly fallen snow, which reminded her of sleigh rides in Chicago with her parents when she'd been a kid. She kicked a few inches off the top stair as she went down from her porch to her car.

"How far is Felicity House?" her mother asked, buckling into the side passenger seat of the Pilot. She'd pulled her white hair back with a red and green hair clip.

Since her mom was coming along, there was no chance of driving by Bella's to see if Vincent was there, on the pretext of fund-raising, but mostly to ask questions about David. Maybe later this afternoon . . . "Ten minutes."

"What do you know about this girl? I hope you told her not to wear that piercing in her nose."

"I didn't say anything about it, actually. Piercings are

very common these days. You have to get with the times, Mom."

"Good taste never goes out of style."

Charlene reversed out of her driveway, which Will had already shoveled—he must have been up at dawn. "Tastes are subjective. She's sixteen, you're in your seventies. Now, I want you to be nice, okay?"

Her mother huffed. "As if I wouldn't! What will they do without that money?"

She glanced at her mom. "When I went over there on Monday, you could see that they're overcrowded. They'd wanted to use that large chunk of cash to expand their building."

"Where are you at in asking for donations?"

"I haven't had much success." Charlene recapped what she'd done so far. "I'd like to hit up Archie at Vintage Treasures." The end of the alphabetical online directory. "It's where I spend my extra money—you'll love it there, and he's a character. If *I* ever won the lottery, Archie would likely get a big chunk of my winnings."

"Playing the lotto is a waste of time," her mom stated.

"If it gets big enough, I'll buy a ticket. Why not?" Charlene pumped her brakes in preparation for the stop sign at the bottom of the hill. The Pilot's tires crunched to a slow halt. The snow was steep in some places but not icy.

"There's something about having a lot of money that makes people a little crazy. Me, I don't want the trouble, so I never buy a ticket. Never have, never will. I don't want all the problems, people out to get me—or to actually *get killed* for a few million bucks? No sirree."

When you looked at it like that, she thought about curtailing her own sporadic buys. "Don't blame you, Mom,"

Charlene replied with a tolerant smile. "Whoever killed David deserves severe punishment, and I'm sure that Sam will see they get it."

"I like that Sam."

"So do I." Her fingers clenched the wheel. "A hit-and-run driver. It's close to home, Mom. I mean, what if Jared's killer had never been caught? There would be no closure for me. I'd never stop thinking about that person still driving around, still being a threat on the road."

"I understand. It gave me peace, too, knowing she's behind bars." Her mom shifted so she could look at Charlene without turning her head. "I figured Tori for it, but how could she, when she was inside? Now, I've changed my mind about the body builder too. Even if Tori promised that big lover of hers some money . . . Maybe Zane or Tori hired someone to do it. As a couple, they had the most to gain."

This subject hadn't been far from Charlene's thoughts. "How could they have? Neither of them knew David was going to hightail it out of the restaurant at that precise moment." Unless Zane had been in the parking lot, waiting?

"I hate not having answers," her mother said. "There has to be a clue left behind . . . there usually is."

"In your books, sure. Otherwise nobody would read them." Charlene lowered the heat in the car. "Statistics show that a hit-and-run accident is usually a *random* act of violence." But not always.

Her mom opened her purse and offered Charlene a peppermint candy, then had one herself.

Charlene unwrapped the candy at the stop. "Do you remember anything from that night?" She glanced at her mom as she drove through the intersection.

Her mom shook her head. "No, it all happened so fast."

She made the turn on the corner of the street for Felicity House as a Lexus SUV passed her on the left. Charlene's tires spun out a little before she regained traction.

"Careful, Charlene," her mom said, holding on to the side of the door.

"Relax, Mom. I'm used to this." Driving on snow didn't bother her after years of practice in Chicago.

Charlene stopped the car in the driveway of Felicity House. The old farmhouse/office was to the right, but the sign in the window said, CLOSED.

"That's odd," Charlene murmured. "Why would it be closed?"

"Were you supposed to pick her up here?" her mom asked.

"I thought so."

Charlene got out, heading toward the fence. On the opposite side, some giggling kids were playing in the snow, making an igloo. Perhaps Avery was with them?

A young man with a mustache and brown glasses, bundled up in a brown wool jacket, hurried over. "Can I help you?" he asked.

"I'm here to pick up Avery," Charlene said, and introduced herself. "That's my mother in the car." Brenda rolled down her window and gave a little wave.

A look of confusion settled on his face. "She's over at the teen house. Have you checked this out with Ms. Winters? The office doesn't open until ten."

"Yes, she knows—I've offered Avery a job at my bed-and-breakfast."

"Oh, nice. Let me give you the address—it's just a few blocks away."

"How many kids do you have here?" Charlene asked.

"Well, let's see. The ten and under group live here." He indicated the building with his gloved hand. "With twenty munchkins, we're running at full capacity. The tweens"—he shuddered with mock horror—"have their own house. Alice has another place for the teens." He considered her with interest. "Are you thinking of adopting?"

Charlene's mother made a snorting sound, and the young man glanced through Charlene's open window as if to make sure her mother was all right.

"No," Charlene answered quickly. "I'm here for Avery, and to help with fund-raising." Her cheeks stung from her mother's chortle.

"Well, it's a shame you missed Pamela, but she had an appointment." He pointed to the road where Charlene had passed the Lexus SUV. "She's in charge of all that."

"We talked on Monday—she had great ideas."

"Yeah, she works really hard." He gestured to the playground. "Felicity House wouldn't have all of this new play equipment without her, not to mention our new roof." He rubbed his hands together and stomped his feet, looking half-frozen.

A cute girl with braces lobbed a snowball at the young man and he laughed and shook off the snow. She couldn't stop herself from searching the children for Tamil—the girl was rolling a ball of snow and didn't see Charlene.

"Duty calls," he said. "Here's the address—you'll have to go in and sign Avery out. Thanks for helping Felicity House."

Charlene carefully drove past the happy kids and when they reached the street, she pulled into a drugstore parking lot, coasting to a space and turning off the engine.

"Why did you laugh when that man asked me if I wanted to adopt?" Hurt emanated within her. Her mother was cruel at times, but this was over the top.

Her mom's brows furrowed in confusion. "Being a mother is very hard work, Charlene. You don't have time for your own parents—how could you have time for a child?"

"That isn't fair." Her mouth tightened and she felt a pain in her chest.

Her mom lifted a finger. "You don't get holidays or sick time. Santa's coming? You have to pretend you don't have a hundred and three fever and smile through the pain."

Charlene thought back to past Christmases, wondering when that might have happened. She shook her head.

"That's right—you didn't know." Her mom self-righteously patted her chest. "Turned out to be pneumonia."

"When your friend Sheila came to stay for two weeks?"

"Yup."

Charlene turned the car back on. "Why didn't you say anything?"

"Why bother? When you have children, they become your life. It's not a hardship, because you love them, of course." Her mother sighed, her jaw clenched as she looked out the window and the blinking holiday lights around the store. "No matter how much you want to protect them from the world, they are independent—and moderately ungrateful. Don't call, don't write." Her mom peeked at Charlene to see how her diatribe was going.

Charlene's defenses rose. "That's unfair!"

"You're right! You spend your life nurturing that person and before you know it, they don't need you anymore."

Charlene's eyes stung. "That just means you did a good job. It doesn't mean I don't love you and Dad."

"Motherhood is the hardest, yet most rewarding job I've ever had. You broke my heart when you left after Jared died. I wanted you close, to help you. . . ."

Shoulders high, Charlene said, "And here comes the guilt."

Their breaths fogged the inside of the Pilot. Her mom bowed her head, her white hair falling forward. "I know what it's like to lose babies, Charlene. I cried with you each time, and it also broke my heart. You never should have given up."

Charlene felt her mouth open and shut in shock. "Given up?" When she thought of all that she and Jared had gone through, she wanted to scream.

"Maybe if you and Jared had . . ." her mom said in a trembling tone. "Well, you wouldn't be alone now."

Charlene somehow managed to put the car in gear, her emotions in limbo between disbelief and anger. "I can't believe you said that, Mom." Of all the things she'd forgiven over the years, she wasn't certain that this would be one of them.

"I am going to drop you off and return for Avery without you." Hopefully that would be enough time for her to cool off.

The ride back to the B and B was made in painful silence.

"I'll be home soon," Charlene said coolly, letting her mom off at the door. She noticed the snowman in the side yard, cap askew, but couldn't appreciate it right now. Later, maybe.

Her mom hesitated before opening the passenger side.

"You don't understand," she said. "I told you it was hard to be a mother."

Charlene bit her tongue to keep from saying words she would regret. "I don't want to talk about this again."

Her mom sniffed and slammed the door, slowly climbing the porch steps. She didn't look back as she entered the house.

Charlene reversed out of the driveway, promising herself one thing. She would never, ever turn into her mother.

Chapter Twelve

Charlene concentrated on the snowy drive to the teen center, pushing the hurt of her mother's words aside. The woman had zero filter, but she'd deal with that another time. Now, she wanted to meet Avery.

Slowing the Pilot to twenty miles an hour, Charlene admired the neighborhood. It was a quiet, tree-lined street, recently plowed with snowbanks on either side of the road. She spotted a few neighborhood children making snowmen or firing snowballs at each other, and it eased the tension across her shoulders.

Another half mile later the yellow house entered her line of sight—the two-story home was much nicer than she'd expected. The GPS announced her arrival.

She parked in the driveway and checked the clock on the dashboard, realizing she was ten minutes late, thanks to the fiasco with her mother. Not the best way to start.

She hoped Avery hadn't gotten the wrong idea. Charlene marched up to the door and knocked.

A woman well into her fifties, with short brown hair and a warm smile, opened the door. "You must be Charlene." She stuck her hand out and they shook. "I'm Janet. Come on in."

"Sorry to be late."

"The roads are slick—I told Avery not to worry. She's in her room. I'll let her know you're here."

Charlene followed Janet into the foyer, and instead of running up the stairs to get her, she used the intercom and punched in the room number. "Avery, Charlene's here."

There were some squeaking sounds coming from the intercom, but Charlene heard her reply. "I'll just be a sec."

The women shared a look. "Teenagers," Janet said.

"My fault for keeping her waiting."

"This is a very nice thing you're doing for her. It'll give her some spending money, and hopefully some self-esteem."

Alice Winters had told Charlene in confidence that Avery's mother was an addict and couldn't take care of her daughter. She'd handed her over to the authorities when Avery was nine. Her father had never been in the picture.

"I'm sure she's nervous." Charlene showed Janet her damp palms. "I am too. I want her to like our place and feel comfortable working with us. It's too big for just me and my housekeeper to do everything, and I could really use her part-time help." She glanced up the stairs. "Unfortunately, right now I have my mom and dad visiting for Christmas, one family booked for a week, and another couple arriving tomorrow. The guests are not a problem. It's my mother."

Janet ruffled her short brown hair. "Say no more. I have one of those too." She gave her a sympathetic smile. "You'd think at my age that my mother would stop offering advice. No! She doesn't understand my commitment to this place. Always telling me I'm going to get murdered in my sleep one day."

Charlene's jaw dropped at the realization that she and Janet really did have the same sort of mother. "What a terrible thing to say. Your kids here—they aren't dangerous, are they?"

"They come from broken homes. Some have lived on and off the streets and seen way too much violence in their short lifetimes. Yes, they have challenges and are troubled. But would they harm me? I should hope not." She lowered her voice. "I keep my door locked at night, but I'm always available by intercom."

Avery tripped down the stairs, long legs in tight jeans with both knees cut out and a heavy-knit brown sweater. No jacket. "Hey."

"Sorry to be late, Avery." Charlene lifted her hand. "It's not a regular thing, I promise."

"Oh, okay. No problem."

"I was getting acquainted with your House Mom."

"She's cool." Avery gave Janet a shoulder hug. "Hope you didn't tell her the truth about me," she said with a sassy grin.

"No, I didn't want to scare her off." Janet walked over to a desk in the corner of the foyer. "Charlene, I just need you to sign in, and again when you return Avery."

"Like preschool," Avery said.

Charlene filled in the details, thinking it did seem elementary, but if it kept the kids safe from parents with a restraining order, or other trouble, then she was glad to do it.

"I'll have her back on time, don't worry. It was a pleasure meeting you." Charlene glanced down the hallway, noticing the kitchen on the right, the living room on the left. Through the pane-glass door, she could make out a fireplace and a decorated Christmas tree. Homey, and a comfortable place for teens to hang out. The rooms she could see were painted a boring builder's beige, but Janet had added bright throw rugs and artwork that perked the place up. "This is very nice." She nudged Avery.

"Yeah, it beats the streets." Avery grabbed a black ski jacket from the hall closet and shrugged into it. "I hear you live in a mansion. What do you want me to do, polish the silver?"

Charlene laughed. "Well, I wouldn't call it that. It's my business as well as my home. But I do love it very much." She opened the front door. "Lucky for you, I have very little silver. A few serving plates that I haven't used in years. Too much of a bother, don't you think?"

"Well, in my parents' home, our maid only used silver. Silver teacups, silver plates, even silver water glasses." Avery quirked her pinky up, the nail painted black.

Charlene raised an eyebrow. "Well, I'm not that fancy, but I do have a cat named Silva. And guess what? She's silver."

Janet snickered as she waved from the doorway. "I can see you two are going to get along just fine."

Charlene waved back, thinking the same. Avery was witty and had spunk. She enjoyed those qualities in a person, so long as the banter didn't turn mean. Her stomach tightened as she thought of her mother. She climbed into the driver's seat, waiting until Avery was buckled in, and backed out of the driveway.

"Let me warn you about my mother," she told Avery

on the short drive home. "She can be extremely outspoken and not very tactful."

Avery shot her a glance. "You're worried she'll say something to piss me off?"

Charlene bit her lip. "It's more than likely."

"I'm sure I've seen and heard worse than anything your mom can say." She crossed her arms and stared out the window. "Do I have permission to beat her up if she gets on me?"

"No, you do not!" Charlene gave her a sharp look and noticed Avery's lips twitching. "You were kidding, right?"

"That depends . . ." Avery looked down at her knees and began picking at one of the holes.

"On what?"

"On your answer. Besides, I don't pick fights, but I do end them."

Charlene couldn't help but wonder what she was in for. "My parents will be leaving in a few days—you'll have to hold off until then."

Avery shrugged but made no verbal promise.

Ten minutes later, she passed the elegant black and ivory Charlene's Bed and Breakfast sign and pulled into the driveway. Avery whistled. "Holy Camoli! This *is* a mansion! You must be really rich or something."

Charlene wondered if she should hide her silver after all. "No, not by any stretch of the imagination. I got it cheap. Seems nobody wanted this monstrosity. Too much upkeep." Not to mention a resident ghost. Dear Jack. She hoped he would behave himself now that she was bringing home a new stray.

"You married? Divorced?"

"Widowed." She swallowed hard. "My husband died in a car accident almost two years ago."

"You miss him?"

"Very much, but it's getting easier every day." She parked and removed the keys.

Avery appraised the size of the house. "Well, I can see why this place keeps you busy. What exactly will I be doing?"

"Helping my housekeeper, Minnie. Changing sheets, mopping floors, dusting. It's never ending, and I know she'll appreciate an extra pair of hands."

"Sounds like it. Glad I'm only working four hours."

They got out of the car, and Charlene led the way up to the porch to the front door. "Minnie's a sweetheart, you'll like her."

Jack was waiting for them inside. As Avery tentatively entered the foyer, he winked at Charlene and whispered in her ear, "Who's this? She looks frightened half to death, and I haven't even levitated the cat yet."

She shot him a warning glance. "Avery, Minnie's in the kitchen preparing lunch. I can smell something in the oven. Let's go see."

From the hallway, Charlene saw her mother put her knitting down on the coffee table and get up out of the chair next to the window. Her father asked, "Where are you going, Brenda?"

"I want a word with our daughter."

Charlene would drive her mother to the airport this minute if she dared to make a scene in front of Avery.

"Sit down, Brenda. Now is not the time."

Her mother glared at Charlene, who glared right back. She returned to her seat and resumed knitting.

Avery stood like a stone statue in the hallway, her eyes big as they took in the front of the house. Jack was right, she did seem scared. Could she see or sense Jack? "What's the matter?" Charlene asked in a low voice.

"I'm clumsy. And you have so many beautiful things. Maybe this job ain't for me." Avery twirled around. "Look at that pretty thing next to the doorway. If I polished it, you might find it in pieces."

"Accidents happen, but I'm sure you'll be careful. I wouldn't blame you or be angry. I'm not perfect either." Charlene heard a "humph" from the living room and ignored it.

Jack arched his brow in her mother's direction. "Just say the word, Charlene. I can make her bed shake like she's Dorothy on her way to Oz."

"Minnie," Charlene called out, and rushed down the hall to the kitchen. "Here's our new helper, Avery."

Minnie had been putting something in the oven and turned around with a smile on her plump face. "Welcome, Avery. I'm delighted that you've come to work with us."

Feeling a chill pass by in the air, Charlene noticed Jack had taken "his" seat at the kitchen table. She'd been so busy with her family and guests, and speaking to business owners for donations, that she hadn't had much "Jack time" lately.

Avery had her eyes downcast, looking shy with the housekeeper, but Minnie dispelled it quickly. "I just love the orange in your hair," she told her. "I've been blond, and red once, but this is my favorite and a lot less work." Minnie fluffed her gray strands.

"I like it," Avery said. "So, what exactly can I do?" She glanced around the narrow, long kitchen, trying to absorb everything at once. Her gaze skimmed right over Jack, thank heavens.

"Everyone has to start learning somewhere. Right

now, our guests, the Garcias, are out on a sleigh ride, so I need to go tidy their room. Charlene, would you like to help Avery, or want me to?" She put her hands on her plump hips. "I'm done here in the kitchen. Made a chicken pot pie for later, and we still have some beef barley soup left from yesterday."

"You are amazing as always, Minnie. Thank you." She patted Avery's shoulder. What she wanted most was the freedom to be herself without her mother's judgment. "I'll give Avery the grand tour. Minnie, why don't you take my car and show Mom and Dad . . . the harbor?" Anywhere but here.

"Certainly. They might enjoy a stroll while the sun's out. The weather report is calling for more snow later." Minnie washed her hands and left the kitchen.

"Would you like something before we start, Avery? Some water or tea? A slice of Minnie's delicious applesauce cake?"

"No, thank you. Maybe later." Avery jumped sideways and then looked down with a laugh. "Your cat. She was rubbing her head against my legs." She bent down to pet her. "Why, you are beautiful, aren't you? What's her name again?"

"Silva. She acts very regal and the name suits her."

Silva purred and arched her back, preening under the attention. Then, head in the air, she pranced off toward Jack, who was making kissing noises to her. Jack encouraged Silva to jump into his lap. The Persian did, then hissed because he wasn't there, and used her paw to scratch at Jack—all of which just seemed like the cat was pawing at the air to anyone else.

"What's she doing?" Avery asked.

"Persians are very high-strung—don't mind her." She

shot Jack a look, reminding him to behave himself, and bit back a smile. "Come on. Let the tour begin. We'll start from the top and work our way down."

"Great!"

Like an excited kid, Avery ran up the two flights of stairs, while Charlene took a more leisurely pace. "This place is amazing! Who did all this?" She pointed at the festive greenery and bows wrapped around the railings on both floors. "Sheesh, it's awesome, but that must have taken a lot of work."

"Minnie's husband, Will. He and his son put up all the outdoor lighting as well. I also had him help me with the tree in the living room. It's twelve feet high. I couldn't do it by myself."

"Wow. Everywhere I look there are more decorations." Her face lit up with excitement. "It's like being in a palace or something."

"Well, thank you. It's certainly not a palace, but it's very special to me." Charlene paused when they reached the third floor. "Here we have three single rooms that are unoccupied right now. Go see, and then I'll show you the widow's walk and one of the best views in Salem."

After peeking into the rooms, Avery returned, and they took the few remaining stairs up to the walk that led them to an outdoor balcony. The air was chilly, but the sights of the city and the glimpse of the sea were definitely worth it.

"Go ahead," Charlene said as she stroked the brass and leather of the telescope. "You'll be able to see the Peabody Museum and The House of the Seven Gables."

The girl stood up to the stand and peered out with her left eye, taking in everything as she rotated the telescope on its base. Her face was flushed with excitement, her eyes sparkling. "I can't believe that you invited me to work for you. This place is so freaking amazing. I could sit up here for hours."

Charlene laughed. "Well, that wouldn't get the work done, would it?" She linked her arm with Avery's. "But you're welcome to come up here if you like on your break."

"Really? That's awesome."

They headed inside. "Now, let's go freshen up the Garcias' room so they'll have it clean on their return."

Charlene instructed Avery on how to make the beds correctly, and collect the used towels and replace them with fresh ones from the upstairs linen closet. She showed her how to fold them, and to replace the toilet tissue if needed, and to tidy up the counter spaces, but not to remove anything. "They are paying guests, and they trust us, which shouldn't be taken lightly."

Avery's eyes narrowed and she blushed. "I get it, Charlene. I promise that you can trust me."

She had the feeling that Avery *could* be trusted, and that this conversation was all that they needed, not a rehashing of things in the girl's past.

"I do." Charlene had Avery run a cordless vacuum from the broom closet over the carpeted areas.

Avery worked quickly and seemed to enjoy her menial tasks. When everything was completed to Charlene's satisfaction, they moved back down to the first floor. She showed her where the pantry, downstairs bathroom, dining room, and living rooms were. To her surprise, Minnie was in the laundry room.

"Your dad insisted he could drive himself and promised to be back by quarter past one to return the car." Minnie looked at Avery. "Well?"

"I love everything," Avery said.

Charlene smiled at her energy. "Thanks, Minnie." She led Avery to the living room and the Christmas tree.

"This is the most amazing tree I've ever seen, except in the town square."

Charlene eyed the tree, her hands behind her back as she peered up to the top. "I doubt that you'll show the same enthusiasm for the tree and the decor when it's time to take it all down."

"Oh, I won't mind a bit." Avery glanced at the door at the end of the hall. "What's down there?" she asked.

"My suite of rooms. Want to see?"

"Sure."

Charlene showed her the small sitting area where she had her TV, sofa, and work space. "And this is my bedroom." She opened the door. Avery didn't enter but gave it a quick glimpse.

"Does that lead outside to the backyard?"

"Yes, I love it, come see." The big oak tree with the snow-covered wooden swing had been made for a summer day, which this was not. She swallowed a laugh as Jack appeared from behind the tree, in a black top hat like Frosty wore, with a snowman's corncob pipe in his mouth. He gave the swing the tiniest of pushes, daring Charlene to say something.

"This is like a fairy tale," Avery said in a wistful tone, not noticing the swing, or Jack. "Especially with the snow on the branches."

"It adds a magical layer, doesn't it?" Charlene turned her back on her playful ghost, checked the time, and groaned. "All right, Cinderella, let's get to work."

Chapter Thirteen

Charlene dropped Avery off at the teen house, with the promise to see her bright and early the next day. The teenager had given a hundred percent, whether when folding towels or sweeping the kitchen. Her mother hadn't dared make a single snide comment, and Jack seemed willing to give Avery a chance—but if one thing went into her pocket that shouldn't, he'd let Charlene know.

Avery didn't bad-talk about David, even though he'd let her go on her first night of work, and that said a lot to Charlene about the girl's character.

Charlene had received a text earlier from Linda—curt and to the point, asking why Charlene had shown up at her house. Charlene explained about collecting donations, but Linda hadn't texted back.

Her phone *dinged*. From Linda. **We have a lot of chil-**

dren on the wards that need presents—the hospital staff donates here.

Charlene made a note to self to return the text later. First, a stop at Bella's to see if Vincent was in his office, and if he would donate cash to Felicity House—while she slyly asked where he'd been that night. Then, she'd skip the online directory and hit up Archie at Vintage Treasures, and Kass, and Kevin . . . she'd even see if Sharon at Cod and Capers could dig a little deeper into her pocket. And how could she forget Brandy? Or Ernie, her real-estate agent? She was much better at this in person than cold calls.

Charlene entered busy Bella's, and Laura, who was usually a hostess when David wasn't at the podium, waited on tables too. The place was hopping due to holiday business. The city was crawling with tourists and would be until the first week of January when people had to return to their jobs.

She'd had a tuna sandwich and a cup of soup at home with Avery and Minnie, but still the Italian spices tempted her. Charlene waved to Jessica, who passed by with a full tray of lunch plates and couldn't wave back.

"Is Vincent here?" Charlene asked.

"Either in the kitchen yelling at Dalton or in his office," Jessica said in a low voice. "He's not in a good mood, so be warned."

Charlene made her way to the back of the restaurant, near the kitchen, and almost got smacked in the nose by a swinging door as a waiter hustled out with steaming platters. Shouts from the chef sounded, and the clamor of dishes.

Chaos.

Jessica whooshed by with her now-empty tray, pushing the kitchen door open with her palm. "Good thing you aren't eating—we have a forty-minute wait for food and Vincent is losing his mind. He's like one of those Sopranos on TV, always yelling at everyone—David managed people. I sure miss him." Jessica looked at the closed office door. "Did you knock?"

"I was gaining my courage." She needed to just do it—she'd be knocking on a lot of doors in the next few days.

"I would say his bark is worse than his bite, but these days? He just threw a sauce pan at Dalton. What a mess." Jessica disappeared into the kitchen, the door swinging shut behind her.

Charlene crossed the hall and was about to rap on Vincent's door, but paused to listen, in case someone was in there with him.

"She did what?" he asked in a loud voice. "Why would she come to your house? Does she suspect Kyle?"

She couldn't hear the reply, but her heart raced and her throat tightened. This wasn't good. Was he discussing her? It had to be Linda he was talking to. She lowered her hand.

"Why would she be sticking her nose into other people's business? Kind of new in town. Runs a B and B, that's all I know. What? Friendly with the cops? Well, you might want to get Kyle lawyered up." A pause. "No, I don't think he did it, but he had reason, that's for damn sure. Hell, so did I. David left me holding the bag here. The restaurant's falling apart. Now, I'm in business with Tori for Chrissakes."

Laura walked over with her arms crossed. "Do you want to speak with Vincent?" she asked pointedly.

Busted.

"Yes, thank you. I was about to knock, but it sounds like he's on the phone."

"Only one way to find out." She knocked firmly on the door and waited until Vincent opened it. "Charlene would like a word with you."

He ended his call without a goodbye. "Fine, fine, but make it short," he huffed, red in the face. "Come in. I haven't got all day."

"Thank you for seeing me. I understand that things have been hectic around here since David's death, but I thought I should just go ahead and ask anyway."

He drew back, defensive. "Ask me what?"

"I'm trying to help out Felicity House. Now that the checks are useless, a lot of children will be hurting this year. As a fellow business owner, I'm knocking on people's doors to ask if they'd kindly donate a little money or some new toys so that every child will get a gift or two. They have around forty kids, averaging from five to seventeen."

His mouth pursed and she could tell he was going to say no—at the least.

She rushed on. "I'm going to give a hundred, and I'm hoping that if everyone chips in, we'll have enough to give them all a nice Christmas."

Overhearing Vincent's conversation regarding Kyle made her think of where Kyle worked. She added another note to her long mental list—surely the Green Market would donate turkeys or something? Charlene would ask first thing. How could they say no to putting food in children's mouths? "If you could do more than a hundred, that would be appreciated."

Mrs. Morris and the Ghost of Christmas Past 161

He puffed out his chest. "More? It's a tough time for me right now. David's death left me in a bad way. He managed the place, but I footed the money." Vincent scowled. "I'm going through the books, and it doesn't look good. Somebody either had their hand in the till, or David mismanaged the cash. We're nearly bankrupt. No wonder he wanted to sell me his 'share' and get the hell out of Dodge. Probably afraid that my accountant would uncover his theft."

What? Charlene couldn't believe it and leaned against a hardwood chair. "David was taking money from the restaurant? That's quite an accusation. I thought he was an honorable man." She regretted saying so; it might not have been true.

"You calling me a liar now?" Vincent snarled.

"No, of course not."

"Honorable men don't cheat on their wives and ditch the kid. Did you know he only paid alimony for one year? Of course, you don't! Nobody does. But one year, then nothing—after she moved here from New York for him. Linda had to take him back to court to get his child support payments for a couple of years. Kid's nineteen now and those payments stopped the second Kyle had his eighteenth birthday."

Charlene hid her shock by looking down at Vincent's desk. It was a mess and stacked with receipts and file folders. There was a purple pamphlet tucked beneath a phone bill for Provenance Casino. She saw the commercials on television for the new and improved card room all of the time. The only time she'd ever gambled had been poker in Las Vegas on a company trip with Jared.

"That's really sad, David treating his wife and son like that. He seemed like a better man."

"Used to be. Back in the day. That's why I went into business with him. He was a hard worker, honest, or so I thought."

"Did you go to college with him and Freddy? The guy with the football jersey?"

"No, I met David after—never met Freddy until that sap showed up at the church. If what Linda said is true about their college days, then I highly doubt David would have wanted him around—or would have invited him here. Who knows, maybe he was the one who ran him down. Wouldn't put it past him."

"You think?" Charlene adjusted the strap of her purse on her shoulder. "He did seem a little shady, I'll admit. Did David ever talk about his college days to you?"

"Nah, he managed two restaurants for me in New York—did a great job and I was impressed. When this opportunity came up for Bella's, I gave him a chance."

She thought back—Kyle would have been in ninth grade—maybe eighth—and starting over with new kids and new schools. That might explain some of his troubled behavior. It wasn't easy as a young teen trying to fit in.

"Linda didn't mind moving here?"

"I told you, that woman is a damn saint. She found a nursing job pretty quick, and things were moving along—until he took up with Tori. Maybe that was the beginning of the end? David couldn't keep up with her demands. She always wanted more. Fancy things. Trips to Hawaii. Luxury cruises. David went broke trying to make her happy." He shook his head and spat out a piece of his cigar. "Guess that's what got him stealing from me. Damn shame, but gotta admit I'm not sorry he got what was coming."

Did anybody care that David was dead, other than Jessica?

"Thanks so much for talking to me, and I'm sorry I bothered you. Obviously, you have enough to worry about—we can forget about a donation this year." She turned to leave.

"Wait a sec. I might have something in my wallet." Vincent reached into his back pocket and pulled out a twenty-dollar bill, and a casino receipt fell to the floor. "There you are. Buy something nice for one of the kids."

"Thanks, Vincent. I'll do that."

"Oh, one more thing. I heard that you paid Linda a visit. Talked to Kyle. I'd consider it a favor if you'd leave them both alone. This is a hard time of the year to lose someone close to you. They might not think too highly of David, but he was her husband and Kyle's father—for better or for worse. If they'd hoped to gain anything from his lottery win, well, that hope died along with him."

She put her hand to her heart. "Certainly—although, maybe you could pass along the message—I know what she's going through, having lost a spouse myself. If she needs a friendly ear, I'd love to buy her a cup of coffee."

Vincent's jaw clenched and he looked at her as if he figured she was lying. Then his shoulders relaxed. "Fine. I'll tell her that—if she's interested, she'll get back to you."

"Thank you." She left his office and passed the kitchen, hearing a shout before the sound of breaking dishes.

Vincent flew as if on wings from his office to the kitchen. "Dalton! That is coming out of your paycheck!"

She hustled toward the front podium, hoping to catch

Jessica's eye to say goodbye. Had David been pulling money out of the restaurant to satisfy Tori's greed? He hadn't paid his wife alimony and had pretty much turned his back on his only son.

What kind of man would do that? Poor Kyle. He wasn't that bad of a kid. He'd been polite to her and certainly didn't have to be. His mother had brought him up well. The two of them had so many reasons to hate David, and yet they'd both defended him. She remembered the way Linda had jumped up to battle Freddy. She'd been in protective mode for her son, as well as for her late ex-husband.

Charlene wanted to know why.

Laura joined her at the podium, her cheeks flushed from the extra hustle. "Did you get what you wanted?"

Charlene narrowed her eyes and thought how to answer. What was Laura digging at? Did she know something?

"I'm asking business owners around town to donate a little cash or a toy for Felicity House, since they didn't get the check they'd been promised." She smiled. "Vincent helped a little, which is all I can ask."

"Oh? I'm glad—things have been really tense around here. I usually work as a part-time hostess, but Vincent asked me to step in until things get settled. David always made the staff relaxed, joking around, ya know? It was fun to work here. But not now." She lowered her voice and glanced toward the office door. "Everyone's keeping their heads down, coming in early, leaving late. Worried about being fired."

Jessica had said the same—David had been a better people person, while Vincent had handled the cash. So how had it gone missing under his watch?

"Did Tori ever work here?"

"Teaching yoga was her life—I have no idea what her and David had in common. I shouldn't say that—sorry." Laura scrunched her nose.

"Did you know Zane?"

Her brows rose, and she whispered, "You know about them?"

Charlene nodded.

"Salem is not that big of a town to hide an affair. Everyone at the restaurant knew—but David didn't talk about it. I don't think it's fair that Tori ends up with everything." Laura reached beneath the podium for a bottle of water she'd stashed and took a drink, checking the time on her watch.

"I'm glad I'm not dependent on this—just making extra cash for Christmas so I don't rack up a big debt on my MasterCard." Laura blew out a breath. "I work at one of the tourist shops on Essex Street."

"By Pedestrian Mall?" Charlene jingled the keys in her pocket. "It's always busy there. Do you know Kass Fortune? She runs the tea shop?"

"Yes, but not well. I love that goddess fountain in her shop. I get my chamomile tea from her."

"I had no idea there could be so many kinds of tea. Do you know Kyle and Linda, David's first family?"

"A little. Kyle was behind me a few years in school. Kinda sullen, always getting into fights. It was hard for him when David hooked up with Tori."

"Yes, I can imagine. Vincent and Linda are close. I hope he's good to Kyle; someone needs to be on that boy's side." Charlene zipped up her coat and pulled her keys from her pocket, touching the twenty from Vincent. "Happy Holidays."

"Same to you."

Charlene left Bella's and drove down Duval toward Brews and Broomsticks, where she could speak to Kevin.

He'd donated at the auction, like she had, but maybe he could do a bit more. The parking lot was packed, but she found a place near the road; slipping and sliding on the mushy snow, she tread carefully to the front door.

Instead of Christmas music, country blared from a small stage to the right. A trio of old men with scruff on their faces and ponytails were playing guitars and singing about honky-tonk women.

A few couples danced; though there wasn't a dance floor per se, they had a little room between the band and the nearby tables. One couple did a two-step, and another swayed to the music, thigh to thigh, hands clasped.

Charlene crossed to the long bar and snagged a stool, waiting for Kevin to notice her—he was at the other end, watching the music. The song ended and he turned around, seeing her. His eyes crinkled as he smiled in welcome.

"How's it going, girl?"

"Well, other than my mother, things are okay," she managed somewhat cheerfully.

"That sounds like you need a drink. What can I get you? Beer, wine"—he leaned close to whisper—"bottle of scotch?"

She laughed. "A glass of wine would be fine. I'm actually here on a mission. First stop was Bella's to see Vincent."

He poured her an ice water, adding a slice of lemon before showing her a Pinot Grigio. She nodded.

"What did you see him about?" He moved as gracefully as a dancer behind the bar.

"I'm asking business owners for money to help buy presents for Felicity House. Doesn't matter how much or little, but I want to make sure they have a merry Christmas."

"That's a great idea. I'm in for a hundred. Will that do?"

"Yes, it's very generous. Thank you." She sat back and nodded at the band. "Great music."

"They're a traveling band, do mostly Willie Nelson and Johnny Cash."

"I like it."

"Have you decided to celebrate our Winter Solstice on the beach tonight? Amy hopes you're going to come."

"I don't think so, but thank you for the invite. I'll celebrate good fortune in the new year, indoors by my fireplace." They shared a smile. "So, tell me about Amy? When did you two meet?"

"A long time ago. We dated oh, maybe ten years back; then she left Salem and moved to California. Hadn't seen her since, though she kept in touch for a while on social media—she's an actress but spent a lot of time waitressing between decent roles in a few Netflix movies and TV. Played some meaty parts, kind of dark—always about a troubled woman in danger. She was real good too."

"Aha! So you kept track of her. Watched her movies." Charlene put a hand over his. "That's really sweet. Is Amy the reason you never settled down?"

"She might have something to do with it." Kevin delivered drinks at the opposite end of the bar and then returned to Charlene. "She's back for good, or so she says. Now she's in one of those reenactments for the witch trials. That should keep her busy."

She hoped for her friend that it was true. She didn't want Amy or any woman to leave his heart bruised; he was too nice of a guy to do that to once, let alone twice.

"I hope so." It was good to see him happy. "Thanks for the donation. I'll collect until Friday, then take it to over to Alice on Christmas Eve morning. Can't let Tori ruin Christmas for the kids, now can we?"

Chapter Fourteen

Charlene sat at the bar, too amped up to go home. She had so much to accomplish if she wanted her goals to be met, and time was limited. Where could she ask for the most donations in one spot?

The mall. Once she'd finished her wine and paid her bill, she'd go shopping. Win-win.

She pulled her Christmas list from the side pocket of her purse, along with a pen, as she waited for Kevin to have a moment free to bring her check. She sipped her wine and glanced at the purchases she had on her gift list. So far it included a gift certificate for Minnie and Will to a romantic restaurant in Boston. Also, for Minnie, a cute antique box she'd found at Vintage Treasures.

Charlene put a check mark by their names. A royal blue cashmere sweater for her mother that she could keep for herself, but wouldn't. An e-book reader for her dad—she wasn't sure if he would give up his physical books, so she'd wrapped the gift receipt inside. A fruit basket for her old college friend Brynne and her husband. Check, check, check.

She'd bought stockings for her parents and her guests to hang from the fireplace, and now that she'd met the Garcias, she'd like to put a few little things under the tree, especially for the girls. The Chilsons would arrive Friday, so they would need stockings too. It was fun to play Santa. Should she get a stocking for Silva?

She doodled Sam's name. What about a little something for him, in case he came over Christmas Eve? What would he like? She thought him insanely attractive, but she didn't really know much about him, so far as likes or dislikes.

A familiar voice inside her mind suggested a date would be a good way to get to know him.

Jared?

Her body broke out in goose bumps and she dropped the pen to her purse. The voice had been so clear, so dear, that she actually looked around the bar's interior to see if he was there.

Of course not. She took a ten-dollar bill out of her wallet, put it under the wineglass, and headed for the door, waving to Kevin as she fled. Outside she shivered, uncertain if it was from the cold or the shock of the familiar voice she'd heard.

Starting the car, she attempted to make sense of the illogical. Had the voice been her subconscious thoughts? Charlene turned up the radio, blaring Christmas music all the way to the mall.

She battled holiday shoppers, driving down one lane

after another until she gave up and settled for a spot at the far end of the shopping center. The plows had cleared the pavement, leaving mounds of snow in random mountains. Charlene cautiously picked her way through the snow and the slush, not wanting to fall.

"You asked for snow," she reminded herself, putting the hood of her coat over her head to ward off the cold. She entered the mall's ground-floor main entrance, overwhelmed by Christmas carols blaring in surround sound, shrieking kids in line with their parents for Santa, the powerful scent of coffee, mixed with popcorn and candied nuts from a kiosk by the doors. The scents and sounds of Christmas.

The woman at the first retail shop let her know that Charlene needed an actual letter requesting donations and to take it to the mall office, not the individual stores.

It was a huge disappointment, knowing that she'd have to return another day, but not to be defeated, she decided to get her stocking stuffers done. She was grateful that her big gifts were all bought—the mall was a madhouse. Nothing really caught her attention enough for her to bring out her wallet—until she reached a toy store with a hundred-pound stuffed gorilla in front of it.

Toys—maybe they'd have something for the kids?

Her mood lifted as she brought her cart up and down the aisles—and when she found an end cap of classic board games two for ten dollars, well, she loaded up. She bought an assortment for Felicity House, as well as for her guests.

And books! Gorgeous copies of *Little Women* and *Tom Sawyer*. And for the younger children, she got the entire series of *Diary of a Wimpy Kid*. Charlene bought a book on the history of the Yankees for Sam—nothing too personal that could be misconstrued. She also found a Rangers coffee mug and wondered if he enjoyed hockey.

To her surprise, she was actually singing along with Mariah Carey by the time she rang up her purchases.

On the return loop of the interior of the mall, she passed a body lotion store—it would be just the thing for the ladies. She stocked up on nice-smelling lotions, and manicure sets for the guys, adding extras to the pile for the older kids at Felicity House.

With her last purchase, her anger at her mother had dissipated to a manageable level, and Jared's voice was buried beneath holiday cheer and retail therapy.

"With a holly jolly Christmas," she sang as she pushed her loaded cart through the snow, to the far end, where her car was parked. It was dark now, and streetlamps illuminated the parking lot, which was still packed with last-minute shoppers.

She unloaded her bags and shut the back of her Pilot, turning to search for a place to return her cart. Her gaze was drawn to the last shop at the end of the strip mall—a gym. The glass walls allowed the shoppers to see inside as the fitness enthusiasts beat themselves up on the treadmills and bikes—huffing and puffing their way to better health.

Finding a spot to return her empty cart, Charlene had half turned toward her car when someone inside caught her eye. She swiveled around so fast she almost lost her balance on the snow. Those broad shoulders and bulky biceps, visible now in a sleeveless workout top, belonged to Zane Villander.

Charlene locked her car again and was already stepping toward the gym before coming up with a plan. Her boots crunched against gravel and hard-packed snow.

Saying she wanted donations for Felicity House from the gym probably wouldn't be believed, and he was a trainer, not management.

She nibbled her lower lip. Maybe a gift certificate?

Pausing by the front door, she peered inside. There was no Tori. Had she already quit? This could be Zane's workout spot, not where they both trained. What did it matter? She was going in to ask some questions, it was too good an opportunity to miss.

With a deep breath, Charlene pulled the door toward her and entered.

The scent of sweat hit her in the nose and she brought her scarf up to act as a filter. Glistening bodies, male and female, attacked the machines—as if looking good already was a prerequisite for working out. Charlene scanned the twenty or so people inside and didn't see an ounce of "extra" on any of them.

This was a lifestyle. Some people golfed, others drank wine, and these folks were dedicated to their bodies.

Zane was helping a man in his twenties bench-press, coaching him through the lift by chanting, "Go, go, go," in the man's ears—the guy put his all into the weights, his face flushed, his arms bulging, his brow dripping sweat.

With a last grunt of effort, the man raised the weights to full extension and Zane clapped his approval, then had his hands out, ready to assist on the descent, as the guy's arms trembled. "You did it, man," Zane said.

A platinum-haired woman in her early twenties bounced toward Charlene with a wide smile. Her hair was up in a high ponytail, she had no jewelry except silver peace symbol stud earrings, and she carried a clipboard. "Welcome to Ultimate Fitness. I'm Sabrina. Are you interested in a membership, after gaining a few holiday pounds?"

Put off by the assumption that she needed to lose weight, Charlene kept her jacket closed. She would not be showing Sabrina anything—but maybe she needed to watch Minnie's cooking.

She cleared her throat. "I would love a brochure," she said, her gaze going back to Zane.

Sabrina noticed and sighed. "Isn't he wonderful? And so good to his clients—if you hired Zane, he'd give you a full-body workout." Her brow arched the slightest bit. "He's *very* popular with women your age."

Wait a minute. Had Sabrina alluded to Zane giving more than just gym instruction? Maybe, since they'd been having an affair themselves, Tori didn't care if Zane was faithful.

"Does Tori work here?" she asked in a conversational tone.

Sabrina lowered her clipboard. "Noooo, she and her husband won the lottery and David insisted she quit. Lucky! Can you believe it?"

"Oh yes . . . but didn't her husband just pass away?"

Sabrina leaned in to Charlene. "Yes, that was very sad—but he was much older than Tori, from what I understand."

"He got hit by a car." This girl had an age phobia—well, she'd learn in time that if you were fortunate, you got to live long enough for wrinkles. "The hotline has been all over the news. A hit-and-run driver."

"Oh," Sabrina said dismissively. "I don't watch the news. It is waaaaay too depressing. I work very hard to keep my endorphins up."

Had Zane been working the night of the auction? He had reason to want to keep Tori to himself—if Tori had shared David's plan to move them into hiding, maybe

Zane had panicked—running David over in an act of desperation.

"Do you have more information?" Charlene perused the enormous gym, filled with machines and men and women pumping iron. How could she find out if Zane had worked that night? She saw bathrooms marked—women to the right, men to the left—and a white wooden door with OFFICE printed on it, in the rear left corner.

Sabrina held up a finger and went to the reception desk by the front door, picking up a glossy Ultimate Fitness brochure. "Here you are. You can pay by the month, but we're running a special. If you pay for a full year in advance, you can take advantage of two free personal trainer sessions." Sabrina smirked. "You can always request Zane."

As if he'd heard them talking, Zane looked up from where he was finishing with his client.

Sabrina waved him over. Charlene, stuck, decided to go through the motions of being interested in a possible membership.

"How'd you hear about us?" Sabrina asked. Bright and chipper.

"I was shopping and saw you from the parking lot, actually. I just moved here from Chicago a few months ago. I run a bed-and-breakfast but want to keep fit."

Sabrina's smile didn't move, and Charlene could tell she didn't really care.

"Well, we are open twenty-four/seven, so if you find yourself in need of a destressing workout after a rough day, Ultimate Fitness is here when you need us. Zane, this lady is interested in our gym packages."

With another hike of her bleached brow, Sabrina gave Charlene a finger wave and rushed off to speak to another gym member—male, lean, and the same age as the fitness goddess.

Zane crossed his arms, adding a flex. "You look familiar—have we met?"

"I don't think so," Charlene said, which was the truth—they hadn't. She knew who he was because he was—what did Sam call it? A person of interest. "I'm Charlene Morris." They shook hands. "Oh—wait, were you at the service for David Baldwin?"

"Yeah."

She noticed he still wore his Rolex. Was he mad that he still had to work, while Tori had the luxury of quitting? There was only one way to find out. . . .

"It was so sad about David, and poor Tori. She seemed very upset."

He shrugged. "She'll be fine."

"Are you a good friend of hers?"

His lips lifted in a smug smile. "You could say that."

Charlene fanned her face with the brochure. "Sabrina just told me that Tori no longer works here. I don't blame her, right? Winning ten million dollars is pretty fabulous—a real game changer. I know I wouldn't work either."

"Why not?" Zane rubbed his smooth-shaven chin with agitation. Charlene noticed that he was shaved all over or waxed. No hair on his arms, legs, or chest. Ouch. His skin gleamed with oil. "When you work at what you love, it isn't work."

She actually agreed with that. "What's your schedule? Do you work mostly nights or days?"

"I make my own hours. Interested?"

Crap. "Maybe. I'm not sure." How was she supposed to check his schedule?

"If you want, we can get your paperwork started. Did you want to pay for the year?"

She wondered if they got bonuses for signing new clients.

"I wouldn't be starting until early January—if I can make the time."

He waited, then said, "Tell you what, sign up now and I'll throw in an extra one-on-one training session." Zane rubbed the back of his hand down her arm.

Revulsion made her step back. But she really needed to see the employee schedule, if there was one. She glanced at the office. "Well, I guess it wouldn't hurt to do the paperwork."

"I can get it," he said, striding across the gym to the office.

Rather than wait, Charlene followed him and stood at the doorway, wondering what he would do if she simply told him she wasn't interested in a membership, but was here for some answers.

Before she had a chance to gather up her courage, the desk phone rang. Zane perched his ass on the edge of the desk and reached for the phone. His eyes widened in surprise when he saw her standing there. He pointed to the chair next to the desk.

Having little choice, she stepped forward and slid in. His rock-hard thighs—oiled to a sheen—were right next to her face. She scooched back.

"Ultimate Fitness." His demeanor changed. "Oh—hey, Miguel. Sure, I can come by—I'm off at nine." Zane moved around the desk, his back to Charlene. "I'll grab some beer. Who called?" He stiffened. "I gotta go—I'm with a customer."

Zane rubbed his watch in thought before looking at Charlene. "Sorry about that."

Here she just wanted answers and more questions kept popping up. She sat on the edge of the metal chair. "No problem. Zane, can I ask you a personal question?" Her success rate wasn't high with this method, but it was better than batting zero.

He placed his palms on the desk and faced her. "What?"

"I know that you and Tori are more than friends. . . ."

His face drained of all color. "It's a lie."

Charlene shook her head. "I was at the auction, that night David was killed, and David mentioned your name."

"What are you talking about?" Just as suddenly as he'd paled, his forehead and throat flushed crimson. "Why are you here? You a cop? Did you call Miguel?"

Charlene swallowed quickly. Did he have a temper? She eyed the open door. She could call for help, or run for it, if needed. "No, no. I'm a B and B owner, just like I said."

He rolled his head around his thick neck before asking, "What did David say?"

Good—she'd nabbed his curiosity. "He demanded to see Tori's phone—she didn't give it over, and he said it better not be Zane."

"What do you care? Nothing nobody can do for David now."

"He was a friend," she said, stretching the truth. "I want whoever ran David over to be caught—do you know anything?" *Did you do it?* What would she do if he actually confessed?

He sat back, biceps bulging. "You aren't interested in a gym membership."

Charlene had her body poised to make a dash for the door. "I'm not," she said in a soft voice. "I just want David's family to be at rest." Finding who was actually responsible would protect Kyle, who was still on Sam's list. She thought Zane had more reason. "Especially his son. He's only nineteen, and his dad just died."

His body relaxed. "Tori and I had a thing, but she called it off after David won the lottery—for obvious reasons."

Money, Charlene presumed—as in, Tori wanted David's. "But now that he's gone?"

Zane lifted his watch. "She gave me this—figured it was a kiss-off. Lucky me, I get to keep this lousy job."

His tone held a hint of fear and Charlene played on his emotions. "If she really loved you, why wouldn't she want you to quit and run away with her? Keeping you here doesn't seem right."

"She says to keep the cops and insurance people at bay—but I told her, my alibi for that night is solid as those dumbbells out there." He shrugged. "She should know me better than that."

"Oh?"

"I was at Miguel's, watching a game, and I got a dozen alibis. Besides, I've already talked to the cops."

"Well, knowing you're innocent, she might change her mind." The two deserved each other—all about image and flash. She looked into her purse and saw her cell phone screen light up. "Oh—I have to get this call. Take care, Zane. Good luck."

He didn't see her to the door but stared morosely at his watch.

Chapter Fifteen

Charlene stepped out of the stifling gym to the brisk winter air with a sigh of relief and answered her phone. "Hello?"

"Hi, Charlene, this is Linda."

She checked the parking lot for traffic before hustling across the slick, packed snow toward her car, using the key fob to unlock it when she was five rows away.

"Thanks for calling me back, Linda. I understand completely about keeping those donations at the hospital for your own group of kids."

"Good—I wanted to make sure I didn't come off as bitchy. Vincent called and said you had a nice chat?"

Charlene reached her Pilot and got inside. Turning on the engine, she blasted the heat to defrost the snowy windows. Is that what he'd told her? "We did."

"How long ago did your husband pass away? You seem so young for that, if you don't mind my saying."

"It's been two years, just about—he was killed in a car accident." In the spring.

"I'm so sorry," Linda said.

"Me too. Every day."

She heard a sob and then Linda sniffed. "I know we were divorced, and that David had moved on, but my love for him never completely died. He was the father of my son. Not knowing who's responsible is tearing me apart."

She could very much appreciate needing closure. "I understand and would feel the same. The woman responsible for Jared's death had been drinking and is serving time in jail."

"Do you hate her?"

The ugly question hit Charlene in the solar plexus. She thought carefully before answering. "Sometimes. I know I'm not supposed to—to forgive is divine, or whatever that saying is, but I'm working on it."

"We are all works in progress," Linda said with a tired laugh. "That's what our minister says, anyway. Vincent mentioned that you wanted to meet for coffee? I think I'd like that."

Charlene turned on the wipers to clear the frost on the front and back windshields. Could be she was finally making friends in Salem. "Just let me know when is good for you."

"I'll have to tell Kyle that he was right about you—he said you seemed like a nice lady. Figured that you were on our side. Are you?"

"Yes, and that was very sweet—you've raised him well."

"He's coming around, but the last few years, with the divorce and everything, well, it's been tough."

"You moved from New York, right?"

"Yeah, I should've stayed in Long Island—but when Vin gave David the chance to be part owner of his own restaurant, it was too good of a deal to pass up."

"That was supportive of you to move. I would have done the same for Jared. Gone anywhere in the world for him. We met at college, then ended up working in the same advertising agency. What about you? Where did you guys meet?"

"He was managing an upscale steakhouse in the city," Linda said, reminiscence in her voice. "It was my twenty-fifth birthday, and David was so handsome. He bought me a birthday drink and slipped his number to me on the cocktail napkin. Where did the time go? In two years, I'll be fifty."

"So, you've known Vincent all that time?"

"No, I didn't get to know him until he sold his restaurants in New York and moved to Boston—he has a place there that serves American fare."

"In addition to Bella's? That's a lot of work."

"Restaurants are money pits—but David had a talent for bringing in repeat customers and making his places successful. He's a people guy, can talk to anyone."

That didn't jibe with what Vincent had told her. Maybe Vincent didn't want to let Linda know the restaurant was in trouble. "The food is good, which also helps. Dad loves that pasta fagioli soup."

"So do I. I have the recipe, if you want it."

"That would be awesome. My dad would be thrilled."

"No problem. I hope Tori gets what she wants and

leaves the rest of us alone. You know? I want this over with and to move on."

"I don't blame you for that. I'll be in touch soon—night!"

Charlene put her phone in the cell phone holder on her dashboard. Who knew that Linda would end up being so nice?

She drove home, her mind sorting through everything she'd learned today. She wished that it was just her and Jack, so they could discuss it all openly, but her house was nearly full.

It was seven thirty when Charlene entered, laden with shopping bags from her retail therapy. The Garcias were out, and her parents were in the living room watching a Hallmark Christmas movie.

"Hey!" She peeked in and waved at them.

Her mom got up and her dad paused the film to ask, "How'd it go, sweetheart?"

Charlene showed off the bags. "Success."

"Did you eat?" Her mom watched her warily.

She smiled, letting the incident from earlier go—but not forgotten. "Nope. What did you guys have?"

"Roast beef sandwiches," she said. "Can I make you one? With some soup?"

"That would be nice, Mom. I'll go put these in my room. I bought stuff to fill the stockings and little gifts for Christmas morning."

Her mom smiled. "How fun!"

Her dad followed them to the kitchen, getting out a can of soup from the pantry and a pan, while her mom pulled the sandwich makings from the fridge. Jack gave her a welcoming smile from the open door of her bedroom suite, then walked up behind her.

"I was getting worried about you, because of the snow," Jack said softly.

She couldn't answer Jack per se, so she said to her parents, "The roads were slick from the slushy snow that's frozen over—I saw a lot of tow trucks pulling cars from the ditches."

"You are a very good driver," her dad said. "I didn't worry at all."

Her mom huffed as she lathered creamy horseradish on a slice of wheat bread. "Normally I would agree, but you don't know these roads here like the ones in Chicago. It won't hurt you to be cautious."

"It's not her driving we need to worry about," her dad insisted. "It's those other idiots on the road."

"I like your dad," Jack said, his image wavering at her doorway, "and yet I find myself agreeing with your mother."

Charlene arched her brow at Jack, her back to her parents. "Give me a second to put these away." She hurried into her sitting room, shutting the door behind her, and put the bags on the love seat.

"I wish I could help you wrap," Jack said, eyeing the bags wistfully.

"You do not," Charlene laughed. She went into her bedroom to kick off her boots and exchange them for slippers. "I can't wait to tell you everything I found out today. Do you know football teams, by any chance?"

"Sure."

"College football, I mean."

"Not as well, but I love the sport."

"Think of teams with red and black colors. This jersey was predominately red."

He rubbed his jaw. "That narrows it down," he joked.

"Well, think back to David's college years."

"How old was he?"

"Fifty-three."

Jack leaned against the doorframe between her sitting room and bedroom as she sat on her bed and snugged her feet into warm argyle slippers with rubber soles.

"So mideighties?"

"We can search online later. After my soup and sandwich. I am glad I'm not meeting Kevin and Amy down at the beach for the yule log burning—brr!"

"The bartender has a girlfriend?"

"A long-lost love—I hope she doesn't break his heart."

"I'm glad he isn't hanging around you."

"Oh, Jack." She stood and smoothed her jeans down her legs. "Do you think I need to tone up?"

Jack burst out laughing. "What?"

"Part of my evening was a stop at the gym, meeting with a very fit instructor."

"I think you look great." He eyed her backside with approval, and she blushed.

"I think Zane offers 'extras' to his personal clients." She shivered with distaste as she recalled the rock-hard waxed thighs at her eye level.

"Now that is a story."

A knock sounded on her door and her mom opened it to call, "Your dinner is ready."

Jack's laughter rumbled behind her as she went out to eat.

After her meal, which she ate in the kitchen with her parents, she brought out some of the lotions and manicure sets for Felicity House. "I'll take these over in the morning when I pick up Avery."

"I was thinking," her mom said, "that I could call

around to some of the places and ask for donations over the phone. I used to be very good at that for the church fund-raisers."

"Would you, Mom? That would be a great help. I am sure that Pamela and Alice would appreciate that too." She could give her the list of people she'd jotted down earlier, with the exception of Archie, who she wanted her parents to meet, since he was such a character.

"Once I lay it on thick about dead David and the trampy wife who is stealing bread from the mouths of babes, I know people will give."

"Mom, you can't say it like that."

Her mother's mouth thinned. "It's the truth."

"It might be slander—Dad, is that against the law?"

"How would I know? I'm an art professor."

"Sam would know," her mom said slyly. "Why don't you call him? You could see how the investigation is coming along."

"Sam doesn't like to talk to me about those kinds of things."

Her mom tensed, her large bosom heaving. "How do you know that?"

Trapped. Charlene evaded the question. "Well, he just seems to be a stickler for the rules, that's all."

"It might be worth a phone call," her mom said, elbow on the table.

"I am not calling to ask him if you can get sued for bad-talking Tori just to get a few bucks."

"For the children, Charlene," her mom stressed. "It's for the kids."

Her dad peered up from his tea and cookies. "It's best sometimes to just let her do what she wants. She's like a terrier—one of those yippy ones with sharp teeth that won't let go of your pant leg."

"Michael Woodbridge," her mom warned. "Neither of you appreciate me."

Charlene exchanged a look with her dad. Things were back to normal—as much as they could be.

The Garcias returned at ten, their faces rosy from a day out in the snow.

"We tried to stay up until midnight for the bonfire, but we couldn't do it," Andy said, Maddie draped over his shoulder, sound asleep. Emily leaned against her mom's legs.

Teresa waved and took off her gloves, urging Emily toward the stairs. "What a day—we're going to sleep in tomorrow for sure."

"I hope you had fun?"

"We did!" Emily perked up for a minute. "We saw snowmen and a giant log on fire."

"Did you go down to the beach?"

Andy nodded. "People were singing and drinking hot cocoa—but it was time to get these girls home."

"There was music and everything," Teresa said. "But it was too much at the end of a long day."

"Can I get you anything? I can put on the kettle if you want tea. . . ."

"No, thank you," Teresa said, following Andy and Maddie up the stairs. "We are going to sleep well tonight. Night, everyone."

Charlene and her parents returned to the living room. "On that note, I think I'm going to hit the sack myself. Good night. Love you guys."

Her parents resumed the Christmas movie they'd been

watching, and Charlene hurried to her sitting room, closing and locking the door behind her.

Jack appeared in a burst of cold, his form sharply delineated in jeans and a green Christmas sweater. He turned on the television for her with a flick of his fingers, creating a blue arc of power.

"Show-off," she whispered.

His smile showed no lines around his eyes or mouth, his skin ghostly smooth.

She brought her laptop to the love seat, logged on to her e-mail, and checked her website for messages. Two were asking if she had rooms available . . . she quickly e-mailed back for more information, wishing they'd left numbers.

"So, what are we doing?" Jack sat next to her on her love seat and stretched his legs before him. Silva crawled out from under the armchair and jumped between her and Jack with an annoyed tail flick at Jack's illusion of a body.

"I'd like to know more about Freddy and David in college. Why would Freddy show up all of a sudden?"

"Well, David had just won the lottery."

She shook her head. "So he arrived in Salem with his hand out? I don't know. No offense, Jack, but David looked like he'd seen a ghost that night."

From his seat next to her, he deliberately faded in and out—full-color Jack to barely there, and back again. "Boo!"

"Don't waste your energy with tricks," she said. "Flickering the lights or switching the TV on and off. I need you to help me find out what college David went to."

"All right, all right, but you don't understand that I get bored without you." He smiled with charm that made it impossible for her to be mad. "Did you check his social media pages? People sometimes fill out that information."

Charlene tapped her search bar. "I checked Facebook and Twitter."

"What about the business one?"

"Oh—yeah, let's check LinkedIn." At the website, she typed in David's name. The search was a bust. David hadn't done more than a cursory profile ten years ago and then never updated it.

Jack scratched his clean-shaven chin, his fingers not really touching his face. "Why don't you search colleges with football teams in New York—do you know where he lived?"

"No, which means that it was probably around the city—New Yorkers from there seem to think that's the only place in New York—I noticed that in my ad days in Chicago."

"Good point," Jack said. "David was just a few years older than me, so when I was in college—"

"Did you play, Jack?"

"No, no. And risk my doctor's hands?"

Charlene admired his large hands. "Really?"

"No, while I loved the sport, I can't run and catch at the same time. Thankfully I found that out when I was twelve, so I didn't harbor any illusions."

Charlene sensed a story and faced Jack with a smile. "What happened, Jack?"

"During practice, I tripped over a cone on the sideline, arms outstretched to catch the pass, and almost broke my nose—the good thing was that all the girls showered me with attention, making the bruises all worth it."

She could see it now—Jack already a ladies' man before entering high school.

"I'm sure you made it worth their while."

He gave a bashful, oh geez shrug. "So what else do you remember?"

"The jersey had some kind of animal on it, outlined in blue. Snarling."

"A wolf?" he asked, leaning forward.

"Maybe. I didn't get that good of a look. Uh, today Linda said that she wished she hadn't left Long Island. Does that help at all?"

Jack snapped his fingers, though the movement didn't make a sound or disturb the sleeping cat between them.

"What?"

"Check out Stony Brook. They had a decent football team." He frowned. "But I don't remember what division they were."

Charlene tapped "Stony Brook" into the blinking bar. The red and black colors of the school popped up, as did a cartoonish wolf's head outlined in blue. "The Stony Brook sea wolves."

"Sea wolves—that's right," Jack said. "Can you do a search of their alumni?"

Charlene navigated through the Stony Brook website and discovered David Baldwin, in 1986. Linda hadn't been wrong—David was a hottie back in the day.

"Played on the team," she said. "Let's check Freddy Ferguson."

Jack's cold energy as he moved closer to see the laptop screen made her reach for an afghan and wrap it around her shoulders.

"There he is—tall and skinny—smiling wide," he said.

She searched for a year of graduation—Freddy hadn't graduated, it seemed. Curious now, she put in David's name again.

"Graduated 1988." She scrolled down his achievements, but football hadn't been listed after 1986. "Linda mentioned an accident, where David had gotten hurt, and claimed Freddy did it on purpose. David was definitely better looking. Maybe he was a better player too."

"Freddy was jealous?" Jack sat back.

"Linda said David *had been* the quarterback, past tense."

"Can you find a newspaper article on the accident? I want to help. . . ."

While Jack had a knack for moving things and playing with power sources, he wasn't always able to be specific with his actions, like searching online for something in particular or turning the page on a book, which was why he enjoyed television so much.

"You do help, just by talking this over with me." Charlene Googled all Stony Brook articles around the time of the accident, but it was hard to zero in on the information she wanted. A half hour later she was about to call it a night when she found a single line relating to the incident and recited, "Quarterback David Baldwin injured in car accident, driver Freddy Ferguson suspended from play."

She closed the laptop and turned to Jack. "If Freddy had been out to injure David before because he was jealous, then maybe he showed up in Salem after David's lottery win to finish the job."

Chapter Sixteen

Charlene didn't want to think about David's death anymore for the night. Jack, being perceptive, left her alone and went to wherever he went when he wasn't with her. He had no name for it, but Charlene guessed that it was half in this world, half in another. It made her sad for him to be caught in the middle somewhere. She hoped with all her heart that Jared was at peace and in Heaven.

She had her nightgown on and was ready to climb into bed, when her house phone rang. She used it for business purposes so quickly picked up.

"Good evening. Thank you for calling 'Charlene's.'"

"This is Gary Kramer. I e-mailed earlier to see if you had any available rooms?"

"Yes, I'm sorry, but you didn't leave a number for me

to call back. We have three single rooms on the third floor. No elevator."

"Not a problem. Please hold one for me. I'll drop by in the morning, if that's all right?"

"That's perfect." She grabbed a pad and a pen and wrote down his name. "I'll make sure the room is ready. Just bring your things. Thank you, Mr. Kramer."

She clapped her hands with satisfaction and then slipped into bed after turning off the lights. When the house was quiet, she thought back on the day and wished she could tell Sam what she'd learned.

If he was as agreeable about her interest in solving this case as Jack, they would get along much, much better. Maybe even go out on a date or two. What would they talk about? He wasn't impressed with her insights, but people seemed to enjoy talking to her, and she learned things. She also noticed things that others didn't and was a good judge of character. He shouldn't blame her for that. She wasn't nosy. She was *involved*.

She punched her pillow and nestled in, finding sleep at last.

The morning came with heavy showers. Rain pounded on the roof and hit her window pane. She stayed in bed an extra fifteen minutes just listening to the sound, not in a hurry to start her day. It wasn't a weekend, so she didn't have breakfast to serve. By now, her dad was probably up and had started the coffee. He was the kindest man in the world to put up with her mother all these years. Sainthood waited for him in Heaven. She smiled, thinking of him with angel wings still doting on his Brenda, the love of his life.

The thought reminded her of Jared, but she didn't want

to think of him now, so she climbed out of bed and went in to shower.

Refreshed and dressed in jeans and a long-sleeve red tee, she headed into the kitchen. Her parents sat at the table eating slices of Minnie's applesauce cake and drinking their coffee.

"Morning," her mother said cheerfully. "Did the rain wake you up?"

"It did." She peered out the window, noticing most of the snow had washed away with the rain. "Looks like it's letting up now." She poured a cup of coffee and then walked over to the table, rubbing her dad's shoulder as she passed.

"Did you both have a good night?" She helped herself to a small piece of cake and nibbled on it.

"Yes, your beds are great." Dad studied Mom. "We've had that hard, old mattress going on twelve years. We should get one of these soft, pillow-top mattresses as soon as we get home."

"And waste more money? We've been comfortable sleeping on that all these years, why should we change now? If it's not broke, why fix it, I always say."

"You always say too much, and that's half the problem." Her dad's eyes met hers over his wife's shoulder.

Charlene gave him a warm smile—and didn't dwell on the bickering. "Avery will be here again today."

"What's that girl going to do with her life? She wants a good job, she'd better get the ring out of her nose."

"Mom, I don't want you speaking down to her, okay? I mean it. You've criticized me most of my life, but I won't have you doing that to my employees."

Her mom picked up her fork and waved it at her. "I've

loved you from the moment you were born, and if you don't know that by now, it's time you did." She stood up. "I'm going upstairs."

"Now, now," her father reached for her as she brushed by. "Charlene didn't mean anything. Sit down, Brenda. Have another cup of coffee."

"I'll get it for you." Charlene took her mother's cup and filled it as she sat back down, exuding annoyance.

"Thank you," her mother said coldly, as she accepted the coffee.

Ignoring her mom's icy tone, Charlene said pleasantly, "I have a new guest showing up in half an hour. He'll be staying upstairs in a single on the third floor. Once he's settled, I'll run over and pick up Avery." Charlene glanced at her dad since her mother wouldn't look at her. "Would you two like to get a ride into town? I can drop you at the wharf or down at the Pedestrian Mall. I think the sky is clearing."

Michael tapped his wife's hand. "What do you say, Brenda? Want to go out on the town with me?"

Her mom's mouth curved in a half smile. "Why, I'd love to." She picked up her fork for another bite of cake. "I still have some gifts to buy for the bridge group. And my knitting club will expect something too."

Charlene's dad groaned. "I thought you got the mugs?"

"What are you talking about, Michael?" Her mother shook her head. "I just bought a few. I saw some really cute souvenir thimbles at the Witch Museum, and I should have picked them up then. And everyone likes fridge magnets. They're easy to pack."

"Sounds like you'll have a full day. I'll drop you off and pick you up at two. Have lunch at Sharon's restaurant, Cod and Capers, or better yet, try Sea Level—it's near The House of the Seven Gables. Let me know where you are, and I'll meet you there."

"Oh, this is going to be fun!" Her mother laughed, their tiff forgotten, sounding twenty years younger. "Charlene, if you make a list while we're out, I can start calling the businesses around town as soon as we get back. By dinnertime you should have a lot of pledges on your hands."

"That's great, Mom. Thanks." Charlene watched her parents leave for their room, feeling happy for them. In spite of everything, they had a good marriage, and it made her sad to think how unfairly she'd lost hers.

But that woman who stole her happiness was serving time, and David's driver was yet to be found. Maybe she'd make a quick call to Sam just to see how things were coming. He couldn't fault her for that, could he?

At ten to nine she was putting the dishes away when the doorbell rang. She wiped her hands on a towel and went to answer it. "Hi! You must be Gary Kramer—I'm Charlene. Come on in."

"Thanks! Sorry if I'm a little early." He was around fiftyish, she figured, not much taller than her, with a clean-shaven face and lines around his eyes.

"It works perfectly—I need to step out for a few minutes, so this is fine." She glanced down at his duffel bag. "Do you have more luggage in the car?" She gazed beyond him to a brown Camry parked in the drive.

"No, I'm only here for a couple of days to see my brother and his family for Christmas. I literally just need a bed for a couple of nights. Left all the presents and stuff at their house."

"Well, that makes it easy, then. Follow me, and I'll show you to your room."

As they mounted the stairs, she gave him a rundown of what to expect. "My parents are visiting, and their room is on the second floor. On the other side of the stairwell is another family, the Garcias. I haven't seen them yet this morning. They're either sleeping in or out already."

"I won't be around all that much myself," he told her.

"Well, we do breakfast on the weekends; the other days we offer pastries and fruit. If I'm not around, help yourself to anything in the fridge."

They reached the second floor, and Charlene pointed down the hall. "My mom and dad are from Chicago. Here for ten long days and nights," she said with a grimace.

Gary chuckled and paused, his hand on the banister. "I get it. Why do you think I'm staying here? Love my family, but getting everyone together with all the kids, well, a man could use some quiet time."

"I understand completely." She glanced down at his ring-less hand. "No wife or children?"

"My wife passed from cancer five years ago. The kids are out of college, both working, and they decided to spend Christmas with their friends instead of family. What can I do? They're old enough to make up their own minds." He shrugged. "Okay, lead on."

They went up the last flight of stairs, and she showed him his room. "There's a single bathroom on this floor, but you'll have it all to yourself."

"This will do nicely. Thank you."

"You're most welcome. If you're interested in getting some air and seeing the view, a few more steps up through that door will lead you to the widow's walk. I highly recommend it."

"Sounds nice. I might do that later."

"Can I get you some coffee? Or would you like a light breakfast?"

"Sounds great, but unfortunately I stopped at McDonald's on my way over."

"Oh, that is unfortunate! Well, tomorrow then." She turned to leave. "I'll let you get settled. There's a set of keys on your table. The big one opens the front door, the smaller one is for your room. You can come and go as you please."

"Thanks, Charlene. I really appreciate it. Do you run this yourself? Or is there a Mr. Morris somewhere?"

"No, Mr. Morris was killed in a car accident two years ago. But I'm never lonely; that's one good thing about running a bed-and-breakfast."

"Maybe later we can have a nightcap together."

Charlene felt a chill in the air. She didn't turn around, but she could feel Jack's presence.

"Let's see what happens," she said, and walked past Jack, ignoring him completely. His arms were crossed, and he had a petulant look on his handsome face. He had to get used to the fact that single men could rent a room, and she enjoyed the occasional company of real men too.

By nine fifteen, Charlene and her parents were seated in the Pilot, listening to a cheery station on the radio. The weather report was for cool temperatures and clear skies. Her mother chatted happily, and Charlene defrosted a little. Whatever cruel words her mother had spit out, deep down she knew her mother loved her and her dad more than anyone or anything in this world. That was never in doubt.

"Have a great time." Charlene slowed before the Witch Museum. It was on Washington Street, and from the outside passersby might take it for a church, instead of a place that had reenactments of the twenty women burned at the stake. "Let me know where you're having lunch and I'll be out front at two." She parked, waved as they exited, and then drove the short distance to 18th Street and the teen house.

She pulled into the driveway and hopped out. Avery opened the door, already dressed and waiting. "Hi, Charlene!"

"I didn't keep you waiting this time." Charlene nodded at Janet, who gave her a thumbs-up. "I'll just sign this, and we'll be on our way."

Janet thanked her and told them both to have a good day. She closed the door behind them, and Charlene gave Avery a small hug. "What are the other kids doing today? With school out, do they go to Felicity House, or the youth center?"

"Everybody does their own thing. Some take classes like pottery or painting. One girl likes to make jewelry, so she's helping out at a shop in town. One of the guys likes to bake, so he was out of the house real early, working at the bakery."

"What about you, Avery? You interested in anything in particular?" They climbed into the Pilot, did up their seat belts, and then Charlene backed out of the driveway onto the street.

"Hmm, not sure. I don't have any great talent hiding inside of me. But I kind of like music. I write a little bit. Used to make up songs and play a guitar, but I don't have it anymore."

"What kind of music do you like?"

"Country. Rock. I don't know. I just dabble, playing around." She tapped her fingers on her knees. "Look at

Taylor Swift. That woman has it all. You know she started writing her own music as a teenager? She moved to Nashville at fourteen and hoped to become a star. Isn't that amazing?"

"She is pretty awesome. Most people don't get that kind of success in life, but she seems to handle it all pretty well." Charlene took her eyes off the road for a sec to look at her. "That what you want? To be the next Taylor Swift?"

"Sure. Why not? I mean, who wouldn't?" Embarrassed at her confession, Avery blushed and looked out the side window.

"Well, why not? Dream big. That's the only way you'll ever reach the stars."

"What about you?" Avery countered. "Did you wake up one day and say, 'Gee, I want to be a bed-and-breakfast owner'?" She rolled her eyes. "I mean, you got a mansion and everything, but was that your dream?"

Charlene laughed. "No, it never occurred to me. My father was an art professor, and we used to traipse around museums together. When I was younger, I thought I'd like to paint something famous. I loved Monet and most of the Impressionists' artwork. Renoir, Paul Cézanne. The landscapes were so dreamy and romantic, I just fell in love with it."

Avery stared at her like she had no clue what she was talking about. "So, did you paint?"

"Basic stuff. But I didn't have any real talent. It was just a period in my life. A few years later—when I was fifteen or so—I decided I wanted to be a curator."

"What's that?" Avery wrinkled her nose, the gold ring sparkling.

"It's the person who's in charge of the museum, an administrator—the collections are under her care. It's a pretty important job."

"I guess. I've never been to a museum. Sounds boring," she said, picking at the hole in her jeans.

"Well, I didn't end up doing that either. I went to college and became interested in commercial work. I have an advertising, marketing, and management degree."

"You made commercials?"

"Well, not just me. We worked in teams, and yes, I helped develop some commercials."

"So, like what?"

Charlene turned onto Crown Point Road. They drove around a curve and she saw her home in the distance. It still gave her a thrill to see the widow's walk, and the grounds, and know that it was hers. She wondered if that thrill would ever go away.

Avery shifted her leg in the passenger seat, facing Charlene. "Come on. Tell me! What commercials did you do?"

"Uh, you know the one where the guy in a white plastic suit comes and sits by a housewife? The house looks like it's just blown up, and only she and the sofa are there. Soot everywhere, even on the poor woman's face. And there he sits—Mister Bright?"

Avery shook her head in disbelief. "That was, like, the dumbest commercial ever."

"Mine!" Charlene pulled into the driveway, turned the car off, and looked at Avery with a big grin on her face. They slapped hands in a high-five. "Yeah, that one really sucked."

Still laughing, they went into the house.

Minnie put Avery to work, and Charlene was determined to tackle the fund-raising list. She went to her room and clicked on her laptop at her small desk, resuming where she'd left off. Over two hours later, she'd managed to make it to the letter *F* but only a measly hundred dollars to the good. She printed out a list for her mom to call that afternoon—hopefully she'd have better luck.

She was about to text Sam when she heard from behind her, "How's it going?"

Hearing the familiar voice, she shifted in her chair. "Jack! I didn't know you were there."

"You were so busy, I didn't want to bother you."

"Jack, I thought it would be easy asking people to donate, but by the time I'm off the phone with some of these folks, I want to give *them* money."

He laughed and scanned the list for her mother. "You really think Brenda will make all those calls? I'd expect most of them to hang up on her."

"You've got a point." She showed him the sheet. "Which is why I've written out exactly what I want her to say—if she goes off-script, that's it—she won't be allowed to help." Truth was, her mom couldn't do any worse.

He settled his hip against her desk, without budging it at all, and gave her a sardonic smile. "You like that guy?"

"What guy?" She pushed her chair back. He was too close. Much too close, and yet, Jack could never, ever get close enough. Damn him for being a ghost!

"You know the one. About your height. Lost his wife. Room nine."

She hadn't numbered her rooms—and Jack's tone was heavy on the sarcasm. "Gary Kramer?" He seemed like a nice enough man, certainly not someone for Jack to be jealous of. "I like him very much. I like *all* my guests. They keep me in business, Jack."

"So they do. I just don't like you drinking with them. I prefer you drinking with me."

"So do I! But I will be polite, even if you can't be." Annoyed, she got up to leave, not in any mood for her jealous roommate.

Chapter Seventeen

Charlene jumped as her bedroom door slammed shut before her and the lock tumbled. She whirled around, but Jack was not visible to her as he played his tricks. The TV flickered off and on.

"Jack, this isn't funny." She folded her arms and searched her room—then swiped the air around her, looking for a certain chill that would give him away.

Her fingers brushed something and a shock of cold—like an ice bath—went through her, zinging right to the bone. She shivered and gasped for breath. "That wasn't nice."

Reaching for her blanket on the love seat, she wrapped it around her shoulders. Jack's laughter echoed and he slowly appeared, but not in strong form. Her nose scrunched and her fingertips had a pins and needles sensation. "I touched you?"

He burst out laughing, the sound an echo only she and Silva could hear. "You should see your face." The television blared static.

Her teeth were still chattering, and the blanket didn't erase the chill. She rubbed her arms.

His laugh faded slowly. "Sorry. You're shivering. Are you all right? Did I hurt you?"

"No, it felt . . . weird . . . that's all. Like jumping into the snow after being in a hot tub."

"I won't do it again." He had the good grace to act ashamed of himself. "But I didn't like you agreeing to see Gary for a drink. We have so little time together as it is."

"I understand—but don't lock the door on me! You don't get to act like a jealous husband. Not to mention that Gary is not my type."

She ran in place, trying to get warm again.

The TV settled on the hotline for David Baldwin, but the news reporter didn't spend much time on it. "David's been gone five days already. Old news, I guess."

Jack fluttered her list up from the desk. "I had a thought about Stony Brook—and Freddy Ferguson. Is there a way for you to Google Freddy and see where he did his jail time? For how long?"

Jail time . . . that would be public record. Charlene returned to her desk and sat down in the office chair. "Sure." Her fingers flew across the keyboard. Freddy Ferguson. Then Stony Brook. Long Island, New York.

Jack reminded her of what they'd read before. "David graduated in '88, but there is no record of Freddy after '86."

"Hmmm. You're right." She typed in both men's names and added the phrase "car accident."

A list of suggested websites came up and she scrolled down, Jack peering over her shoulder.

"There it is!" he said.

She dropped her gaze to where he pointed. The bottom article was about a DUI involving two college students.

Charlene brought up the article with a tap of her finger—it had been published in a small paper. She zoomed in to enlarge the print.

She read out loud, paraphrasing, "Sophomores Freddy Ferguson and David Baldwin involved in collision involving alcohol, yada, yada. David Baldwin was taken by ambulance to the hospital. Freddy taken to jail." Charlene turned to Jack. "Is that where he injured his knee?"

"It doesn't say. Is there more?" Jack asked.

"This is before the Internet, so maybe not." She went to the next search page and scrolled down.

"Oh—what's this?" Charlene clicked on the article. "Freddy Ferguson, charged with manslaughter after another DUI, involving David Baldwin and freshman *Doug* Ketchum." Charlene's pulse skipped. "Doug is the other name that David had called out—he'd said that Doug was supposed to be dead."

Dead? And now David was too. Her phone rang, startling her, and she gasped, her hand to her wildly beating heart. She eyed the screen. "Mom." Tempted to ignore it, she remembered that they were downtown and she had to answer.

"Hello?" She checked the time—only noon.

"Charlene! We're having lunch at the Lobster Shack. Are you sure you can't join us?"

"Positive, Mom. I'll see you at two—text me the address?"

"Okay—but I wanted to let you know that we have dinner plans with that detective tonight."

"You do?"

"You too, don't be silly. He's very nice and was so helpful when he gave us a tour of the police station."

Her stomach tightened. "What? A tour?"

"I wanted to know how the investigation was going, and you're right, Charlene, he wouldn't reveal a thing. Tight-lipped, like he was guarding national security or something."

She cringed, envisioning the scene. "How did that end up as dinner plans?"

"Well, I think he felt bad and so he suggested that we make a date for dinner."

A date, huh? Very sneaky, Sam, she thought. "I have guests and I need to be at the bed-and-breakfast in case I'm needed."

"I thought of that, so we're going to order barbecue from a ribs place that is supposed to be amazing."

"Mom!"

"It's a done deal, Charlene—he'll be over at six, after he gets off work. He has to run home and feed his dog, and it won't take long, he assures me. We ordered extra in case you have other guests—already paid for."

Charlene sat back in the chair, not sure if she was angry at her mom for being so pushy, or at Sam for outmaneuvering her and getting a date. But she liked ribs as much as the next red-blooded American, so she decided to just roll with it. "See you at two—send me the address."

She ended the call, realizing with the coconspiracy between Sam and her mom she'd been outplayed.

A knock sounded on her door, and she answered quickly.

Minnie waited on the other side. "Sorry to bother you—I heard you talking?"

"Yes, Mom. She invited Sam over for dinner tonight, and she's ordered ribs."

Minnie hid a smile. "Barbecue is delicious—but I don't know that I'd consider that date food."

"It isn't a date."

Jack's presence chilled behind her. He hadn't been privy to her mother's conversation.

"I think your mom is taking matters into her own hands." Minnie snickered. "I like Sam, and you're a single woman. A little flirtation won't hurt."

She thought about Jack's wrath. "That's true, I suppose. Only five more days, right?"

Minnie winked. "Anyway, I just wanted to let you know that I have to leave early—one of the grandkids caught the flu, and my daughter asked if I could sit with them—she has to work."

"Oh sure, that's fine. Where's Avery?"

"I've got her dusting in the living room. She's on a ladder, doing the higher shelves. I told her to leave the mirror." Her grin revealed her side tooth missing. "Sweet thing is being so careful."

"You like her then?"

"I do."

"Me too. Go take care of your grandchild. I hope everyone is feeling better before Christmas."

Minnie thanked her and hurried out.

Charlene found Avery safe on the ground, studying the books on the shelves she'd dusted. "You are welcome to borrow any that strike your interest."

She tugged her earbuds out—they dangled down the front of her shoulders, attached to something in her back pocket. "Really? I love to read, but I get most of mine from the school library. Have you read all these?"

"Pretty much, some were my husband's. I tend to buy most of my books online, but once in a while it's just nice to browse a library. How's school going? Pamela, Mrs. Avita, mentioned you were doing a project?"

"I have to, for extra credit, or else I won't pass." Avery rolled her eyes. "Math. My worst subject." She lifted her shoulders with a shrug. "Why do we need to know that stuff? I mean, everybody has a cell phone."

"You do?"

"Yeah." She smacked her back pocket. "It's not a cool one, but I can text, that's all I need it for."

"That, and math?" Charlene teased.

Avery giggled. "You know what I mean. Math is going to be like learning cursive—not necessary anymore. And when is someone like me gonna use geometry or algebra?"

"So, what's your project? Can I help?"

"Nope, I got it done. It ticks Mrs. Avita off so bad that her kid is in the same remedial class as me."

"Why would that make her mad?"

"Her kids transferred this year from private school—like they were so smart, but her son is a junior, like me, and needs tutoring. She doesn't like the public school and expects them to be head of the class or something."

"Does she have two sons?"

"Nope—her daughter is a freshman. She's pretty and popular and has all the best stuff—she had *no problem* fitting in." Avery twirled an earbud. "Even her dumb son has friends. Amazing what having money can get you."

"Not everything," Charlene promised. "And real friends don't care about that. Do you have anyone that you're close to? I saw that you knew Kyle the night of the auction."

"Yeah, we used to hang out and smoke."

Charlene's brow lifted.

"Don't worry, I can't actually afford cigs—and I don't like them, anyway, but it was cool to sneak around the back of the school building and share a cigarette."

Charlene hadn't had a chance to do any parenting, but she was pretty sure that Avery had really wanted a pal. "Do you still see Kyle?"

"Sometimes at the beach on the weekends—but he's working now, at the Green Market, so he doesn't have time to hang out as much. He's kinda cute, I think." She shifted her feet, her sneakers black and white Converse. "I can't *believe* I dropped that plate. Of course, he saw it."

Did Avery have a crush on Kyle? A rebel with a motorcycle—probably Kyle was popular with the teen set. "I felt really bad for Kyle that night. You too."

"I know, right?" Avery ruffled her spiky hair. "David didn't have to be such a jerk—not to me, not to Kyle, and not to all those people he gypped with those checks. I saw Mrs. Winters and Mrs. Avita—they were really bummed."

Charlene recalled looking for Avery that night, but she hadn't seen her and had assumed she'd gone home. "Did you see anything that night, Avery?"

"You mean the hit-and-run?" She shook her head. "Nah, I was pretty upset about being asked not to come back—embarrassed in front of everyone: Kyle, Mrs. Winters, and Mrs. Avita. I was going to help her with the baskets out to the car, but Dalton snagged me back in the kitchen to tell me about Kyle." She chewed her lower lip. "Kyle, well, he blew off some steam about David occasionally, but he loved his dad."

This is interesting. "You know what Dalton said about Kyle?"

"Yeah—he's a major douchebag," Avery informed her. "He let Kyle take the rap for something . . ." She trailed off and didn't say what. "That was high school, right, so it doesn't matter anymore, but you can't trust someone like that. And after this latest thing? I don't think they're friends anymore."

Good, Charlene wanted to say. The two walked to the kitchen and Charlene put on the electric kettle for tea. "Do you like Kyle?"

Avery turned scarlet. "No!" She studied her short fingernails, painted black. "Maybe—but he has a thing for Jessica, even though she's, like, way older."

Young love. "Want some tea or hot chocolate?"

Avery pulled her cell phone from her back pocket—it was one that you could pay for the minutes as you used them and wasn't fancy or a name brand. "I still have an hour of work and a list of things that Minnie gave me to do before I go, so no, thank you. I really like this job, Charlene."

Charlene resisted giving the girl a hug—but just barely. "I'm glad—in that case, I will continue making phone calls to these businesses for fund-raisers. I don't want to let Felicity House down."

Avery popped in her earbuds and gave Charlene a nod before heading back to the living room.

"I can't quite figure her out just yet," Jack said from his place at the kitchen table. "Don't be fooled by a teenaged con artist, okay?"

"Stop it," she whispered. "She's been very hardworking."

"We'll see."

She gave him the eye and he disappeared—literally,

fluttering a stack of paper napkins on the table in his wake.

Charlene made it all the way through the *G*'s on her list when it was time to take Avery home and pick up her parents. Feeling very good about her new employee, she signed Avery in and made plans to pick her up on Friday, then drove to the Lobster Shack.

Her parents were bundled up on the bright, cold afternoon, waiting on the sidewalk for her. Charlene parked. They got in—her dad in the front this time and her mom in the back. "Would you like to check out Vintage Treasures?"

She could see her parents and Archie getting along famously.

Her mom didn't look so good and lay down across the back seat. "Can we go home? I think I overstuffed myself on the lobster rolls—they were soooo good."

"No problem—are you feeling okay, Dad?"

"Right as rain, but I stopped before I burst."

"Just be quiet, Michael," her mother droned.

"Should we cancel dinner tonight?" Charlene asked. Sam would understand. That would free up some time to finish making phone calls for the kids—Christmas was only three days away.

"Maybe we should reschedule for tomorrow," her mom said in a sad voice.

Charlene nodded. Instead of phone calls—what if she appealed to Tori on a personal level? Make her listen to reason regarding Felicity House. And maybe Tori would know how Charlene could contact Freddy. She wouldn't be gone long, and her dad could handle the guests if there was a problem.

"I have some local peppermint tea that will make you feel much better, Mom. And then I can run some errands this afternoon, Dad, if you don't mind manning the place?"

"I'd be happy to," he said.

Her mom groaned, and Charlene actually felt sorry for her.

Chapter Eighteen

Charlene brought her parents home and made her mother the peppermint tea, then got back in the car and drove to her favorite local florist. She knew she could do better fund-raising in person than over the phone.

Witches Bloom was decorated festively with fanciful wreaths and garlands, and she was hit by the smell of evergreen, pine, and cinnamon. While she waited to speak to the manager, Margaret Tissel, who was busy ringing up a big order, Charlene chose a centerpiece for her dining room table—long and narrow, with three red candles and greenery, red berries, and pine cones.

She thought of Tori, and how to get the woman to open up to her. Who didn't like getting flowers? And since she wasn't going to the funeral service, it would be appropriate to bring flowers to Tori's home.

Charlene grinned as she picked out a flashy gold Christmas tabletop arrangement and stepped up to the counter with her arrangements. She had a standing monthly order for flowers for the foyer.

Margaret, who had just turned sixty, had a long gray ponytail that dangled over one shoulder and black-framed glasses on her slender face. She was tall, possibly five foot ten, wearing a long, flower-patterned skirt, a long-sleeve tee, and three ropes of multicolored beads, which swayed when she moved.

"Hi, Charlene. These are lovely. Is there anything else I can help you with today?"

"Actually, there is." Charlene took a brochure for Felicity House out of her tote. "A few days ago, this organization was expecting a rather large check, one that would enable them to build a new wing and house another twenty needy children, and it didn't happen."

"God, I heard," Margaret said, lowering her voice. "I know Alice and she told me what happened to poor David, run over that way. Who would do such a thing?" She glanced at the brochure. "How can I help?"

Charlene's shoulders relaxed. "If you're willing, you can either make out a check to Felicity House or send one directly to them. If you'd prefer to donate toys for the children, that would also be appreciated. We want to make sure they don't go without this Christmas."

"Wait a sec. Let me get my checkbook." Margaret wrote it out for two hundred, and Charlene put it into a special brown envelope she kept in her bag.

"Thank you so much, Margaret."

"Do you need help getting your items in the car?"

"No—thanks, though. And Merry Christmas."

A few minutes later, Charlene had the arrangements in the back and drove to Tori and David's address that she'd found in the online Salem directory. Tori's was a modest home, on a very nice street, but not flashy like she'd expected.

Pre-lottery, she thought. It was a two-story with white siding, black trim on the shutters and doors, a double paved driveway, and a pretty walkway framed by dozens of poinsettias and holiday lighting. An oak tree in the center of the lawn had a flower bed underneath, with evergreen bushes poking out of the remnants of snow left over from the rain. A giant metal moving box was to the left of the driveway.

She parked, took out the smaller gold arrangement from the back of her Pilot, braced herself for a heated argument, and knocked on the door.

No one answered, but she saw someone peeking out the framed living room window, so she knocked louder.

Tori opened at last, wearing leopard-print tights and a loose black knit sweater, drooped to expose one slender shoulder. "What are you doing here?" she drawled.

Charlene put on her best Mary Poppins smile and thrust out the floral arrangement. It had red carnations, a gold candle, and gold ribbons amid green ferns.

Tori eyed it warily before accepting it. "Thank you. What's this for?"

"An apology," she said, attempting to sound genuine. "I won't be able to attend the Christmas Eve service. I have a house filled with guests and—"

"Ah, geez. As if I cared." Tori held the arrangement in one hand, her nails a bright blue, her hip jutted forward.

"Tori, you don't have to pretend with me. I saw you the night David was killed. You were hysterical with grief." Charlene poured sincerity into each word. "I know you were planning on leaving together. You're probably heartsick."

"You don't know nothin'."

Charlene stepped back at the poison in her tone.

Tori stared at her. "You want something? I already thanked you for the flowers." She fluttered her hand in the air. "Now you can turn around and say goodbye."

"Tori." She reached for her bony wrist, hoping she could appeal to the Tori who didn't have to work so hard at being perfect. The little girl who maybe knew what it was like to go without. "Can I come in for a moment? I really am so sorry about David."

Tori looked from the flowers to Charlene. "Okay. But no guilt trip, got it?"

"Okay." Charlene realized that she had one chance to reach Tori and maybe get her to fund the check for Felicity House. She followed Tori into the living room. There was a brick fireplace against one wall and two matching striped beige and gray sofas with a large ornate armchair facing the fireplace. A square onyx and glass coffee table sat in the center. There was no clutter. The only personal photo was of Tori and David on the mantel. No books, just a *Shape* magazine that looked well leafed through, under the glass table.

"I just put it on the market, which is why it's so boring."

Charlene knew that to sell the home she'd probably packed up all the personal stuff. Realtors were big on decluttering, making the house more appealing to prospective buyers.

"I like it," Charlene said.

"Seriously? I prefer modern." Tori put the flower arrangement on the coffee table and took a seat on the sofa.

Unasked, Charlene sat down on the edge of the heavily cushioned armchair. Three small round pillows were tucked in the back. "My house goes back a few hundred years."

Tori twirled a short blond wisp around her finger. "To each his own." She gave Charlene a calculated look. "So why are you here? You expect a confession or something?"

"No, you didn't kill your husband."

Tori's bare shoulder eased an inch or two. "So? What do you want with me, then?"

Charlene knew she'd have to tread carefully if she wanted to make any headway with the young widow. She gestured to the photo. "Just an answer to a few questions. I'm curious by nature." She smiled, but Tori didn't join her. "How long were you and David married for?"

"Two years, but what's it to you?"

"I want to know who killed David, don't you?"

"Not really. I just want to get the hell away from here." She sighed, admiring her long, painted fingernails. "I loved him, but we had no passion. When we first met? It was hot and heavy. When you're sneaking around with another woman's husband, things tend to be exciting. All those secret phone calls late in the night . . . meeting in strange places. Doing it anytime you can." Tori raised a slender arm on the back of the sofa and folded one leg over the other. She looked smugly at Charlene, as if daring her to say anything.

Charlene didn't shock easily—not anymore. "I'm sure it was fun for you. Not so much for Linda, though. Probably broke her heart."

"That's where you're wrong. You and everyone else."

Tori leaned forward. "You guys think you're all so smart. As if you know me and get to judge. Well, I might not be a saint, but neither is Linda."

"What do you mean?" Charlene edged closer—she'd liked the nurse.

"I mean that Linda was cheating on David before I ever got involved. Her and Vincent were going at it like two cats in an alley." She gave an ugly laugh. "Yeah, that's right. David came crying to me one night at the gym, and I felt kind of sorry for the guy. One thing led to another. We went out for drinks. Then we started having drinks more and more often. He'd show up at my apartment and we'd get it on. Yeah, it was hot. Affairs always are. Marriage kills passion."

Charlene touched her heart-shaped diamond studs. The last gift that her beloved Jared had given her. And he'd given her so much . . . all his devotion, all his love. "I never thought marriage was boring, not for one second. I loved my husband and trusted him completely. We didn't need anyone else."

"Yeah." Tori pretended to yawn. "That's what you think. I bet he was having a good time when you weren't looking. Did he come home late some nights?" she asked with a sly smile. "Bet he did, huh?" Her eyes sparkled with malicious glee.

Tori was enjoying herself at Charlene's expense.

"We worked in the same office, and we both had to stay late some nights. We were in advertising, on separate teams." She lifted her chin. "We never had to cheat to get our thrills. We had it at home."

"Separate teams." Tori spoke slowly and plucked a red carnation from the arrangement, running it up and down her cheek, never taking her eyes off Charlene. "Hmm . . . now that's interesting. Tell me more."

Charlene stood. "Don't you dare insinuate that my husband would cheat. Your own moral code has nothing to do with mine or Jared's. Our love was pure. Untainted."

Tori laughed. "Who are you trying to kid? Yourself?"

Charlene's fingers turned inward, making a tight fist, but she wouldn't give this woman the satisfaction to know she'd scored a hit. She was here for the kids at Felicity House. "Why was Linda cheating with Vincent?" Charlene moved the topic away from herself as she sat down again. "Did that happen before they moved to Salem?"

"I'm not sure. According to David"—she waved the carnation around and around, looking amused—"he'd get home from work and smell cigar smoke. He didn't smoke, but Vincent sure did. Guess he did other things that David neglected to do too." She broke the end of the carnation off and tucked the flower behind her ear. "But I'm more interested in you. And Jared," she said in a singsong voice. "What was that naughty boy up to?"

Charlene was repulsed by this woman and no longer interested in finding the lost girl inside. The innocent girl was dead and gone. Only bitterness lingered.

She'd come to find out about Freddy, and to see if she could get Tori to honor David's check to Felicity House. Focus. "Why leave town? David's gone, but you still have Zane. I bet that romance is still going hot. With David working nights, you two could get away with murder."

The figure of speech came out of her mouth and settled in the room between them like a ticking time bomb.

Brow arched, Tori asked, "What did you say?"

Charlene dabbed her hot cheeks. "I didn't mean anything—just that you and Zane can be together now."

Tori stood and wrapped the knit sweater tight around her body. "David and I were planning on running away together. He messed that up by getting run over. I had no reason to kill him. He was my ticket out of here." Her mouth trembled. "Now everybody hates me."

"They wouldn't if you did the right thing."

"Right thing?" She snorted. "I'm moving right after the service. The cops will know where I am, but I don't feel safe here in Salem. Not even Zane will know."

She *had* wondered if Zane would make the new move, but Tori was obviously good at looking out for Tori. Why was she afraid? "Tori, do you think that David's death might have been on purpose?"

Her eyes widened with fear. "I don't know! I've asked myself that a dozen times—if someone could kill him—what if I'm next? If I'm gone, then you know who would inherit?" She paced around the coffee table. "You better believe that I asked around, but Linda worked at the hospital until eight thirty that night. One of the ladies I know from the gym is a neighbor of hers, and she said she saw Linda arrive home after that, and that she never left. Kyle got off work at nine and then came to Bella's—you saw how pissed he was when he left. He was home by the time David"—she hitched in a breath—"was hit. The neighbor confirmed that she heard the motorcycle."

Charlene nodded as she listened, remembering how close the houses were together. Linda and Kyle had alibis. So, supposedly, did Zane.

Tori shook her finger at Charlene. "I had nothing to gain, so I didn't kill him. I wouldn't have." She folded her arms across her middle. "I am so done with this town, and these narrow-minded people."

"You checked for Linda and Kyle, but what about

Freddy? I know he and David were in a car accident together, back in college. He went to jail, right? Maybe he had some kind of vendetta."

Tori turned to Charlene with interest. "If he did, I don't know what it was. He dropped by a few times, wanting to talk, but I don't have time to listen to some drunk guy babble on about the glory days—I wasn't even *born* yet."

"Is he staying nearby?"

Her lips curled. "Sleep Inn. I remember because he thought it was so funny—sleeping in. Sleep Inn." She shuddered. "What a dive. He's staying through David's service on Christmas Eve and wants to get together. He asked if David had left anything for him, which he didn't—like David had him in the will or something. He wanted a handout, like all those losers at the auction." She dropped her hands and went back to pacing, her head down as if thinking.

This was Charlene's chance. "They aren't losers, Tori. It's really important to the children that Felicity House gets the check. They want to build another addition, which will enable them to house another twenty children." She stepped in front of Tori, forcing her to look up. "At-risk kids. Please, Tori, you have the rest of the money! Buy a big yacht, have a great life. But do the right thing for these kids."

Tori lifted her chin, her gaze ice-cold. "I will do nothing. I don't owe them anything."

"You were a kid." Charlene kept her eyes on hers. "Maybe life kicked you in the shins a few times. You must know what it's like." She put out a hand when Tori tried to step aside. "Just listen. These kids have had more than a few kicks. They would be homeless without Felicity House. Their parents are either addicts, in jail, or dead. Have a heart, Tori. Do the right thing. Just once."

"Just once? You don't know me. Why should I? Nobody did the right thing by me. Besides, the place is subsidized. I know. I checked. They got that nice house with money from United Way."

"That's the teens' house, but what about the younger ones?" Tamil's bright smile shone in her mind.

"My accountant says it's going belly-up—it's not a good investment."

No matter what Charlene said, Tori had an excuse. She released a weary sigh. "I'm sorry. I'm really sorry."

"You should be. Why are you in my home asking me for money? Shame on you. You're no better than the others. Thanks for the flowers, now get out." Tori pointed to the door.

"I'm not sorry for asking, I'm sorry for you. Whatever happened to turn you into this person?" Charlene walked away, shaking her head. "I just hope these children don't end up the same way. That would truly break my heart." At the door she looked back one last time. "It's a shame you don't have one."

"Let the door slam behind you," Tori yelled. "And don't come back."

Charlene left the vile woman, anger heating her as she returned to her Pilot. Now what was she supposed to do?

CHAPTER NINETEEN

Charlene sat in her Pilot as it warmed, looking from the moving pod to Tori's front door. As much as she disliked the woman, Tori had not driven the car that had run David over.

Should she track down Freddy, if he was still in town? David's service was in two days, Christmas Eve. She recalled Freddy's gaunt appearance at the remembrance, and the button on his shirt misaligned. He'd probably fallen off the wagon, hard.

She could just go home, but Tori's comments about Freddy going on about the glory days, asking if David had left something for him, made her wonder if Freddy was behind the hit-and-run. He'd killed somebody with a car once. Who was to say he wouldn't do it again?

Salem wasn't that big of a place. She plugged in "Sleep Inn" to her GPS and found one only ten minutes away. Freddy didn't have friends in Salem to spend his time with. David hadn't given Kyle, or Linda, good reason to make him welcome, and he'd know better than to expect it from Tori.

Charlene could easily imagine what he was doing to wile away the hours. He'd hit the nearest bar. She opened the search to include bars. Sailor's Roost, Dead Man's Watering Hole, Whistler's Keg.

Had he driven from New York? It was worth a few minutes to question Freddy, possibly get another drunk driver off the streets.

She found the Sleep Inn and parked. At four in the afternoon, the sky was gray and overcast, the clouds heavy with possible snow. Right next door to the cheap hotel was Sailor's Roost. The place was made of timber that listed to the left, and had an old-fashioned sign hanging out front painted with a yellow-slickered sailor, who had a pipe and a bushy beard.

Here goes nothing, she thought, and entered the bar. It smelled like smoke—all kinds, from cigarettes, to weed, to cherry pipe tobacco—though she didn't see anybody smoking.

The place was well-lit, and each of the four walls had a different sport playing on huge television screens.

"Welcome!" A young lady greeted her from behind the bar. Pretty in a hard way, her hair was bleached blond, her face prematurely aged. "What can I get ya?"

"I just have a few questions," Charlene said.

"Sure, you staying over at the Inn?"

"No, but I'm looking for someone who is."

The girl laughed good-naturedly and gestured to the men and women in various jerseys. "We have three-dollar pitchers, and our nachos are good."

Charlene scanned the faces but didn't see Freddy. "Freddy Ferguson—midfifties, thin—oh, that doesn't help. He was a friend of David Baldwin's."

The girl gave her a blank expression, but then suggested, "There's a bar inside the Sleep Inn—you might want to check there."

Dredging up a name from her online search, Charlene asked, "The Whistler's Keg?"

The girl drew back in alarm. "My friend got her purse stolen there last weekend, so if you go, hide your bag under your jacket. I'd try the Inn first, but Whistler's Keg is on the other side of the motel. Be careful, and Merry Christmas."

Charlene left the bar and entered the Sleep Inn. Everything seemed to be made of cheap laminate and colored in mustard and avocado—original to the seventies. An Indian couple studiously ignored her when she entered the lobby. A sign pointed to the bar and restaurant to the left, so Charlene followed her nose.

Cheery holiday faces didn't seem to mind the cheap motel food as they listened to Christmas music and ate their fill—she noticed the ham special was popular, with mashed potatoes and green beans. Advertised as only $6.99 on the sign.

The waitress hustled to the podium, greeting her with a grin and a menu. Charlene smiled back. "I'm looking for someone—Freddy Ferguson? He's staying here at the hotel."

Sunshine, or so her name tag proclaimed, said, "Oh, I know him—he's been here a week or so, and always orders eggs for breakfast. Went next door to Whistler's Keg to get a beer—Jeb's running a Christmas special on Rolling Rock. A buck a bottle."

"Thank you."

Charlene left the diner and eyed the darkening sky. She wouldn't feel safe in this area alone after dark—the streetlamps weren't on every corner like the Pedestrian Mall, loaded with businesses and people. Foot traffic here was nil.

What had Freddy expected David to give him—money, or forgiveness? She had to ask Freddy about why he'd come to Salem. Had David invited him, or did Freddy have his hand out? Why had Freddy brought David's jersey? Why had Freddy kept it? It seemed odd to her.

She raised her head, alert for others, but she was alone as she walked the twelve feet from the diner to Whistler's Keg, a wood structure in need of paint, one window shaded by dark curtains, and a door. A buck a beer, huh?

Just the type of place a person looking to get drunk cheap would hang out.

Her closest brush with addiction was the woman who had killed Jared. Finding out if Freddy had killed David, she figured, was worth the possible danger of going into this seedy bar. David deserved justice, as she'd gotten justice for Jared. She had her phone in her hand, her thumb on Sam's number for speed dial.

She twisted the brass knob of the wooden plank door and paused at the threshold before stepping inside. The interior was darkly paneled and lit by the golden glow of a candle lamp flickering at each of ten tables, the whole room only twelve by twelve, which made her claustrophobic.

No music played, just a television on so low at the bar that she wondered if it was broken.

The bartender, Jeb, had so many wrinkles it was impossible to tell his age. He blinked at her in surprise. "You lost, or lookin' for your daddy?" He cackled at his own joke and the laughter turned into a cough.

She braced herself and stepped forward. "I'm looking for Freddy Ferguson." She peered around the room—three men, three separate tables, two buckets of beer.

"People in here generally don't want to be found," the bartender said. "He your old man?" He laughed again and smacked the counter, startling a fourth gentleman who had been dozing at a table to the left of the bar. Had she finally found Freddy?

"No." Charlene glanced around the space before taking another few steps.

The man who'd appeared to be snoozing blinked blurry eyes and tried to focus on her. "Have we met?"

"Hi, Freddy, I'm Charlene. At David Baldwin's remembrance?" Technically they hadn't been introduced—she'd been watching Linda block him from Kyle.

"Oh, yeah. I got to meet David's kid—gave him David's jersey." He straightened, but then slumped as if that was too much effort.

"Can we . . ." She counted three empty beer bottles at his table, the smell of hops overpowering. "Can we talk?" Charlene pointed to one of the corner tables that was slightly better lit—she wanted to see his face for the truth when she asked him why he'd come to Salem.

"Sure, but the price is a beer." Freddy looked at the bartender. "Save my chair?"

The bartender snorted and waved a gnarled hand to the mostly empty bar. "No worries."

Freddy knocked on the counter and waited for Jeb to drop off a bright green Rolling Rock bottle. "Make it two."

"Can I get you something?" Jeb asked Charlene.

"Coffee's good, thanks." She pulled out a five to pay for the drinks.

Freddy ambled toward Charlene with a wary smile. Up close, it was hard to believe the tall man was in his midfifties—his eyes were red-rimmed, his nose also veined with purple and red, his jowls slack, his hair a dark gray. He could've been mistaken for David's dad, rather than friend.

She matched his square jaw with the one from the Stony Brook yearbook, but only because she was searching for similarities.

"Thank you for talking to me," she said. "I really liked David." Charlene stirred her coffee, knowing she wouldn't drink it—the plastic stirrer stood upright in the burnt-smelling brew.

"Everybody did."

The other patrons were all in their own worlds and paid no attention to Charlene or Freddy. She took her Styrofoam cup of coffee to the cleared table. "Would you like this too?"

"Yeah, sure." Freddy reached for the sugar packets and emptied three into the sludge-like coffee. "How'd ya find me?"

"I spoke with Tori—she mentioned you'd be around until after the service and that you were staying at the Sleep Inn. Did the police instruct you to stay until after the investigation?"

"They hinted it'd be better for me not to leave town. But I was kind of hopin' that David would leave me something." He sniffed and blew his nose loudly in a paper napkin. "Tori won't give me the time of day. Not sure what he was doing with that tramp," he said. "I saw her making out with that blond body builder."

"You did? When?"

He gave a sour smile. "I got here last Friday—dropped by David's place early, to surprise him, ya know? But I got a surprise of my own."

She thought back to how angry David had been on Saturday, the night of the auction, specifically about Zane. "Did you tell David?"

His red eyes welled with easy tears. "That was the last thing we talked about."

"When was that? You'd mentioned that he'd invited you to come for dinner, but something came up?"

He slurped the coffee and made a face, then shrugged. "That wasn't exactly true," he admitted. "He rescheduled for the next night. I could tell he was embarrassed by me." He peeked back over his shoulder and shivered.

"You told him you'd seen Tori with Zane?" That explained Tori's aversion to Freddy—he'd busted her with her lover. "He must have taken that hard."

"Yeah." He braced for a bad taste and took another drink. "We were going to meet up Sunday night. I told him that I couldn't do it anymore. That I *remembered*." He tapped his temple with his forefinger.

"What?"

"About Doug." His yellowed teeth peeked from between dry lips. Was he driven by guilt to the bottle?

Doug had been the other guy in the car. "Tell me what happened," she said, her stomach tight. She was sitting across from the man who had taken a life, and it made her nauseous. This man was a monster of his own making—or was it his addiction? Was that any justification?

Charlene was too emotionally close to be an unbiased observer, no matter how many prayers she'd said for the woman—Jared was gone. The woman was being punished as the law saw fit.

If she was to be fair, then yes, Freddy had also paid for his crime.

"I recognized your jersey from Stony Brook," she said, to prod the conversation.

"Did you go there too?" His red blurry eyes squinted at her.

"No, I grew up in Chicago."

Freddy looked over Charlene's shoulder into the shadows of the dark bar. "Me and David were best friends all through elementary school—our parents were middle class—hard workers but no money set aside for college. We played every sport—started every team—we were magic together."

He drank the rest of the bad coffee with a grimace and glanced longingly toward his untouched beer, but he didn't so much as sip it.

Charlene gave Freddy another nudge to keep him talking. "Did he think he was better than you?"

"It wasn't that. We had college plans—to be better than our folks. David was okay smart, but me, well, I struggled." His voice trailed off before booming back. "We needed scholarships."

Thinking of the jersey he'd given to Kyle, she said, "Sports?"

"They didn't have football scholarships back in the eighties—we had to get merit scholarships. David charmed his way into getting girls to tutor him—nobody could be as charming as David."

She'd heard that many times before and had seen it for herself.

Freddy's hand trembled around the white cup, empty now. "I couldn't keep up and was hanging on by a thread at Stony Brook. One thing I could do better than David was throw a football—he ran circles around me in drills, but I had distance down the field."

His smile peeked through the depressing atmosphere like a hint of sun quickly covered by a cloud. "Another thing I could do better than David was drink."

He rubbed his arms and glanced over her shoulder again. "I'm getting to it," he muttered.

Charlene looked behind her—nobody was there. Who was he talking to? Was he delusional, or haunted by spirits of his past? She recalled David's yearbook photo from college, forever a young man.

"Drinking like a fish is a Ferguson family pastime."

She waited, barring herself from feeling empathy for him.

"Times were different then, and people talked about drinking and drug addiction under their breath, like they were dirty little secrets. Wasn't like now, where everybody is addicted to something, right?"

He looked at her without expecting an answer and kept on. "So, David was talented, getting good grades, and on the starting team. I was popular for drinking and making people laugh. Laughing *at me* for being a dumb-ass. There was no stunt I wouldn't do with enough rum in my gut. Got so that I embarrassed David, which pissed me off, I don't mind saying."

His voice roughened and Charlene slipped her hand into her coat pocket, palming her phone for a sense of safety. "Was the accident why you and David weren't friends anymore?"

"I was the weight around his ankles." He glared into

the dark shadows behind Charlene. "Keeping him down. One Friday night we got into a car accident—I was the idiot drinking and racing on the back roads. David got hurt, and I was the bad guy." He scrubbed a shaking hand over his ravished face. "Kept telling me to pull over, called me a loser, which just made me angrier. My foot jammed down on the pedal harder and harder."

Charlene's stomach did another flip. "Is that when David hurt his leg and couldn't play?"

Freddy's gray skin mottled with red anger. "It was a damn accident. God, I could never live that down. I was put on probation and I knew that if I didn't bring my grades up, I'd be booted out of Stony Brook."

"But you got to take his place on the team?"

He slammed his palm against the cheap wood table. "Is that what you think?" Freddy leaned toward her, gray brows drawn. "We were best friends, lady. I would have died for him." He closed his eyes against some pain that Charlene didn't know—did he feel like David owed him? Is that why he'd come here—for a payoff?

He averted his gaze, once again, over her shoulder. "Way back when, I told David I was holding him back—I knew it. But I didn't hurt his leg on purpose. He knew that, he said, and he told me he wasn't listening to those jackasses who said otherwise."

"Who is Doug?"

Tears spilled down his thin cheeks. "He was my other friend—more like me than a superstar like David. He figured this was his only year at Stony Brook, too—we didn't care. One Friday night, I kind of strong-armed David into partying with us. He got so drunk he saw stars."

Freddy straightened as he retold the tale, accepting his role as he shared what had happened.

"We went back to the scene of the previous accident to race again, taking turns driving my old car. I knew it was the end of something for us, and I didn't want it to be—one more drink, one more race." He choked back a sob and struck his chest. "I was losing my best friend, who refused to read the writing on the wall. He'd go on and be successful, and I'd turn into my old man, dead at fifty from liver disease—if I was lucky."

Charlene said, "You make it sound like you didn't have a choice."

"Did I?" He rubbed his gut. "I'll be gone by this time next year."

Sudden compassion welled inside her, and she squelched it down. What she'd assumed was ravaged features from alcohol could also be illness. "Doug never saw twenty-two—he died with *you* behind the wheel."

"I see Doug every single day," Freddy droned. "You probably think I'm crazy. His ghost never left me. And here's the bitch," he laughed sardonically.

She hunkered into her jacket and stared at Freddy over the dim candle. Was he serious about being haunted? Charlene knew enough now not to discredit the paranormal—she peered around her, eyes squinted, but couldn't make anything out. Freddy kept rubbing his arms, like he was cold, and that was one of the signs that signified when Jack was around for her.

"What?" What could be worse than what he'd shared so far?

"After decades of sobriety and counseling, I discovered that I hadn't been behind the wheel."

What? Not the driver. "What do you mean?" Her voice came out sharp.

"Last month I had a breakthrough in my therapy—

something that I hadn't been willing to accept before my recent diagnosis of liver cancer. I'm dying, right? I've carried Doug's ghost for all of these years." He jerked his thumb behind him, but Charlene didn't see anything. "Figured it was my fault that he'd died, I deserved to be haunted."

He was serious. Jack was not the only ghost, but Doug stayed with Freddy, while Jack was trapped to his house.

Freddy crumpled the Styrofoam cup in anger. "Guilt destroyed my life. I don't own a car; I don't trust myself to make friends. Until last month, I was sober as a church mouse."

"What changed?"

"I found out that my best friend, the man I would have died for, had set me up—got me sent to jail on manslaughter. But it wasn't me." He lifted his hairline to show a jagged pink scar on the right side of his temple. The passenger side of the car. "David Baldwin drove the night Doug was killed."

"No." She sat back in shock, trying to make sense of his words. David had set Freddy up?

"Yeah, my shrink thinks my impending death allowed me to truly recall what happened—the smack of the bumper into the tree. Doug's body flying out of the car as the glass shattered. I was on the passenger side." Tears flowed down Freddy's face. "After we hit the tree, I was passed out, right, but David must've put me behind the wheel and himself on the passenger side. Cops thought it was me, and since I'd done it before and it was my car, I believed it."

Charlene's belly churned in disbelief—this was not what she'd expected to hear. "You came here to confront David?"

"You don't get it, lady." He wiped condensation off the beer bottle, his tone thick with sorrow. "I brought him his jersey as a peace offering. I'd forgiven him, but first he had to confess. Figured I deserved that. We were s'posed to meet for dinner, but he blew me off. Then, he died. No resolution for either of us."

She remembered the horror on David's face when he'd looked out the window, when he'd said the name *Freddy*, then *Doug*.

Charlene asked a question she'd asked before, hoping for the truth this time. "Were you there that night? Be honest. Help me find who killed David. I believe you, about Doug. Maybe telling the truth will set you both free."

Freddy licked his lips as he looked from the beer to Charlene. "Yeah, I was there, but just for a minute. I was havin' a little nip for the guts to confront David—I waited across the road." He winced and glared at the space behind him.

This time Charlene noticed the chill. "He saw you, and ran out. David said the name *Doug*."

Freddy groaned and reached for the beer, taking a hefty swallow.

"What did you see?" Charlene pressed.

"Nothin'. A black shadow, and then I hid."

"A black shadow?" That made no sense.

His hand trembled and he finished the bottle of Rolling Rock in three gulps. "It burst from nowhere. Gin gives me nightmares, so maybe I was seeing things. I hightailed it back to the motel and convinced myself it was the booze."

"Did you tell this to the police?"

He grimaced. "Sure. I told the officer that I saw

nothin'. They quit hassling me—I was drunk. Makes me un . . . unre . . . something."

"Unreliable witness."

"Yeah, that's it."

David must have seen Doug's ghost and known that Freddy had discovered the truth.

David had made a date for dinner with Freddy for Sunday night, when he'd had no intention of being in Salem. How awful.

She pressed her hand to her stomach. "I am very sorry for your losses. I . . ." What could she say? That she believed him, about his ghost? That she felt his betrayal? That she, too, strove to offer forgiveness?

In the end, Charlene stood and offered him a hug.

Sometimes there were just no words to say.

Chapter Twenty

Charlene walked out of the sleazy bar in a complete daze after her meeting with Freddy, but immediately reached for her phone as she recalled the sketchy neighborhood she was in. The broken sidewalk wasn't lit by streetlamps, but she used her flashlight app until she was on the other side of the Sleep Inn and the parking lot. Once she was inside her car, she risked a look at her phone. Three missed calls from Sam.

The dreary bar, Freddy, the reveal of David's lie and cover-up to save himself, tempted to bring on a crying jag.

She deserved some Sam time to hold off the blues. Calling him back, she said, "Hey. Sorry I missed you. Did you get my text? Mom stuffed herself on lobster rolls, so we'll have to reschedule ribs. I was thinking tomorrow?"

"I didn't mean to blow up your phone, but I'd hoped

we might get together for a quick bite, just you and me. Tomorrow I'll be in New York and it might be late when I get back."

For a trial. "That's right! I forgot."

"I won't keep you long—I know you have guests and your parents in town." His rich chuckle made her heart feel lighter. "Any chance I can commandeer your attention for an hour?"

"Hmm. A whole hour?" She pretended to think about it. "How about Cod and Capers? I want to hit Sharon up for a donation for Felicity House. Can you meet me there?"

"Won't say no. I'm going to jump while the jumping's good. How's the fundraising going, anyway?"

"I'll tell you all about it over dinner. I'm looking forward to it, Sam. See you soon."

She parked in front of the harborside restaurant at Pickering Wharf, and upon entering asked to be seated at a booth by the window.

"We're clearing one of the tables now," the hostess replied. "It'll only be a few minutes." The restaurant was bustling with activity, but with the number of tourists in town for the Christmas holidays it was no wonder. The wharf was a popular destination, with charter boats and quaint shops.

Charlene spotted Sharon behind the bar counter, her face pink from exertion, her thick red hair tied in a knot to keep off her face. Sharon had customers at every bar stool and people lined up behind, angling to get a drink. Obviously swamped, Charlene decided to wait until after their dinner to have her chat.

She recognized a few of the locals but surmised that most were tourists or families visiting for the holidays.

Ernie Harvey from Salem Realty sat at an inside table. Should she go over and say hello? He'd sold Charlene her home at a bargain basement price . . . not mentioning that it came with a ghost who'd frightened away several previous buyers. Regardless, she was willing to let bygones be bygones since if he had warned her, she'd never have bought her beautiful mansion, or had the privilege to know Jack.

She gave him a friendly wave and wondered if he was meeting with prospective clients. A couple in their thirties, their daughter seated in a booster chair. She looked about three, with blond bouncy curls and pink cheeks. Adorable.

Charlene turned to see Archie from Vintage Treasures with a plump lady in her midfifties. The woman appeared to be bored to death, and she wondered if it was his wife. Archie always flirted with her when she came into his shop, and she didn't know if he was married or not. The sly dog.

Suddenly, she felt a hand at her waist. Sam.

"Hey." She bumped his shoulder, happy to see him. After the meeting with Tori and then Freddy, she needed gorgeous, good-hearted Sam.

"Hey, beautiful. Glad you could make time for me." Sam peered down at her from his six-foot-four frame, his chocolate-brown eyes filled with warmth. He was wearing his customary dark blue jeans, a Ralph Lauren plaid shirt—she recognized it because Jared had owned the same one—and an open wool coat, black loafers. His thick, wavy hair curled around his ears, and the grin on his face made her pulse jump.

She knew he was interested in a relationship with her, and quite frankly, if it wasn't for Jack she'd be tempted.

But Detective follow-the-rules Sam was a man who believed in tangible things that you could touch, see, and smell. Just as she had once.

He didn't believe in ghosts, so she couldn't tell him about Jack, or their friendship. Nor could she discuss running all over Salem talking to people, which he'd see as interfering in his investigation. She saw it differently. So, so long as they didn't talk about those two things, dinner would be wonderful.

Perhaps searching for David's murderer had opened up that channel for her, and now it wouldn't close. Like a bloodhound, she couldn't stop once she'd caught the scent.

"Your table is ready. Take them to twelve," the hostess told the twentysomething waitress. She had a long blond braid down her back and reminded her of Elsa in the Disney movie *Frozen*.

Sam kept his hand on her back as they followed the waitress to their table, and then sat across from her, his attention unwavering. He was a really good guy. Jared would approve, she knew. Maybe that voice she'd heard earlier *had* been his?

"I'm Michelle, and I'll be your server tonight." She handed them menus. "Can I get you a drink?"

Sam lifted his eyebrow at Charlene. "Would you like wine?"

"Yes, please. But ice water with lemon as well."

"I'll be right back to tell you about our specials."

"She's very pretty," Charlene said, watching the waitress as she dashed away.

"So are you." His eyes made her mouth water. She wished she had the iced glass in her hand to cool her down.

"You're not so bad yourself," she said. She picked up the menu and pretended to find it interesting.

"Why do you look away?" he asked softly.

"Why do you stare?" she countered.

He chuckled. "You like to challenge me, don't you?"

"Not sure what you mean." She fidgeted with her cloth napkin, finally putting it in her lap.

"Sure you do. Why do you hold me at arm's length?" He rubbed his shaved chin, his long mustache framing his mouth. "Never met a woman as stubborn as you."

"I'm not stubborn; well, maybe just a little." She looked directly into his eyes, not wanting to play games. "I just moved in three months ago, and I've been incredibly busy as you well know. I'm not intentionally putting you off. I don't want to lead you on. I find you very attractive."

Michelle returned with the ice waters. "Have you decided?" she asked.

Neither of them glanced her way or answered her.

"Want me to come back later?"

Sam broke the silence. "Charlene, red or white?"

"Red." She cleared her throat and quickly took a sip of water.

"We'll have two glasses of the Pinot Noir, Sonoma-Cutrer." The girl rushed away. He reached across the table and took her hand. "Hope you don't mind me ordering for you, but I think you'll like it."

"Yes, it's wonderful. Jared and I visited Sonoma Valley and enjoyed a few of the wineries." As soon as she saw his face, she wished she hadn't mentioned that.

"I'm sure you have many great memories together." He dropped her hand.

"Sam. I'm sorry. I really enjoy being with you, more

than you know. It's just that things are complicated now, and until I get my life organized, I can't take on anything else."

He nodded and she glanced out the window, feeling guilty for a dozen good reasons she couldn't explain.

"It's so beautiful here," she said softly. "Look at this view. Didn't have this in Chicago, that's for sure."

"Isn't it famous for a river that runs through the city?"

"Yes." She appreciated his attempt to bring back the mood. "I used to love to have dinners there, and we could see it from our office windows." She gave him a smile and reached across the table to touch his hand. She was determined to enjoy this one hour together before she had to go home.

"Well, I've seen this view hundreds of times, but it's much prettier with you in it," he said, his expression serious.

She swallowed hard. "Thank you! You know, I've always loved the sight and the smell of the sea. Ever since I was a little girl. My parents used to take me to Florida for spring vacation. They thought I'd enjoy Disney World, but it was the beach that drew me."

It was just after five, and a pink and purple sky hovered over the stormy gray water that crashed against the rocks and the pier. The movement of the sea never failed to mesmerize her. Perhaps she'd been a mermaid in a previous life? Why not? She was starting to believe that anything was possible.

"What are you smiling at?" Sam shrugged off his coat and placed it beside him on the wooden bench.

"My fascination for the sea. Maybe I was a mermaid in an earlier life."

"Yeah? You'd look good with one of those fanned tails. You know they don't wear shirts?" He used two fingers to smooth his mustache, his eyes steady on hers.

Her pulse jumped into another gear. "Well, the old man in the sea was probably the only one who saw me." She grinned. "In this day and age, I could probably sue him for being a peeping tom. Right?"

He laughed, so she kept going. "What about you? What past life do you imagine yourself in?"

The conversation was interrupted as Michelle arrived with the wine. She had two individual six-ounce carafes and poured a little into Charlene's glass. Charlene tasted the dark red and then pronounced it delicious.

The waitress filled both glasses and said she'd be right back to tell them the specials.

They toasted and both took a sip. "Excellent. Thanks, Sam."

"You're most welcome."

"Okay, back to our previous lives, what were you?" she asked, sliding her fingers up and down the stem of her glass.

"That's easy." He leaned back, puffed up his chest, and put on a bad-guy face. "I was either a bandito or a bootlegger. Maybe a highwayman."

She laughed, shaking a finger. "No way! You were a cowboy. Riding your horse all day, camping out with a can of beans and a mat, your boots on the hard ground where you rested your head. A manly man, didn't need a woman, just driving the steers, as you rode Rusty, your chestnut horse."

"Sounds like a lonely life to me. And I hate rattlesnakes."

"No, you didn't!" She teased him to make him smile. "You made your boots out of their skin and ate their innards in your stew. That's what good cowboys do."

"Okay." He put up his hand. "Enough. You're going to ruin my appetite."

Sharon greeted them at the table. "Well, isn't this a pretty sight? Two of my favorite people. How are you both doing? Your wine okay?"

"Good, thanks," Sam answered. "Caught Charlene off guard and got her to agree to dinner with me."

"We'll have to make it special, then, won't we?" Sharon was one of the first people Charlene had met when coming to town, and she had come to Charlene's home for the grand opening. They were becoming friends—slow but sure.

"I also came here to see you," Charlene said, setting down her wine. "You may have heard that I'm trying to raise money for Felicity House. Since, well, you know." Sharon and her husband, John, had been at the auction that night. They'd shared the tragedy of not only David's death, but Tori's selfishness.

"I already donated a thousand dollars. I can do another hundred, though." Sharon put a hand on her hip and looked at Sam. "It's a good thing you're doing after what that louse Tori did. I overheard my waitresses talking—she's moving?"

Sam shrugged, saying nothing, giving nothing away.

"Can't wait to see the last of her," Sharon said decisively. "We have some good people in this town, and we don't need the likes of her."

"Thanks, Sharon. You can either give me a check to bring to Alice or send one directly to her. It doesn't have to be much. Figure if we can get a few hundred businesses chipping in, we can raise a substantial amount of money. Twenty or thirty thousand at least."

Sam looked impressed. "How much is everyone donating?" he asked.

"A hundred dollars each can go a long way if we can get enough people on board." Charlene was used to working as a team to get things accomplished, which was why she'd agreed for her mom to do the cold calls.

"I'll speak with a few of the divisions around here and see if we can come up with something. I'll hit up the firefighters too. They're big when it comes to collecting for kids."

"Sam. That's awesome. I know most people have already given for the year, but any bit helps. Thank you so much."

"All you had to do was ask."

Sharon's mouth twitched and she cleared her throat. "Not sure if you ordered or not, but we have a lobster special. We can prepare it any way you like."

"I don't think we have time," she said regretfully. "On the other hand, I could give my parents a call and let them know I'll be another hour."

Sam nodded his approval. "I'll have mine steamed, with garlic butter sauce."

"Same for me."

"I'll put the order in and tell them to get it ready, pronto." Sharon brushed a strand of red hair off her flushed face. "I'll get that check made out to Felicity House right now, Charlene. You're a welcome addition to this town."

"Thanks." She savored the surge of happiness that comment brought and shared a warm smile with Sam.

"I bet Sam thinks so too." Sharon bumped her hip against Sam's chair. "Ain't that true, Sam?"

"Why are you women conspiring against me?" He shook his head. "First, Charlene thinks I went around skinning snakes in my first life, and now you're putting wicked thoughts into her head."

"Skinning snakes? I'd love to hear that one."

"No, you wouldn't, trust me." Sam was looking at Charlene again, and she quickly took a sip of water. *Was it hot in the restaurant?*

"Okay, you two have fun." Sharon's cheeks turned pink. "And I'll get to work."

After Sharon left, Charlene sat back, wondering if she dared ask about the investigation. *Let it go,* she told herself. For one hour she could forget her parents, her personal obligations, and banish all thoughts of the hit-and-run driver.

Sam deserved more than a mere hour and so did she.

"I'll just step outside and call Mom and Dad." She touched his shoulder as she passed.

"I'll be counting the minutes," he responded with a wink.

Dang it, he was cute.

She stood just inside the door, as it was freezing cold, and told her parents she'd be home around seven. "Have dinner without me. I'm with Sam," she told her mom, knowing that would make her happy. She only hoped her mother wouldn't start planning a wedding.

"Oh, take your time, dear. He's a lovely man. Wasn't very polite at the station, but away from the office he's actually very charming. Perhaps he'll tell you what's going on with the investigation. I'm surprised they haven't already got that Tori woman behind bars. Zane too. It's clearly a crime of passion."

After what she'd learned from Freddy, her emotions were very mixed on David at the moment. "Or greed, Mother. There's always that."

"True. Well, your greedy dad ate the rest of the chili for lunch, so we'll find something else. No shortage of food. We'll save the ribs; my stomach couldn't handle them tonight."

Charlene could hear her father in the background, telling her to mind her own business, and she smiled.

When she returned to the table, Sam stood and helped her in her seat. He was such a gentleman that she wished she could give him more of herself, but as long as Jack remained a ghostly presence in her home, this was all it could be.

She sipped her wine and told him about the conversation. "My mom asked why you haven't got Tori and Zane locked up. You know that she always knows best. She's announced it's a crime of passion." Charlene rolled her eyes. "So there. Case closed."

"Thank heavens. I was getting worried that it would never get solved." He eyed her sternly. "You're not bringing this up hoping that I'll tell you something, are you?"

"Me?" She gave an exaggerated laugh of surprise. "No way. Wouldn't even enter my head." Of course, she'd hoped, but he wasn't having it.

"That's good, because I want that pretty head of yours thinking about succulent lobster dripping in sweet butter sauce, and oh! Here it is."

Michelle had come up from behind her with a serving cart. She placed the utensils on the table, two little pots of liquid joy, a bowl for the shells in the middle, and two huge platters of pre-cracked lobster. Broccoli and jasmine rice were side dishes to share.

"Would you like a lobster bib too?" Michelle tied one around Sam's neck.

"Sure. I might make a mess, but I don't care."

After she gave Charlene a matching bib, Michelle pulled out a check from her side pocket. "Here, this is from Sharon. She also told me not to put the lobsters on the bill, and to charge you for only the wine."

"That's not necessary," Sam said, eyeing the food. "These lobsters are huge. Cracked even."

"Tell Sharon, thank you very much," Charlene said. "Both for the generous check and the lobsters."

After the waitress left, they toasted again. "At this rate, we'll need to eat here more often," she said with a smile.

"I like the sound of that."

"So do I."

It took them a good half hour to work their way through the delicious meal and finish their water and wine. It had been a long time since she'd enjoyed herself this much.

They'd chatted about his sister and her husband, who lived in California and were already planning a trip back to Salem this spring. They were going to stay with her, and she looked forward to their visit. Jim was a firefighter, Sydney a nurse, and she felt as though they were almost friends.

When it was time to go, he paid the bill, gave a generous tip, and walked her to her car. She turned to face him. "Sam. It was an amazing night. Thank you so much. I needed that."

He took hold of her arms and before she could resist, he kissed her. It was a quick kiss, but it zinged right through her.

"Good night," he said, with a hint of a smile. He opened the door for her and waited until she was in, the car engine running; then he turned and walked away.

Charlene sat in the car for a few minutes, wishing he would allow her to help with the case. If he was open to discussing the file, to solving this mystery together, well, she'd be able to enjoy his company more often. It wasn't just curiosity that drove her—she honestly believed she had a knack for discovering the truth. After all, she'd helped solve Jack's murder, and that of a very unfortunate young witch.

She had a short list on who she thought might have killed David, and she would go through it, name by name.

Sleuthing may be her third career.

Chapter Twenty-one

Charlene drove home from dinner with Sam in a much better mood than she'd been in since David's death.

Sam's kiss had been chaste compared with the ones they'd shared in her dreams, his firm mouth flavored with butter. She stopped at a red light and touched her lower lip. Life was short, she knew that better than most. It was important to live in the now.

With a shiver, she eyed her empty backseat. "I would not want you haunting me, Jared—your memories are enough." Poor Freddy, with Doug's specter always with him. What would it be like if Jack's presence was a constant? She might be driven to drink herself.

Home once more, she visited with her parents until they went to bed at ten, her mom feeling better after the peppermint tea. The Garcias had already retired for the night, though the occasional giggle drifted down through the vents. Gary was still out with his family, and the Chilsons would arrive in the morning.

Satisfied that all was well in her bed-and-breakfast world, she turned on the television in her suite. "Jack?" she called in a whisper.

With a cold pop of air, his apparition slowly manifested to full clarity beside her as she stood behind the love seat. "Brr. Jack, Freddy Ferguson claims to be haunted by Doug, the kid who got killed at Stony Brook—and *David* was driving—he set Freddy up." Her nose stung from the chill and she rubbed it. "I just don't know what to think. How could David do such a thing?"

Jack glowered. "Perfect motive. Did Freddy kill David out of revenge, after all this time?"

"The pathetic man doesn't even own a car—he's dying. Liver cancer. He's here in Salem to forgive David for lying and sending him to jail. If anything, David should have tried to kill Freddy to cover up his secret."

"That's maudlin. How do you know if he's telling the truth?"

Charlene twisted her long hair off her neck. "Freddy had a scar at the right side of his temple, from being on the passenger side of the car when it hit the tree. Said over and over that David was his best friend, no matter what. It's so sad." Sober all of those years, until faced with a hard truth. She couldn't blame him for wanting something to numb the pain. "He kept looking around, talking to himself, saying he was haunted by Doug's ghost. I tried to see it, but I couldn't."

Ghosts and spirits had rules, supposedly, but Charlene had only ever seen Jack and hadn't believed in the paranormal until then. Jack didn't fit into the categories in the books. Ghosts were supposed to be shades of humans replaying an episode in time, without thought, while spirits had ill intent. Jack was just Jack.

"I've only ever been aware of me," he said.

Such a lonely existence.

"I feel awful for Freddy, but there isn't anything I can do. I hate that." She eyed Jack. "Is there a cure for liver cancer?"

"I would have to see his labs before commenting, Charlene. I was watching a documentary on stem cells that make regenerating *anything* seem possible, but that takes money, even with good insurance."

"I wonder if he'd hoped David would help him? I guess Freddy asked Tori if David had anything for him."

"We'll never know." Jack rubbed the back of his head.

"Let me do some checking—there were pictures of him online from Stony Brook with short hair, for football." She sat before her narrow desk and opened her laptop.

"What are you looking for?"

"I just want to make sure that he didn't have a scar before the accident, to see if Freddy is telling the truth."

She quickly found the picture she was looking for and zoomed in on Freddy's forehead and temple. "Nothing, Jack."

Jack leaned over her shoulder. "What do you plan on comparing it with?"

"His mug shot from the night he was arrested—the county will have that on record, won't it?"

"Clever, Charlene." He made to pat her shoulder and her arm broke out in goose bumps.

Ten minutes later, she'd pulled up a bleary-eyed photo of Freddy Ferguson, a gash on the right side of his temple. "He was telling the truth."

"How awful for him," Jack said.

Depressed, Charlene closed her laptop and picked up Silva, who had been dozing on the love seat. "I'm exhausted. Tomorrow is another long day. Night, Jack."

"Good night, Charlene. Good job."

So why did she feel so sad?

The next morning, Charlene woke up to cat whiskers on her cheek as Silva purred and tried to make herself a scarf around Charlene's throat.

Ugh. Cat breath. She laughed and set Silva aside. "Morning, fur-baby. We have got to get you some mint."

Silva swiped her tail from side to side from the center of Charlene's bed, blinking gorgeous eyes as if unaffected by the world around her.

"Lucky cat," she murmured.

Charlene dressed for a day of errands in black jeans and a red, black, and green Christmas sweater; red ornaments for earrings; and her hair brushed back into a high ponytail. Her hazel eyes glittered, and she touched her mouth with a fingertip before quickly turning away.

She opened the door from her living suite to the kitchen and breathed in, checking the time on the stove clock. Eight. "Minnie—I wasn't sure you'd be here today. How're the grandkids?"

"Better, thank you. Nothing my homemade chicken soup can't tackle. Coffee's ready, and I'll warm up the coffee cake." Her rounded cheeks plumped as she smiled. "You look wonderful this morning."

"Thank you." For some reason, she thought of Sam's kiss and took a sip of coffee to hide her face.

"Do we have Avery today?"

"Yes, I am going to pick her up—but I'll leave a bit early to drop off some checks for Alice at Felicity House."

Charlene leaned back against the kitchen counter to enjoy her coffee. That stuff at Whistler's Keg had been a crime against coffeemakers everywhere. The pot probably hadn't been cleaned in years.

Minnie tied on her green half apron. "Have they found out who ran over David?"

"Not yet." She didn't have the heart to share David's secret shame.

"They will," Minnie declared. "Tomorrow it will have been a week."

"I know . . ." Charlene feared that whoever had actually done it might have had a good reason, if there was such a thing. She blew on her coffee to cool it before taking another drink. "This is the calm before the storm. I can't believe tomorrow is Christmas Eve already." She brought her purse to the kitchen table and counted the checks and cash in her little brown envelope.

Minnie handed over a fifty. "As you said, every little bit counts."

"Thank you very much. On that note, I'll get out of here and come back with reinforcements."

Minnie laughed. "I hope Avery sticks around, Charlene. She's a sweetheart underneath all of that wild hair and makeup."

"Yes, she is."

Charlene poured herself a to-go cup and headed out the door, driving straight to the Felicity House office. Luckily, the light was on inside. She'd worried that she might have to make a second trip, having forgotten that the office hours started at ten.

She parked and raced up the four steps to the porch and knocked on the door. Alice let her in, worry around her eyes. She was dressed in another awful sweater, this time of Santa stuck in the chimney with his legs in the air.

"Charlene! Good morning."

"Good morning. Happy Christmas Eve eve."

"Don't say that—I'm not ready. We had a Christmas wrapping party last night, and I think each of the kids got something special—but they need so much more. Socks and underwear aren't all that special, *are* they? Charlene, the stocking stuffers you donated will be perfect additions."

Charlene opened her purse and offered the brown envelope. "Some folks have given twice—Sharon Turnberry mentioned that she'd gifted a thousand last week at the auction, but she was happy to give again."

"She did?" Alice tucked her hand in the front pocket of her jeans. "So kind—I will have the kids send thank-you cards to each person. They'll want to show their appreciation."

"I hope this helps. I'll have my mom on the phones today to rattle the trees. You never know."

"I do thank you—Pamela is our genius at getting donations, but this thing with Tori has really set her back. I've never seen her so upset—she normally has the strength and fortitude of a dozen women." Alice paused. "Her husband has medical issues, bless her—and him. MS. And her teenagers are driving her through the roof!" With a side glance, as if she wasn't quite sure she wanted to know the answer, Alice asked, "How's Avery?"

"I get to be your Christmas angel today," Charlene laughed. "Avery is doing very well, and I hope that she agrees to work weekends after the holiday is over."

Alice closed her eyes and exhaled. "Thank you, thank you. I just knew we needed to find her the right place."

"Speaking of Avery, I better get going so I'm not late picking her up. You've done amazing things for the kids in Salem."

Alice emanated happiness. "Well, it takes a village."

Charlene left with a wave and drove over to pick up Avery, who was waiting outside the teen house, talking to Pamela through the rolled down window of a car. Janet fluttered her fingers, then gave a thumbs-up from the open door before closing it.

Pamela, who probably didn't even *own* an ugly sweater, sat in the passenger seat of a newer-model black Nissan rather than her Lexus SUV.

"Thanks again, Avery," Pamela said, then rolled up the window.

A cute teenage boy was behind the wheel and he barely missed Charlene's Pilot as he peeled out of the driveway.

Avery hopped in. "Hi, Charlene."

"Morning. Who was that?"

"Mrs. Avita's dumb son."

"Hey. That's not nice."

"Sorry. He just makes me so mad. He's so rude—snapping at his mom because he wants a car for Christmas—can you believe that? They're test-driving this one to see if he *likes* it." She fiddled with her earbuds. "Grr. They had to stop by so that he could basically copy my extra credit. He's too cool to actually follow the rules."

"You let him copy?" Charlene puffed up in Avery's defense—what was Pamela thinking?

"Not the answers," Avery grinned. "But he didn't even know what work to do. You should see your face, Charlene. If I was ever in a throwdown, I want you on my side."

She wasn't sure exactly what that meant, and rather than reveal her ignorance she let it go.

"I've got something new to show you today, on how to set up a room."

Avery twirled the hot-pink wires of her headphones around her finger. "I like being busy, and you might think this is work, but being at your place is actually fun."

"Today is payday too," Charlene decided. "Do you have a bank account?"

"Nooo."

"Next week I can help you get an account set up, if you want, and give you cash today?" She'd ask Janet later what the protocol was but for now, to make sure that Avery had some spending money, she'd act, then beg for forgiveness later.

Avery grinned, very much a teenager. "Cash? That means I can buy my friend Jenna something for Christmas—there's this really cool bracelet shop at the Pedestrian Mall, with ceramic beads?" She gave the earbud another twirl. "Having my own banking account would rock."

Charlene arrived back at her house before ten. Jack waited for her on the front porch, teasing Silva with a branch. The cat chased it and leapt for Jack, who wasn't actually there, which confused Silva no matter how many times Jack played his trick.

"Your mom is in fine form this morning," he accused. "Insisting on warming the butter before putting it on the pumpkin bread." He squeezed his finger and thumb together. "I was this close to hiding her slippers."

Charlene glanced at Avery, who was oblivious as she bent down to pick up Silva and bring the silver cat inside. "Can I give her a treat?" Avery asked.

"Sure." She waved at Jack and followed Avery. The

teen hung her coat on the coat tree in the foyer—changing hands so she didn't have to set Silva down.

"I've always wanted a cat," Avery said. "But that wasn't happening. We moved too much, or stayed at places that didn't allow pets."

"You're welcome to lavish all of that attention on Silva—I can hear her purring from here." Silva's loud rumble sounded like a toy motorboat engine.

Charlene led the way to the kitchen and showed Avery where the cat treats were kept.

"She warmed the butter herself," Jack added. "So it wasn't like she put Minnie out or anything. But still . . ."

Charlene bit her tongue about her mother's foibles.

Minnie washed the last dish and turned to greet their new hire. "Morning, Avery."

"Hi, Minnie. How's your family?"

"Better, thank you, hon." Minnie looked at Charlene. "Your parents are chatting with Gary in the living room, and the Garcias are out all day in Boston. Oh, we might have another single rented—I'm waiting for a call back."

Avery set Silva down with a tuna treat and then washed her hands, the spider tattoo on the back of her neck visible beneath her short hair. Done in thin dark blue strokes, the design was actually very feminine.

"Minnie, do you mind showing Avery how to prepare a room for guests? I'd like to get my mom started on the phone. Alice, Mrs. Winters, was saying that the kids still need so much more."

Minnie wiped her hands on a dish towel. "I'd be happy to."

"Last night at teen house, we helped wrap some of the toys for the little ones, which was really fun." Avery brought her headphones from her pocket. "I remember believing in Santa—wishin' I'd get something cool."

"What did you want?" Charlene asked.

"Well, I found out that Santa wasn't real when I was, like, five, so it was dumb—a doll." She shrugged. "My mom thought it would be better if I didn't get my hopes up."

Her eyes burned for the little girl Avery must have been—before the makeup or wild hair or tattoos. "That sounds very practical." It was the nicest thing she could think to say. It was a good thing that Avery had found Alice and Felicity House.

"And here I thought Brenda Woodbridge would win Worst Mother award—I think Avery's mom has yours beat. I'm glad she's here with us," Jack said. "I'll be watching TV." He disappeared in an instant.

"Follow me, Avery," Minnie drawled, "and I'll show you how the magic happens."

Charlene quickly got her mom set up on the phone in the dining room—with the precise wording of what to say.

"Don't ad-lib, okay, Mom? We can really help here, but we don't want people feeling pressured. Everybody has their own things going on for the holiday."

Her mom rubbed her hands together as if warming up for a telethon. "I bet I can get a thousand dollars by two."

"She's good," her dad said. "Go get 'em, Brenda. I might challenge Gary to a game of chess."

"He's still in the living room, I think," Charlene said.

Gary and her dad listened to Christmas music—Elvis—and talked art. The new guest would be going to his sister's later, but he seemed to enjoy hanging out at her bed-and-breakfast. He claimed it was homey, which made her very happy. Charlene had just checked to make sure that everyone had tea or coffee, when a knock sounded on the front door. She checked her watch. Quarter past eleven. It had to be the Chilsons, who'd left a message that they would be here before noon.

She opened the door to see a red-cheeked Jessica on the front porch, her Kia parked askew. "Jessica? What's wrong?"

"I think I'm in shock—Vincent is closing Bella's for good on New Year's Eve. I'm on my way to Dr. Matt's before heading to Philly and my parents' for the holiday, but I thought you should know." Jessica sniffed and pulled a tissue from her coat pocket.

Closing Bella's? "Do you want some coffee?"

"No, I can't stay."

Charlene gave Jessica a hug—she was obviously on her emotional last straw. "Did Vincent say why?"

"Only that he can't put any more money into it—he has his other restaurant in Boston to think about."

Jack materialized behind Jessica in jeans, boots, and a blue plaid shirt, dressed for the cold that he didn't feel. His dark hair fell over one turquoise eye. "Is she all right?"

Charlene couldn't answer.

Jessica's eyes welled. "Charlene, he said that David was stealing money from the till."

After what Charlene had just learned from Freddy, she wasn't sure what to think about David anymore.

"Is it possible?" Jack asked.

"I don't believe it," Jessica insisted, her tissue in her clenched fist.

"I'm so sorry." Charlene opened the door wider. "Are you sure you won't come in? I hate for you to drive when you're so upset."

"My parents will give me some much-needed TLC. I

won't be back until after the first. This was my last shift—isn't that crazy?" She shuffled her boots on the porch.

Charlene had the door open and from behind her Avery said, "Jessica?" She turned to see Avery take the stairs down two at a time. Minnie followed more sedately but joined them all on the front porch.

"Hey, Avery," Jessica said, breathing in to regain her composure.

"This is the best job ever." Avery, like Jack, didn't seem to notice the cold.

"I'm glad you have it—and you're better off. Now *I'm* the one out of a job."

"Oh no!" Avery said.

"I was going to quit anyway, because Vincent is no David, and I hope to get more hours with Dr. Matt. It's just, well, David hasn't even been *gone* a week."

"She's been through a lot," Jack said. "Poor girl. She's always been on David's side, not once blaming him for this mess."

"I agree," Charlene said.

"With what?" Avery asked.

Dang it, Jack. "Uh, that it's very sad—and that it all seems so sudden." She turned so that Jack was behind her.

With the resilience of youth, Jessica rolled her eyes and laughed. "Look at me, being such a drama queen. I'm ready for a break, and some of my mom's Christmas turkey. Merry Christmas, everyone—I can't wait for the New Year—this one sucked eggs." She darted down the porch steps. "Bye!"

Avery laughed nervously and they watched Jessica drive off with a two-honk salute.

"Is she going to be okay?" Minnie asked as they all gathered in the foyer, even Jack.

"I think so. Jessica is a tough cookie. She'll find something better." Charlene thought of the worthless check from David, thanks to Tori, and prayed for a real Christmas miracle.

Chapter Twenty-two

Charlene hesitated in the foyer to gather her thoughts after Jessica left. Was David this terrible man whom Vincent and Freddy accused him of being? She'd always prided herself on being a good judge of character, and she couldn't see it. He'd come across as a nice guy, a charmer for sure, but someone with a good heart. Had she been wrong?

She followed Minnie slowly into the kitchen and hitched her butt on the bar stool.

"I can't believe it," said her housekeeper. "David stealing money? Why?"

Avery shrugged. "Didn't really know him, but he wasn't very nice to me after I broke that plate. Like I did it on purpose." She huffed and helped herself to a smidgen of the banana loaf on the counter.

"No, he wasn't nice to you. It's no excuse, but I think

he had a lot on his mind." Charlene frowned. "More than we'll ever know, that's for sure."

Minnie wiped her hands on her apron and clicked her tongue. "Me and Will enjoyed eating at Bella's a few times. David seemed very proud of his restaurant, so I just don't believe he'd steal from his own till. That wouldn't make sense. Course, hooking up with that Tori woman when he had a nice lady at home doesn't make sense either."

"I didn't like David, and I think Vincent's a wacko," Avery declared. "Did you see how mad he was at the auction? The veins in his neck got huge—he looked like The Hulk. Did you ever see that movie?"

Minnie tapped her lower lip and gazed at the ceiling. "No. Wasn't he a wrestler?" she asked. "Dwayne something?"

Avery rolled her eyes. "No, that's The Rock. Sheesh!"

Vincent had a temper, something to remember. Charlene brushed her hands together. "Okay, let's get to work. The Chilsons will be here before we know it. Their daughter is Nikki, from the veterinarian's office."

"Don't know her." Avery plugged in her earbuds and sang about workin' for a livin' all the way to the staircase.

Minnie shared an amused look with Charlene. "She's a kick."

"Sure is." Charlene sliced a few pieces of the loaf and arranged them on a serving plate with napkins to take to Gary and her dad. They were seated at a small table, the chessboard between them.

"Who's winning?" she asked, placing the plate next to them. Her father grunted in response.

She put a hand on his shoulder and studied the chess pieces. "Gary, my dad's a master. He might be toying with you . . . letting you think you have a chance before he goes in for the kill."

Gary sat back and regarded Michael with interest. "That true?" Crossing his arms, he stared at the board for a few seconds. "Son of a gun." He rubbed his chin. "Dang it. I thought I had you."

Her father chuckled. "They all do."

Charlene patted Gary's arm. "He tortured me for years until I learned better. Now I only play backgammon with him. He doesn't like to take chances, so he's easier to beat." She headed toward the door. "Either of you want coffee?"

"How about some of that hot cocoa?" her father asked.

"Coming right up. Gary?" She felt a chill behind her and knew Jack was there. She ignored him. For now.

"Thanks, but no. I'm having lunch with my family. Michael, good game, but I think I've learned my lesson too. I'll stick to crossword puzzles."

Charlene returned to the kitchen to make her dad's cocoa and one for her mother. Jack had followed her, so she kept her voice low. "Can you believe that Vincent is going to close Bella's? And he's telling people that David stole money."

"I don't blame Jessica for being upset. It seems rash for Vincent to shut it down now, with the investigation into David's death still on."

"I agree." When the cocoa was ready, she poured it into two mugs and added three tiny marshmallows in each. She nodded toward her room. Jack knew what she meant and disappeared. Charlene took the cocoa to her dad and brought the other to her mom, but first, she'd spy on her. She listened outside the door and couldn't believe how cheery and well-spoken her mother was to perfect strangers.

"Just a small donation, a few dollars, whatever you won't miss." Her mother drew in a breath. "Twenty dollars, oh my! That is very generous. Yes, send it to 'Charlene's' or to Felicity House. Here's the address on Crown Point Road. It was such a pleasure speaking with you. Yes, and Happy Holidays to you as well."

Her mother wore a pleased smile as she ended the call. Charlene cleared her throat and entered the office space. "Mom, I brought you some cocoa. Someone is gifting a twenty? That's great news."

"Oh, that was peanuts. Most people are sending a check for fifty or more."

Ah. "Nice work. How much are we at now?"

"Four hundred and twenty-five."

"You're halfway there, Mom. I'm so proud of you." She dropped a kiss on her mother's head. "You are good at this. Better than me, that's for sure."

Her mother actually blushed. "That's a real fine compliment, my dear. You are so competent at everything you do, well, I'm just an old housewife, that's all."

"You're way more than that, Mom. You've made a beautiful home for the two of you, and Dad is real happy. That's no easy thing."

"Why, that's a lovely thing to say. You and Michael mean the world to me."

"I know, Mom. I know." Charlene was already on overload. With Sam's kiss, Jack in the sitting area waiting for her, the restaurant closing, Jessica's fears—and David's killer still on the loose—she couldn't deal with more emotions.

"We have the Chilsons coming this morning. I've got to make sure everything is ready."

"Go. I'll be fine. I have a long list of names to still call. Wish me luck!"

"Luck." Charlene closed the door softly behind her and went into her suite.

Jack stood near the window looking out at the old oak tree, the limbs once again bare of snow. Would she get a white Christmas? He was dressed in jeans and a light-knit sweater, handsome as always.

"How's Brenda doing?"

"Much better than I expected. She's raised nearly five hundred dollars and it's only been a couple of hours. She's genuinely happy. Maybe this is her calling. A fundraiser?"

"Maybe it is." Jack gave her a warm look. "I'm glad she's busy and not on your back."

"Me too. So what do you think about David? Is it possible that he was stealing from Bella's? Why would he? I know Tori was high-maintenance, but still."

"I've been thinking about that, and David might be a fool when it comes to women, but the restaurant seemed to be well managed, at least when I saw it. Is it run-down, or kept up?"

"Clean, like new, with Italian ambience."

"Bella's has a good reputation." Jack walked around the room as he talked. "Showing a profit to his business partner and possibly giving them each a raise would seem more likely."

"Agreed."

He whirled a Christmas ornament in his palm. "Although he must have known that Vincent was sleeping with his ex-wife. That probably didn't sit well." The ball dropped to the armchair.

"That's true. So, is it possible that he did take from the till, as a payback to Vincent for having an affair with Linda? Maybe he wanted the restaurant to go bust?" She pushed her hair off her face. "But that wouldn't help his situation either. The lottery win was a fortunate break that couldn't have been planned."

Jack leaned against the love seat and crossed his arms. "I can't see him taking money from the till—it would be too easy to track. From all accounts, David was a smart businessman—he'd run several successful restaurants in the past."

"Why would Vincent close the restaurant down? He kept saying that the business was in trouble, and yet it was busy every night." She rubbed her temples, feeling a slight headache coming on. "Why? Where's the missing piece?"

"What does your detective say about all of this?"

"Sam hasn't told me anything." Charlene hadn't told Jack about her dinner with Sam, and didn't plan on doing so. Why upset Jack for nothing? "I'm sure they have it narrowed down and might already know who the killer is. Can't make an arrest until they prove it—you know that."

"Oh, poor Sam. It's only been a week. Shouldn't he have more time to solve a murder?" Jack chuckled.

Charlene bristled at the jibe, knowing it came from a place of jealousy. But a ghost had no right to be jealous of a flesh and blood man. She wanted to jump to Sam's defense, yet her relationship with Sam wasn't going anywhere, not as long as she kept her ghostly roommate. Jack had given up eternity to be with her.

"Sam is thorough. He'll present an airtight case, when the time is right." In the meantime, she would continue her own questioning.

Jack pretended to yawn. "Maybe he'll make the big announcement tomorrow night. Christmas Eve. I think he likes the drama, don't you?"

She ignored his comment. "I've got to go, Jack. The new guests will be here any minute. Then I'm going to call Linda and see if she's free for coffee. Tori, for all of her wickedness, did rule out Linda and Kyle as suspects." She'd had to check Tori's story, and she'd called the neighbor, saying she'd heard that the motorcycle had been very loud and asking if they should have a noise ordinance—what time had she heard it? Eleven, the woman was sure, because the nightly news was on. But the lady wasn't complaining. Linda was a good neighbor.

"I'm sure you're not interested in having coffee with Linda." Jack brightened. "What are you hoping to learn?"

"I just have a few questions about Vincent." Charlene clarified her thoughts. "Linda knows him better than anyone. I want to get a feel for what kind of man he is."

"Good luck." Jack turned his attention to the television. "I'll wait here and catch the news."

She made sure to close her door tight behind her. Minnie and Avery were laughing as they descended the stairs, and it did Charlene's heart good.

"How's the room looking?"

"Man, that is one beautiful bedroom," Avery said with a grin. "Minnie showed me how to arrange the flowers and hook the drapes so it exposes the view."

"Did you put out the welcome tray with wine and cheese?"

"No, we ate it and drank the wine," Avery smarted off.

Minnie swayed exaggeratedly. "I think I had too much of that fine merlot."

"Very funny." Charlene was delighted at how well the two of them got along and, like Jack, almost a little jealous. She wanted to have fun with Avery, too, and not do all the worrying.

"Doorbell," Minnie said, taking a step toward the door. "Want me to get it?"

"You two drunks go to the kitchen. The lady of the house will greet her guests." Head raised, she walked past them as regally as Silva.

Opening the door, she put on her welcoming hostess expression. "Hello. You must be the Chilsons. Welcome to 'Charlene's.' You flew in from San Diego? Nikki must be so excited!"

The husband was perhaps in his late forties, lean and average height. His wife was a petite brunette, thin and tan, wearing skin-tight jeans, her hair pulled back in a single braid. Charlene hadn't seen Nikki since the vet tech had helped her with Silva but didn't recall a resemblance to either parent.

"Yes, she's called a few times already," the man replied. "We'll be meeting her for lunch." He shook her hand. "I'm Tom, and my wife is Marlene."

"And I'm Charlene." She shook their hands and led them in. "How was your flight?"

"Fine—it seems odd to leave sunshine for snow, but Nikki loves it here," Marlene told her. "Your place is just amazing. How long have you been here?"

"Three months."

Her father left his chair in the living room and greeted the couple. "I'm Michael, Charlene's dad. My wife and I are spending Christmas. You'll meet her soon."

Minnie and Avery came out of the kitchen.

"This is our fabulous chef and housekeeper, Minnie, and our delightful Avery, helping out for the holidays."

Avery grinned. "Nice to meet you. Can I take your bags to your room?"

"That's not necessary," Tom said, not relinquishing his grip on the large suitcase. "It's heavy, trust me."

"Okay." Avery gestured to the stairs. "Follow me."

Charlene wondered if Tom hadn't trusted the young girl with her spider tattoo and nose ring, or if the bag was really too heavy. She was so used to Avery by now that she might have overlooked the obvious.

Marlene followed Avery up the stairs, commenting on the beautiful wooden banister heavily decked out in garland for the holidays. "It's spectacular. The staircase alone blows me away. Like something out of *Gone with the Wind*. And the decorations are gorgeous."

"My husband, Will, did that," Minnie said proudly.

"Thanks for the warm welcome." Tom shook Michael's hand, then lifted the large bag and carried it up to the center floor. He looked down at the little group in the foyer. "This is some place you've got, Charlene. I bet it's completely booked."

"Getting there," she told him. "Just two singles left."

After everyone was settled, Charlene drove to the hospital for a quick coffee with Linda. She parked in the visitor's parking lot and entered the main lobby, asking directions to the cafeteria from the middle-aged man at the front desk.

She followed the corridor around a few bends and entered, looking for a glimpse of Linda. The room was crowded with visitors and hospital staff, but being lunch hour that was no big surprise. The nurse had agreed to meet her, wondering if Charlene had any new information.

Charlene had told her no, but that she knew Sam Holden, the detective on the case, and expected a break very soon. Well, that part was true. A lot depended on Linda's answers.

After standing in line to pay for her coffee and bottle of water, she grabbed an available seat near the entrance and waved at Linda the moment she walked through the door.

Linda nodded at her, straightened her shoulders, and marched over. "I haven't got much time. What is it you wanted to speak with me about?"

"Can you sit for a minute? Please? I promise it won't take long."

Scowling, Linda reluctantly sat down. "If it's about Bella's closing, I assure you I don't know more than you. Vincent's been on a rampage lately, but he won't talk to me about any of this. I had no idea it was going to happen."

"I'm so sorry, Linda. How's Kyle doing?"

"As well as can be expected." She wet her bottom lip and wrung her hands in her lap. "We'd both like to see an end to this, and whoever is responsible put away."

"Of course you would. I know I felt the same after Jared's death. It helped some, but nothing can bring him back." She uncapped her water and took a sip. "Sorry. It's still hard to talk about. Only two years."

Linda relaxed and covered Charlene's hand with her own. "Yes, you know what we're going through—only for you it was much, much worse. David and I hadn't been friendly the last few years. Kyle got a card from his dad at Christmas and his birthday, and David took him shopping before he died, but they argued about Tori, and so Kyle was home early."

"I'm sorry. I thought he was a better person than that." Charlene stirred her coffee with a plastic stir stick, wondering how to ask. "Jessica came to the B and B this morning. She not only told me Vincent was closing the restaurant, but that David had been taking money from the till. That surprises me. Is that the David you know?"

"No." Linda's fingers trembled as she grabbed for a paper napkin. She wiped her palms, her cheeks sickly pale. "No, it isn't. He wasn't fair to us, but he did the best he could, I suppose. He paid what he was required to pay and not a penny more. I honestly believe he would have if that nasty wife of his wasn't a greedy, money-hungry . . ."

"I know. Tori is all that and more. I don't think I've ever met such a heartless woman." Charlene's mouth twisted in a half smile. "She's like a cold-blooded serpent that would bite your head off just because she could."

"Wow." Linda sank back in her plastic chair. "You really don't like her."

They both laughed. "I really don't." Charlene tasted her coffee. "Not bad."

Linda checked her watch and stood up. "I probably should go."

"Just one more minute, please."

The nurse's eyes held shadows. "What is it?"

"Linda, are you safe? You could be in danger."

She shook her head, understanding what Charlene implied. "No, Vincent would never hurt me. I don't think he would have hurt David either, but if he thinks David was stealing from him, I'm not so sure."

"His temper?"

Linda covered her mouth with her fingers. "I've probably said too much. Please don't tell the detective about Vincent. He helped me through a difficult time and we've had some fun together. But, I don't like the anger I see in him now. He didn't used to be like this." She jammed her hands into her scrub pockets. "I don't know what his problem is, but he's spending a lot of time in the casino lately. Maybe it's an escape. When he wins? Things are great. But if he loses—which seems to be happening a lot—he gets all worked up. Shouting, breaking things."

"Linda . . ."

"Kyle doesn't want him coming around anymore. I usually go over to his place in Boston instead—it's only thirty minutes away. More often than not, I don't bother." Linda shrugged.

"Thanks for talking with me—please, just be careful, okay?"

"You too." Linda held her gaze, then hurried out of the cafeteria, the large doors swinging behind her.

Had that been a warning? Charlene tossed the coffee and headed down the slick corridors toward the parking lot in the rear of the building. Someone close to David had killed him. That someone wouldn't like her asking questions.

The question was, who?

CHAPTER TWENTY-THREE

Charlene left the hospital with Vincent on her mind. Why was Linda willing to accept the status quo?

The nurse was attractive, smart, and self-sufficient . . . maybe she got what she wanted from Vincent, a sometimes-companion, and that was enough. She seemed to be an involved mom who loved her son and put him first.

How did Vincent feel about that?

On the pretext of bringing some of her dad's favorite soup back to the house, she decided to drop in and see how things were going at Bella's. She knew from the auction that the restaurant planned to be closed Christmas Day.

The parking lot to Bella's was full when she arrived. Why wouldn't Vincent want to find another manager and keep the money coming in? At least throughout the season, when things were busy.

Charlene lucked out with a space. She scanned the vehicles in the parking lot for what Vincent might drive. He'd left early that night, furious with David. Why hadn't David handed his share over, since he no longer needed the money? Ten million was a lot of cash to start over with. And to kill for.

Linda had mentioned Vincent's recent temperament and being quick to blow a fuse. Had he been mad enough to leave, then came back to talk things over, or worse, to wait for David and run him down? But that would be a dangerous plan. Tori would likely be with him. Other diners might see. Vincent wasn't a fool.

Freddy had mentioned something dark barreling toward him but had blamed the vision on the gin he'd been drinking—she believed he hadn't killed David, but he'd been there all right. It was the only explanation for David seeing Doug's ghost—she'd witnessed the horror on David's face before he ran outside.

Her head hurt thinking about it. Tomorrow was David's service, and the more time that passed, the harder it would be to find David's killer. Charlene opened the door; the restaurant was outwardly festive with an underlying somber tone.

Laura greeted her from the podium, wearing a crisp white shirt, black slacks, and Christmas tree earrings. "Welcome, Charlene," she said, and looked behind her.

"Just me. I'm not eating, but I'd like two quarts of pasta fagioli to go. I heard the news that Bella's is closing New Year's Eve?"

Laura gestured to the dining room. "We've never been busier. I don't know what Vincent's thinking. He called in some employees from his other restaurant to help out so at least we're decently staffed. Tomorrow will be twelve-hour days for some of them. Not me. I'm off at two, and I am very tempted to not come back." She sniffed. "I will, because I said I would, but . . ." She shrugged and left the podium. "Let me go get your soup."

"Thank you."

Charlene waited until Laura had disappeared into the kitchen, the door swinging closed behind her, and bee-lined for Vincent's office.

She knocked and he answered, his cheeks ruddy, his gray mustache untrimmed. He didn't look so good.

"Hi! I just wanted to say that I'm so sorry about the restaurant closing."

Vincent yanked her inside and slammed the door. "That's been spreading like wildfire. How did you hear?"

"Jessica told me. I'm going to miss this place. A lot of people will."

He paced the office, the air around him vibrating with nervous energy. Charlene backed up and glanced across his desk—like before, it was piled high with receipts and manila folders.

Two purple poker chips were barely visible beneath the mess. Linda was concerned about his gambling problem, saying he was losing heavily lately. He was a man on a downward slide.

"Bella's is busted." Vincent wiped his face with his palm.

"Business ebbs and flows," she said. "Maybe if you give it time . . ."

"The flow ain't strong enough to keep this ship afloat." He sat down with a squeak of springs on his office chair and opened the drawer of his desk. He rifled through the contents until he pulled out a wrapped cigarillo.

"Are you okay, Vincent? This has to be stressful."

"I'm fine, fine."

With his red eyes and unkempt appearance, he seemed far from fine. Was guilt eating at him? Charlene said a prayer of thanks when Vincent pulled a lighter and his keys from his front pocket—a silver Ford key fob.

Freddy had told her that the black shadow had come toward him, across the street from Bella's parking lot. "Any chance you'll change your mind? Lease it out, or hire someone to manage it?"

He ripped off the wrapper of the cigarillo and a vanilla cherry scent rose toward her. He started to light the end, but then thought better of it and dropped the lighter to the desktop. "'Cause that worked out so well last time?" Vincent sneered before chomping on the end. "No, I'm done with Bella's. Salem too."

Her intuition screamed that Vincent was not being honest. "Will you go to David's service tomorrow? I talked to Freddy and he's go—"

"That guy's a washout."

"He's dying."

Vincent scrubbed his palm along his bristly jaw. "Yeah, I know. He told me that David was going to help him out. Not sure what he meant by that. He's got liver cancer—if he thought David would give him part of his, he's crazy."

He shuffled the papers around on the desk and then dropped them, overwhelmed.

"Have you talked to Tori about buying this place?"

Vincent's brow tightened. "That piece of work told me to kiss her sweet derriere. I'm turning it all over to my lawyers. It won't be the first time I've filed bankruptcy." He sat back and exhaled, protruding his round stomach. "It's the risk of running a restaurant."

Charlene nodded, but didn't agree. Bella's had prospered under David's management, according to Jessica. Why was it only now—after David's death—that Vincent was openly accusing him of stealing?

She could think of only one really good reason—to cover his own theft.

Maybe David had discovered Vincent's dipping into the pot. That might explain why David hadn't handed over the deed. That would sure piss off a man who thought he was getting away with something.

A man with a temper, and a gambling addiction.

What if he'd decided to kill David in order to cover his losses? Charlene knew she was right—but now what? She would need proof . . . her gaze was drawn to the poker chips. But what would that prove exactly, other than the fact he liked to gamble? It wasn't a crime.

A knock sounded on the office door and Vincent hollered, "Come in!"

Laura entered, a brown paper bag in her hands. "Oh, there you are, Charlene. Here's your soup. I added some breadsticks."

"Wonderful!"

Laura waited expectantly, and Vincent gave her the eye.

Charlene accepted the bag and started to back out. "Thanks, Laura. Bye, Vincent."

She followed the hostess to the register and gave a good tip. "Merry Christmas to you and yours."

She left Bella's with the brown paper bag. Rather than go straight to her car, she walked behind the two rows of vehicles, past her Honda Pilot, a Kia Optima, and a Kia Soul. Both seemed in average condition and had snow tires on.

The night that David had died there had been no snow, but it had been predicted. Her tires were all-terrain. There hadn't been any skid marks. David had been hit by a car going less than thirty-five miles an hour. She looked to the road.

It had been plowed and salted, and the asphalt was bare. She stood in the parking lot and tried to imagine how David had been killed, his neck broken. She hadn't heard a screech of tires or the rev of an engine. It happened so fast that there'd been no sign of a car.

She walked by a Town and Country minivan in crimson—wasn't that a Dodge? Vincent didn't seem like the minivan type. She'd pegged him to be a truck guy. There were four of those.

She kept going, reading license plates, checking—she didn't know for what, but hoped she would know when she saw it.

Two of the trucks were Chevys, both brand new. The other was a Ford, but probably ten years old. The tires were worn.

Her pulse skipped a little as she saw the last truck in the lot, parked away from the front door, like a good business owner would do. It was a Ford. Midnight blue.

The tires were brand new. So new she could see the sticker price outline of adhesive against the black.

Why would Vincent need new tires?

Just because she hadn't seen skid marks didn't mean that Salem's police department couldn't have discovered something; she'd seen the computer program herself. What if Vincent was covering his tracks, literally? Ditch the tires, buy new—and sell the restaurant to cover up his gambling losses? Adrenaline raced through her body, causing her soup bag to shake.

It was entirely possible that Vincent had been waiting for David to come out that night, and acted on impulse, ramming into him before driving away, as if nothing had happened.

She turned toward the front of Bella's and saw Laura and Vincent staring at her from the doorway.

Chills trickled like a fall of snow down her back.

Charlene had no good reason for being out in the parking lot, checking cars, so she ducked her head and hustled back to her Pilot, got in, and started the engine. She studiously avoided looking at the front entrance of the restaurant.

She had to call Sam and make sure that he questioned Vincent about David's death. Remembering that he was in court all day, she sent him a text. Sam was probably already on it, but if not, this might point the police department in the right direction.

She drove home, the smell of the soup making her queasy. From now on, she would associate pasta fagioli with turmoil. The clock on the dashboard read two p.m. She parked and raced the soup inside the house, knowing she was late taking Avery home.

Her mom waited with a victorious smile. "I did it—eleven hundred dollars."

"Mom, that is so terrific. Thank you."

"I know Mrs. Winters will be so happy," Avery said, getting her coat from the coat tree by the door.

"Dad, here's your soup—I bought two, and you might want to stick one in the freezer." She swallowed down the nausea in her tummy. "I stopped at Bella's and Vincent confirmed that he's closing it down."

She wanted to share with them her suspicions that Vincent had killed David, but not in front of Avery. Better yet, she'd wait to hear back from Sam. She'd grown in many ways since moving to Salem.

Her dad clutched the brown paper bag to his chest. "Thanks, honey. That was sweet of you. I'm sorry about the restaurant. I know you enjoyed it."

"It's all right." David was not the man she'd thought he was, and her goal now was the kids. "Mom, when can we get the money for Felicity House?"

"I told them it was urgent, and so most are dropping it by today—I figured we could bring what we have over in the morning?"

She didn't blame her mom for wanting to deliver the money and toys. It felt good to help other people. Why didn't Tori see that? Her selfishness was at the root of her own unhappiness. No matter how much money she had, she would always be miserable.

Speaking of money—she'd told Avery that today was payday. "Hang on!"

She hurried back through the kitchen to her closet, and the box of cash she kept for emergencies in the safe, taking out three hundred dollars. Twelve hours of labor didn't equal much money at all, and Charlene wanted to make sure that Avery had a special Christmas too. A guitar! Avery had enjoyed composing music with the one she'd had, but now it was gone. Or an iPhone. Maybe she could get an older model. Or she could spend it on whatever she wanted.

"What are you thinking?" Jack asked from the doorway between her bedroom and the living room. Silva stalked past him with her tail high, flicking it through the illusion of Jack's pant leg.

"Jack!" Charlene sank back on her heels with a gasp. "Good. You can help—Avery is a ward of the state, so that means paying her needs to be official. Probably not cash. She doesn't have a bank account yet, and I want her to have spending money and . . ."

"I see." He tapped his chin. "You *can* pay her for these past few days in cash—because you haven't officially hired her yet, right?"

"True! We're on a temporary basis." She grinned up at him. "Which means I can even give her a holiday bonus." She fanned the twenties.

"Avery wants an iPhone, like the other kids. And she mentioned a guitar . . . that would be a great gift for a sixteen-year-old. Should I give her more?"

"Be careful of sending the wrong message," Jack cautioned. "Working for you, she can have all those things by earning them soon enough."

"You're right." Her parents had made sure that she'd had a very comfortable life, but she was a hard worker by nature.

A knock sounded on her bedroom door. Charlene rose, bumping into her dresses hanging behind her in the closet. "Thanks, Jack."

All told, she was gone only a few minutes, but there'd been no time to tell Jack about Vincent and the tires.

"We have to talk when I get back," she said.

"I hate it when you do that!" He pleaded with her, using his blue, blue eyes, to convince her to stay a bit longer.

"Patience, Jack." She slipped into the kitchen. Her dad shut the refrigerator door and she passed him on the way to the foyer—he gave her an apologetic shrug. Mom was restless.

Avery waited with her mom by the coat tree, the two

discussing her mom's true crime book. Avery seemed captivated.

"You can have it when I'm done with it," her mother said.

"Thanks!" Avery zipped her jacket. "I read a lot. Mysteries, thrillers."

"I hope they don't give you nightmares," Charlene warned.

"I love scary movies. Nothing scares me. I'd love to see a ghost." Jack manifested himself behind the teenager as she said, "I think connecting with the other side would be soooo cool."

Jack grinned and blew a strand of her spiky orange hair. Avery leapt forward and rubbed her head, her eyes wide.

"Let's go." Charlene urged Avery outside. "Behave," she whispered to Jack, who stood next to her mother.

Her mom huffed. "I've been nothing but good today, Charlene." A sly look crossed her wrinkled face. "Have you heard from Sam yet?"

"No, he's at a trial, Mom." Charlene escaped and climbed into the Pilot—Avery buckled up on the passenger side. Sam still hadn't texted her back. Was he angry at her for interfering?

When they stopped at a red light, Charlene handed Avery the envelope with cash. "Here you are—thank you for all of your hard work. I gave a little extra for Christmas."

Avery peered inside and started to laugh. "A *little*? Thank you! I can't believe it. I didn't think I'd have any money to spend for Christmas, and now I do. Thanks, Charlene."

"You're very welcome. Now, if you decide that you want to work with me after Christmas, then we'll need to make it more official, with paystubs and everything."

"I do!"

"That's really great." The light changed. "Will you get to see your mom during the holiday?"

Avery's face saddened. "Haven't heard from her in a while, and she doesn't live at that same apartment anymore." She eyed the envelope and Charlene could see the wheels churning.

"It's okay for you to take care of yourself. Buy clothes, or makeup, books. Music even."

"That seems like a waste of good money," the girl said. "I'd like to get something for my mom. It's not her fault she's . . ." Avery stared out the window.

"I am not judging, believe me." Charlene squeezed Avery's forearm through her black ski jacket and kept her opinion to herself. "I'm here if you want to talk or if you need a friend. Okay?"

Avery lowered her eyes, running the pad of her thumb over the white envelope. "When do I get to come back?" She peeked at Charlene between spiked bangs.

"Do you want to work a few days next week?"

"Yeah!"

Charlene smiled. She'd accidentally driven to Felicity House rather than the teen house. "Oops. Oh, well, there's Mrs. Avita." The fund-raising queen—although her mom might give her a run for her money—was standing outside the black Nissan her son had driven earlier and waved to Charlene. She pulled into the driveway and rolled her window down. "Hi, Pamela!"

Dressed in impeccable holiday attire, from her emerald cashmere coat and black gloves to her leather boots, slightly scuffed by age, Pamela's smile almost matched the brightness of the diamonds at her ears. Her husband must be very successful, or had been.

"Charlene!" She fluttered her gloved fingers at Avery, a small rip at the wrist of the fine leather. "Avery. I spoke to your teacher today to let her know you gave us the assignment directions, thank you." Her attention returned to Charlene, behind the wheel. "Alice said you've been hard at work—we appreciate that."

"My mom, actually, has been on the phone. People have pledged another eleven hundred."

Her mink lashes batted. "Just in time. If I could get that Tori," she exhaled. "But I suppose any forward legal action can't happen until after the first of the year. Everybody takes this next week off."

Legal action? Charlene hoped with all her might that there was something the lawyers could do. "The sooner the better—Tori has plans to leave Salem after David's service."

Her gaze sharpened. "Really? I'll have to put a call in. Let me go tell Alice the good news." Pamela blew kisses at them and backed up to the four porch steps, then went inside Felicity House.

"I'm so glad we're able to help," Charlene told Avery as they drove away. "Those two women really make a difference."

"They're nice. I should get them something, and Janet too." She tapped the envelope. "You wouldn't think it to look at them, but Mrs. Winters is the tough one who enforces the rules. Mrs. Avita is just so sad to me. Like all she has to be proud of is the money they used to have. She can't let go of the past, or something."

"That's very observant." And compassionate. They arrived at the teen house and Charlene walked in with Avery.

"Have a great holiday," Avery said, giving Charlene a hug.

"Merry Christmas. Don't forget—call if you want to talk. I'm a pretty good listener."

Chapter Twenty-four

Charlene returned home feeling pleased with the result of her fund-raising for Felicity House—and her mother's participation in it. They'd done some good, and the children would have a nice Christmas. The big money hadn't poured in yet from her GoFundMe page on the website, and their plans for a new wing might be put on hold, but with help from the community it would happen down the road.

Charlene turned into the driveway, admiring the sight of the half dozen three-foot crystal reindeer with sparkling antlers that stood proudly under the stately evergreen trees. She and Jared had never gone all out on their house on the hill. They would work late right up to Christmas Eve, as the holiday season and Super Bowl ads kept the teams busy.

But "Charlene's" deserved glitz and glamour; nothing less would be appropriate for such a splendid home.

And to think it was hers.

Oh, Jared. Can you see me now? If you do, I'm sure you're smiling with pride, knowing what a good decision I made. Yes, I still miss you, and always will. But I'm happy, too, and this year will be the first for me where I will actually feel joy. Be happy for me; I am living for both of us now. I also hope Heaven is as wonderful as we believed it to be and that your heart is full. Merry Christmas, my darling husband. I will always love you.

She climbed out of the car, feeling peace and calm inside. Her parents' visit would soon be over, and she'd have the house back to herself. She would actually miss them, she knew, and might invite them back again during the summer months.

A tingle of excitement spread through her as she entered the house. She just knew that Vincent was behind the hit-and-run. The new tires combined with his gambling debts and the sudden closing of Bella's made him her number one suspect.

"Hey, Mom, Dad." They cuddled by the fire, each with a book and a cup of cocoa. Minnie had left for the day.

Charlene shrugged off her coat and took it to her suite of rooms, hanging it in her closet and swapping her boots for slippers. She returned to the living room and sank into the sofa. "So, you two look cozy. Is Gary gone?"

"Yes, he left right after you did," her dad said. "He'll be out most of the night."

"I hope he's having a nice visit with his family. He's a pleasant man." Charlene snuggled back against the cushion of the sofa.

"Oh." Her mom looked up with a raised brow. "Any romantic interest?"

"No, Mom. Not even a flicker." She felt Jack's presence, and it made her smile. "Although he's kind of cute," she said to tease her special ghost.

"Seriously?" Jack frowned. "Thought you only had eyes for Sam."

"Sam's more handsome," her mother said.

Jack threw his arms out to his sides, the air around him whirring and causing the fire to pop.

Her mom scowled at the drape-covered window. "I'm calling someone to check your seals on this place before we go home."

Her dad looked up from his book. "What does Sam's attractiveness have to do with it? Charlene will find the right man when the time is right. I think she's got plenty to do without worrying about a guy."

"Thanks, Dad. I agree."

"So do I." Jack stood in front of the fire, the flames behind him semi-visible.

"What time will Sam return to Salem?" her mom asked. "There's a big snowstorm in New York City, according to the news. Travel's a nightmare."

Charlene dug her phone from her pocket and checked her messages. "I hope he's all right." Sam had texted but she'd missed it, so she eagerly scanned his message. No mention of her tip on Vincent, but the trial had gone long, and his flight had been delayed. She groaned.

"Is that from Sam?" Her father put down his reading glasses.

"He's trying for standby on a different airline, since his flight's delayed by five hours."

She sent a message for him to travel safe and keep her posted. He responded with a thumbs-up emoji followed by a Santa blowing her a kiss.

Charlene put her phone in her pocket, then clasped her hands, her stomach knotted with worry. "I won't relax now until I know he's home."

"Detective Sam will be just fine," Jack said dryly. "I hate to see you upset." He raised his hand toward the fireplace and a few sparks lit up, making her mother flinch.

Silva had been asleep in her dad's lap, and the cat jumped down and hissed, then pawed the air toward Jack with a meow. "What got her in a dither?" her dad asked.

Amused, Charlene gave Jack a look, and he smiled sheepishly. "We've got a bunch of ribs to eat by ourselves," her mother said. "With all your guests out."

Her dad picked up his book once more. "Love a nice rack of ribs with slaw and beans." He glanced down at Silva. "Too bad she's not a dog. All those bones gone to waste."

Charlene got off the sofa and stretched. "I'm going to do a little paperwork in my office, and I'll catch you back here at five thirty or six. Cocktail hour. We'll throw the ribs in a warm oven and eat around seven."

"I might take a wee nap." Her dad covered a yawn with his novel.

"I'll call some of my friends back home," her mother said. "Tell them all the comings and goings around this place. We're helping solve a murder! They'll get a kick out of that."

"Yup, you solved it all right. Told that young buck of a detective that he didn't know his ass from his front, and that everybody knows the husband was killed by his wife." Her father stood up. "Nappy time."

"Be careful when your eyes are closed," his wife told him. "You push my buttons enough, you might be next."

Charlene could hear him chuckling as he went up the stairs. She stared at her mom. "How's he going to sleep after that?"

"Like a babe. He knows I couldn't hurt a fly."

Jack floated through the door just as Charlene entered her suite.

"You were naughty again," she fake-scolded.

"I do it to make you smile. You know Sam will be just fine. Even if he has to stay over in New York, he's on official business and the department will cover the cost of a nice hotel. Worst case, he won't be here till tomorrow."

"Thanks, Jack." He stood next to her, close enough to touch, but all she felt was a chill in the air. Not the warmth from his soul, and that was sad because it was definitely still there. "I might have upset him though . . . I sent him a text about Vincent." She took a seat and gestured for Jack to join her. "Vincent has a motive to kill David."

"You thought that might be the case when you went to have coffee with Linda." Jack sat in the chair across from her. "What happened?" He draped one leg over the other. His face was animated, eyes bright and alert.

"We know that Kyle and Linda have alibis; the neighbors heard them at home. Plus, both Linda and Kyle had more to gain by David living than his dying." Charlene folded the afghan over her lap. "Freddy had motive to kill David, because he'd been framed for the vehicular homicide that put him in jail all those years ago. I think he'd resent David's new wealth. But he doesn't have a car. I doubt he had the money or the time to find someone to do the dirty deed for him."

"Unless he planned this and hired someone before he arrived in Salem, or met someone at that bar his first night in town. It wouldn't take much cash to get a junkie to do something despicable . . . even murder."

Charlene thumbed the crease between her brows. "He seemed genuinely sorry about David's death. Said he loved the guy and wanted to forgive him, even though David had framed him."

"He's dying—what if he wanted hush money from David?" Jack tapped his lip with a long, ghostly finger. "Enough to buy the latest cancer treatment?"

"Yeah . . . And if he didn't get it, maybe he hired one of those creeps at the bar to wait outside Bella's until David came out. Maybe Freddy *lured* him out with Doug's ghost and the other guy ran him over?" The idea made her sick.

"We won't cross Freddy off our list," Jack said. "And if Tori actually checked out Kyle and Linda's alibis in fear of her own life, then she probably didn't do it."

"I don't think so, dang it. I'd like for her to spend some time in jail to reconsider her sins."

"Your mother is wrong. And not for the first time."

They shared a smile. "I don't think Tori plans on keeping her good buddy Zane around."

"So where does that leave Zane?" Jack stood up and paced, not making a noise as he crossed the room. "He knew Tori planned on leaving the next day, running away with her husband and his money. That had to be very disappointing . . . perhaps motivating."

"I know," Charlene said, remembering how he'd looked at his watch. "He's the biggest loser in all this. He has twelve alibis that say he was with them that night. A dozen people wouldn't swear to it, no matter how good of friends they were. So, it can't be Zane."

"And that leaves . . . who?" Jack faced her, the television on behind him, the sound on low. She could see shadowy movement through him and averted her gaze from the reminder that Jack was not human.

"Vincent! Vincent took off angry, saying that the amount of the check wasn't enough. David claimed it was and that Vincent knew why." She stood up, feeling agitated.

Jack watched her, his arms crossed. "Why would Vincent be unhappy about the check David gave him?"

"Not sure—but Vincent loaned him the start-up costs to be a partner in the restaurant. Why would David pay back less than what was owed?"

Jack shrugged.

Charlene reached for her notepad and pen. "Both Tori and Linda told me that Vincent had been acting strange lately, and when I stopped in I saw it for myself. He seems about ready to fall apart. He had poker chips on the desk, next to his key chain, so I checked the parking lot after I left. Brand-new tires on a dark truck, Jack." She gave a short laugh. "That's why I texted Sam—once he gets back to Salem, I bet he'll arrest Vincent for hit-and-run felony."

Jack considered this. "He gambled, you say?"

"Yes, at the Provenance Casino. Linda told me that he'd been losing a lot, and his temper has become volatile. If he has a really bad gambling debt, he might have set David up by saying he had his hand in the till, to cover his own hide."

She could see it so clearly.

Jack rubbed his chin, his blue eyes shining. "It's a

solid motive." His form began to shimmer and fade, and she knew this mental exertion had tired him. "Promise to . . ." he whispered, "stay away from Vincent."

"I am not going anywhere tonight, Jack. Tomorrow we'll celebrate Christmas Eve with Vincent's arrest and David's killer caught. It'll probably be on the news when we wake up."

He grinned and then he was gone. She caressed the chill from her arms.

Her mother knocked. "Charlene? Why is your TV so loud? Can I help you get dinner started?"

She opened the door to her sitting room and her mom peered in with a shiver. "Is your heater broken?"

"I think this room is just colder because of the shade from the oak," Charlene said. "Ready?" She urged her mom backward.

"Don't you want to shut off the television?"

To keep her mother from worrying about high power bills, she used the remote on the coffee table to turn it off. "Better?"

"Sorry to nag." Her mom gestured to the counter and the ribs covered in foil.

Charlene set the oven to 350 degrees. She pulled her phone from her back pocket and set it on the kitchen table. Nothing from Sam.

Her mom put the ribs on a tray in the middle rack and closed the oven door. She caught Charlene looking and asked, "Any news?"

"Not yet. I have a good feeling, though, Mom." Sam would come home safely to Salem, and arrest Vincent for murder. "How about a Christmas martini?"

"Ooh, that sounds interesting. Why not? I like to live dangerously."

"I think we should celebrate." Charlene flipped through her cookbooks and found a thin laminated recipe book for fancy cocktails. She'd bought it on a whim, after moving here, in case her guests might like something different.

"Here's one. It has vanilla vodka and white crème de cacao. How does that sound?"

"Delicious. Better make one for your dad as well."

"I will." Charlene showed her mom the picture. "Can you crush a candy cane for me? We need to decorate the rim, and then I need three more to use as stir sticks." She grabbed three martini glasses from a cabinet that she used for her special glasses. "I'll get the liquor from the wine cellar downstairs."

"Aren't we fancy?" her mom teased, primping her short white hair.

"For my mom and dad? Only the best. And if we like them, we can have them again tomorrow night for Christmas Eve. Or try another," she added with a laugh.

She ran down to the cellar knowing she wouldn't see Jack—if she was lucky, he'd be back tomorrow. What would the holiday be without him? She found the two bottles of alcohol and carried them upstairs, where her dad, awake, read the instructions out loud as her mom crushed the candy canes.

She plunked the bottles on the counter and gave her dad a hug. "How was your nap?"

"Glad I had it, so I can party tonight." He waggled his brows.

"Mom's got the candy cane done, so why don't you dip the rim and let's hope it sticks."

"How does that look?" Her dad held one up in the air to admire.

"Good job! It's perfect."

Using a shaker, she added ice, four ounces of vodka, two ounces of crème de cacao, and a splash of cranberry, then gave it a good shake. She strained the cocktail in all three glasses and made a toast. "To having a very Merry Christmas, my first in my new home, with my wonderful Mom and Dad. I love you guys."

"Love you more," they said in unison, and then clinking glasses, they each took a sip.

Smelling the ribs, she turned off the oven to let them sit. "I'm kind of glad it's just the three of us. You'll only be here for a few more days."

"We could always stay," her mother offered.

Charlene choked on her martini. "Maybe you should come back in the summer when the weather will be nice and we can do more outdoor activities." She sipped on her cocktail, thinking up plans for the summer. "We could do Plymouth Rock then."

"That's a nice idea." Her father got the beans and the coleslaw out of the refrigerator, while her mom set the table. They decided on a date in July when they'd return, then enjoyed a family dinner of barbecue ribs and baked beans, with a tasty slaw on the side.

A perfect ending to a hectic day—killer was no doubt caught, David's family could be at rest, and the fund-raising had gone well. She and her mother weren't at each other's throats. If only she'd heard from Sam.

Chapter Twenty-Five

Charlene dreamed of Jared, at their last Christmas, smiling warmly at her as he gave her the heart-shaped diamond earrings. He had loved her, and she'd loved him, and the memory comforted her without sadness. She turned over in her bed, snuggling into her pillow.

Her blanket flew off her and she woke abruptly.

Alarmed, she sat up straight and searched for Silva, but the cat had been caught in the covers and now poked her silver head out with a disgruntled expression. It would be funny if she wasn't freezing.

Freezing—the chill that usually accompanied Jack. "Jack? What are you doing?"

Charlene's forest-green plaid flannel pajamas were no match for Jack's cool energy, and she leaned down for the comforter. She couldn't see Jack, but the cold gave him away. This was breaking the rules—he was not to be in her bedroom unless invited. The door separating her sitting room and the bedroom was open, when she knew she'd shut it.

"Jack!" she whispered loudly.

"Get up, Charlene. Look at the news."

"The news?"

"I'm sorry for waking you." Jack had the television on, the sound low. His form wasn't as solid as he usually made it for her—she noticed that he hadn't visualized the details of his buttoned shirt, and the outline of his jeans was blurry.

"What is it?" Charlene hurried from her bedroom to the sitting room love seat and wrapped the afghan around her. "Did Sam arrest Vincent? We called it, didn't we, Jack?"

The weather was on—more snow predicted for a white Christmas. Yes!

Jack's frenetic energy made his voice crack. "Tori is missing—Zane appealed to the news station—look! This is from twenty minutes ago."

Charlene couldn't tear her eyes away from the screen as the buff blond body builder was interviewed live. The brunette reporter had streaks of gold in her hair and kept peeking at Zane's biceps straining his tight leather jacket.

The reporter finally looked at the camera. "We have here Zane Villander, who claims that the newly widowed lottery winner Tori Baldwin is missing."

Zane jumped in front of her to talk to the camera. "The cops won't do nothin' because she hasn't been gone long enough. How stupid is that?" He gestured to the camera as if expecting an answer. "That wacko Freddy Ferguson's gonna kill her—you hear that, Freddy? The whole town'll be after you now."

The reporter put her hand on Zane's arm. "Why don't you tell us what happened? And please remember, you can't accuse someone of murder—it's defamation of character, all right?" she chirped brightly.

Zane wasn't impressed. "But that's who came by yesterday afternoon, Freddy Ferguson, threatening Tori that he was going to the police if she didn't 'help' him out. Said he had evidence on her, but that's bull, man." He rubbed his thick, bulky fingers together in the sign of money. "Everybody wants something from my baby, and will the cops do a thing about it?" He grimaced. "No."

"Poor Sam." Charlene tucked the crocheted blanket tight around her lap. "He has to deal with this soap opera drama." Had he gotten home safely? Her phone was by her bedside.

"When was the last time that you saw Tori?" the reporter asked Zane.

"I worked at the gym last night til seven, and when I came back later, she was gone. Cops say there's no sign of a struggle, and she probably left herself, but *I know* she didn't leave 'cause her jewelry's all in the safe." He poked another finger toward the camera. "Take that, Salem PD!"

Jack, now fully filled in so that he had buttons on his shirt and loafers on his feet, took a seat to her left and laughed so hard his image wavered. "Is he for real? Sounds dumber than a doorknob."

"That's Zane. I bet Tori slipped away under the radar. But he's right; she wouldn't leave her jewelry behind." Charlene glanced at Jack. "Should I go by the motel and see if Freddy is there? I know where he's staying—not exactly what room, but . . ."

"It's too dangerous. Tell the police," Jack suggested. "You don't know what this guy is capable of. Freddy's a drunk, he's dying, and desperate."

"You're right. I'll call Sam. I still think Vincent killed David, but Freddy frightens me, because he has nothing to lose." She would be smart this time around, rather than act impulsively as she had before in these situations.

Zane beseeched the camera. "Tori, I won't stop looking for you, babe."

"How are you related to the missing woman?" the reporter asked with a sniff. "Her husband was the man killed a week ago today by a hit-and-run driver. Are you a relative, a friend?"

"Say what you want, but that hit-and-run ain't solved either," Zane snorted angrily. "The cops in this town are useless!"

"Tori Baldwin, please call this station if you hear this report." The reporter turned to Zane, putting a hand on his chest as if she had to touch it to see if it was real. "It would be an awful tragedy if something happened to her too." The camera zoomed in on Zane as she asked, "She was a fitness trainer. Did you work together?"

"Yes, yes we did. We're good friends." Zane crossed his arms, daring the reporter to probe any deeper than that.

With a smirk, the reporter cleared her throat and faced the camera and her viewers. "Well, if you have any news on the whereabouts of Tori Baldwin, please call this number." A sequence of numbers ran the length of the screen, and an image of Tori popped up on the lower right. Zane must have been inside Tori's house because it was David and Tori's wedding photo. "There is a reward."

The camera panned out.

Holy smokes. "You know, I wonder if this is Tori's get-out-of-Salem plan? She'd said she was going to leave after David's service." Which was today. "Maybe she decided to leave early and avoid the drama. She didn't have any friends here, other than Zane."

"I almost feel bad for Freddy, who'll likely wake up to the cops at his door," Jack said. "Unless he has her, and then Zane's gambit worked."

"Freddy didn't kill David, although he was there that night. David saw Doug's ghost, which made him run out of the restaurant. He was hit within minutes. How could anybody have planned that?"

"A crime of opportunity," Jack agreed.

"Vincent was waiting for him, I know it." Charlene warmed her feet beneath her rear on the love seat. Every fiber of her being screamed the restaurant owner was lying. So why hadn't Sam arrested him yet?

She didn't know what to think about Tori missing. If Freddy *had* threatened Tori, and now the young woman was gone? It didn't look good. What could Freddy want from her?

Charlene got up for her phone and read the waiting message. "Sam texted—he didn't get home until four in the morning, yikes. I hope he's sleeping." It was just seven. She wouldn't bother him until at least noon—he knew she wanted to talk to him.

"The man's a detective," Jack said. "He should be fine on an hour of sleep and coffee. Let him arrest Vincent, and *then* he can crash."

She rolled her eyes and changed the subject. "I get to drop more items off at Felicity House today. I understand why David had wanted to play Santa. It feels good to give."

"I'm sure the kids are excited," Jack said wistfully.

Charlene waved toward Jack—careful not to actually touch him or she'd be cold for hours. "I wish you could come. Doug travels with Freddy. I wonder how?"

Jack smoothed his dark hair back from his pale forehead. "Maybe I'll find out in the research I'm doing on ghosts. You know I feel stronger after watching television? I saw a documentary which suggested that ghosts were electromagnetic waves."

"A documentary? I'd like to see that too."

Jack grinned—was that a ghostly blush? "Fine. It was really *Paranormal Investigators,* which is not quite as legitimate as a documentary."

Charlene burst out laughing. "I'd still watch it with you, Jack."

A knock sounded on her door and she gasped—had she been talking too loudly with Jack?

"Coming!"

She jumped off the love seat and opened the door. Her mother, wrapped in a red robe, handed Charlene a cup of coffee. "Merry Christmas Eve," Mom said. "I could hardly sleep, I was so excited for today."

"Thanks, Mom. Let me get ready—I know exactly what you mean."

Charlene hated to disturb Sam, who had to be exhausted. She tried Officer Horitz's number and left a message about Freddy staying at the Sleep Inn. She showered and dressed festively for the day in a sage-green sweater that brought out the green in her hazel eyes, and gathered her long brown hair in a loose twist with a sage-green clip. She put in her earrings with a smile, warmth spreading through her as she remembered her dream.

She gathered the money and items for Felicity House and jumped when her phone rang. Salem Police Department. Not Sam.

"Hello!"

"Good morning, this is Officer Bernard, returning your call about Freddy Ferguson and Tori Baldwin? Officer Horitz is away from his desk."

"Yes, I'm not sure if you saw the news or not, but Zane Villander has offered a reward for Tori Baldwin's return."

"We're well aware," the officer said glumly. "'Take that, Salem PD!'" He sighed. "We have no information regarding Tori Baldwin or Freddy Ferguson. I will send a car to the hotel you mentioned to see if he's there."

"I worry that other people might go looking for Freddy too. I don't suppose you could let me know what happens?"

"No, ma'am. I can't do that."

It was hard to accept that answer, but she would not, she told herself, under any circumstances, go to the Sleep Inn herself.

Jack watched her carefully as she ended the call. "Well?"

"What? I said I would stay out of danger, and I will."

He lifted his brow in disbelief.

By ten that morning, the postman delivered another five hundred bucks in checks. "Let's go, Mom. We can drop these off, and maybe Alice can get them to the bank before it closes."

"The bank is open on a Saturday?" Her mom reached for her red coat on the coat tree.

"Yeah, only until noon because it's a holiday."

"My bank isn't open," her mom argued.

"That's because you have a credit union. It's different." Her parents had been with the same bank for fifty years.

Her mom stopped arguing once she saw the bags to take to Felicity House, her earlier joy returning. "The kids will be so happy."

Jack walked with them out to the porch—her boots crunched, his made no sound at all. Five inches of fresh snow had fallen and now covered her yard. "Have fun, Charlene. Straight there and back." He tapped his wrist as if he had a watch.

She wouldn't go by the motel. It was in the wrong part of town, anyway.

They drove down the hill to the intersection and passed Bella's—the parking lot was full. Vincent's truck was gone. Maybe Sam had him in for questioning? Better yet, behind bars.

"I can't believe it's been a week since David was killed," Charlene said. She'd told her parents about Tori going missing and Zane's appeal to the public.

"I thought that detective of yours would have caught the perp by now."

"The perp?"

"Perpetrator." Her mom peered at her over the top edge of her glasses knowingly. "The killer. I don't blame Zane for trying to find Tori. That's his golden goose."

She happened to agree with her mom. "I just don't see Freddy taking her. I know she's tiny, but she's very fit and could probably kick his butt. He's not a well man."

Her mom hummed. "Desperation can give people added

strength—you've heard the stories about mothers lifting cars to save their children."

Charlene didn't argue, determined to keep the mood pleasant and not have a repeat of the last time she and her mother had gone to Felicity House. Though she'd buried her hurt, it was still there.

"Here we are," Charlene sang, pulling into the driveway next to Pamela's Lexus SUV. She could see stacks of wrapped gifts shadowed through the tinted windows, and a large red Santa sack tied in the back. A dozen children in coats, boots, and hats rolled snowballs, shouting with joy. She waved to the young gentleman in the glasses—his nose was red from cold.

Her eyes were drawn to the little girl who'd asked to be adopted, and found Tamil with a trio of friends, building a slide from what had been the igloo. This would not be a one-time-only charity for Charlene, and she welcomed the challenge to make a difference.

"Come on, Mom. Alice is expecting us. Looks like Pamela will be here, too—how fun. I wouldn't be surprised if they asked you to join the fund-raising team on a permanent basis."

Her mom blushed and tucked her short white hair behind her ear. Red Christmas lights twinkled at her lobes. "I'm much too busy," she protested.

They got out of the Pilot and walked up the four stairs to the narrow porch. The drapes were closed, which Charlene thought was odd. Every other time they'd been here the curtains had been open to reveal the Christmas tree and lights.

She checked the time on her phone. Ten thirty. "Alice should be here," Charlene said, and knocked on the red door before twisting the handle. "Merry Christmas," she called out. She pushed at the door, but it was locked.

There was a muffled sound, and a minute passed. Footsteps shuffled toward the door. Charlene and her mom exchanged a smile. They waited—but nothing happened. Charlene knocked again. A slam sounded from inside.

Her pulse raced. She tried the knob a second time and it opened. Someone had unlocked the door, but didn't answer it?

"Odd," she said. Charlene wondered if the adults were creating a surprise for the children and proceeded cautiously to not give the game away.

Once she and her mom were in the front room, she shut the door. Something didn't seem right, besides the drawn curtains—it was too quiet. "Alice?"

The tree, unplugged, was to the right and the desk and phone on her left. The central hall led to a tiny kitchen on the left and two offices on the right. Everything was dark.

A back door, out of sight from the front room, slammed closed.

Her mom grabbed Charlene's arm. The presents remained under the tree, so it couldn't have been a thief. "Alice? Pamela?" She waited at the edge of the area rug. Danger crackled in the air.

There was a loud thump coming from Alice's office, and Charlene cautiously walked down the hall, expecting someone to jump out at her any second. The tidy kitchen had a single mug on the counter that read, ALICE.

"Stay there, Mom."

"No chance."

"Alice?" she called loudly. "It's Charlene. Are you here?" She rapped on the office door before slowly opening it. She scanned the room—closet, two armchairs, a desk, an office chair—the top of the desk was stacked with accounting books, a laptop, and a bank bag.

No sign of Alice or Pamela. "I heard something—didn't you, Mom?"

Her mom nodded, her grip on Charlene firm. She shuffled to the desk. The blue money bag was open and empty.

Dark house, slamming door, empty bag. "They've been robbed," Charlene said in disbelief. "Who could do such a thing?"

Her mom didn't offer an opinion, for once.

Charlene hurried around to the side and saw the drawer open—and Alice Winters stuffed beneath the desk, bound with red and green packing tape, a toy reindeer protruding from her mouth. Her eyes flashed fury.

"Alice!" Charlene cried, bending down to help.

Her mom went to the open office door to stand guard, arms crossed and looking mighty fierce in her red down jacket and boots.

Charlene removed the reindeer from the older woman's mouth. "What happened? Where's Pamela?"

She flashed back to Avery saying that Alice was the tough one, but classy Pamela had problems of her own . . . Pamela could be over her head in possible debt, if the frayed gloves and the kids in public school meant anything. Her stomach rolled. What if Pamela had reached the end of her rope when David's check was no good?

"Go catch her!" the director confirmed in a shaking voice. "Pamela."

Her mother raced down the hall like she was sixty instead of seventy-five and opened the front door. "Gone!"

her mom shouted, then quickly returned, her cheeks as red as her earrings. "She tricked us into coming in while she escaped out the back."

Alice drew in a deep breath, and Charlene helped her to her seat.

"She's probably been skimming the profits for years." Alice squeezed the bridge of her nose. "When you told me that Sharon Turnberry had donated a thousand dollars, I noticed it wasn't in the books. I couldn't believe it. I was triple-checking again this morning."

Which explained all of the ledgers. "Did you confront Pamela?"

Alice rubbed her red mouth. "My mistake—I thought I could reason with her, but she's lost her mind. Saying that she would make Tori fix things? Pamela hit me and tied me up. How *could* she?"

"Oh no." Charlene stepped back and accidentally knocked over the money bag. A letter fell down too. She picked it up, seeing a red stamp marked PAST DUE across the top.

She handed the paper to Alice, who looked at it in confusion, then dawning horror as she read the notice of loan default.

"This is due the last day of December, or they'll start foreclosure proceedings," Alice said in a hoarse whisper. She scanned the letter in shock. "Pamela gave *her* name and address to the bank instead of mine. I never saw this before now." The director turned green and swallowed hard.

"Let me phone the police," Charlene said. "Do you think she's going to the bank?"

"Yes—we'd collected another five thousand to deposit." Alice shook her head. "What is she doing with the money?"

Charlene had no idea. She called Sam first, but it went to voice mail—this would be worth waking him up for. Next she dialed Officer Bernard and gave him the details of what had happened. "Did you find Tori?"

"No," the officer said. "She wasn't at the motel. I'll send a car over to Felicity House, but most of our units are dealing with the Freddy Ferguson situation so it might be a while. Zane's there and it's a circus."

"Is Detective Holden around?"

"No, ma'am." Officer Bernard hung up.

If Freddy didn't have Tori, and Zane didn't have Tori, who did? She looked at the picture of Alice and Pamela shaking hands, framed on the wall.

"The poor children!" Alice sobbed. "You have to find Pamela, Charlene, and make her give the money back. We can't lose Felicity House!"

"Me?" Charlene brought her hand to her chest. "It's a police matter." The empty money bag had Salem Federal printed on the outside. How could Tori help Pamela "fix" her situation?

"They will *arrest* her, Charlene." Alice wiped her eyes with a tissue from a box on her desk. "I don't know what happened to make Pamela snap, but she is, *was*, my friend—she can't go to jail on Christmas. I know her husband, and her kids." She dabbed her red nose.

"What am *I* supposed to do?" Sam wouldn't be happy if she was involved.

"Find Pam, convince her to give the money back and then turn herself in." Alice grabbed Charlene's wrist. "Please, Charlene. I'll call the bank right now and alert them to what's happening. I have your number—I'll call you—can you please go find her before she goes too far?" Alice wouldn't let her say no.

Well, she knew where Tori lived, and if Pamela was going to Tori's house to somehow convince her to give her money, it wouldn't hurt for Charlene to relay Alice's message. She checked the time. Ten forty. Bank was open until noon. "I'll have to hurry, but I'll see if I can find her."

Charlene ushered her mom toward Alice. "Wait here for the police." She raced down the hall, out the front door, and got behind the wheel. Her mother was already in the passenger seat before she turned the engine on.

"What's the plan?" her mother asked, sounding like a rookie cop.

"Mom . . . stay here with Alice." She suddenly realized what Sam felt whenever she acted on her own.

"No way," her mom said. "I can help you."

There was no time to argue. "Fine—but you stay in the car, no matter what." She handed her the phone and started the Pilot. "Text Sam that I think Pamela is looking for Tori about David's money, and that Salem Federal closes today at noon."

Her mom typed into the keypad. "Done. Now what?"

"We'll go to Tori's house first. Keep an eye out for a black SUV."

"I warned you that winning the lottery makes people crazy. Good thing is Tori should still be kickin'." Her mom scanned the streets like an eagle looking for prey.

Still kickin'? "We're just going to talk to Pamela."

"To your right," her mom said. "I recognize the car from the parking lot."

They followed and for the second time, the SUV went around the block—was Pamela getting cold feet?

Suddenly, the SUV whipped to the left around a corner. Charlene had no choice but to make a sharp turn behind her—the sound of her cell phone hitting the dashboard and sliding backward beneath the seat made her flinch. The tires on her Pilot spun for a second before finding traction on the packed snow.

"Sorry—should I get it?" Her mom reached for her seat belt.

"No—just leave it." The residential area quickly gave way to an even quieter side street and the back entrance to Salem Federal; the parking lot was a series of five-foot-tall snow drifts between plowed spaces.

Where was Pamela?

Charlene drove around to the front of the bank, where two cars were parked at the entrance of the two-story brick building. Ten after eleven on Christmas Eve.

"I don't see her," Charlene said.

"My gut is tellin' me she knows where Tori is." Her mom pulled a peppermint from her purse. "Want one?"

"No, thanks."

"Try the back?" her mother suggested. She popped the holiday candy in her mouth.

Charlene slowly drove around. Tall snowdrifts had created barriers between the spaces, but her gaze was drawn to the last row. Pamela, parked slightly crooked, was out of her SUV and standing at the back with the hatch up, staring in.

Pulse racing, Charlene carefully turned to the right and parked next to Pamela, the hood of her Pilot facing Salem Federal, her headlights inches from a snowbank. The bank's green, red, and blue lights twinkled from the roof. The fund-raising co-chair did not look up as Charlene peered inside the Lexus but saw only shadows of gift-wrapped packages. No Tori, no passengers at all.

"Stay here, Mom, while I talk to her, okay?"

"Are you sure you don't want me to get your cell phone? That way you could record the conversation and get her to admit she stole the money."

"You've missed your calling, Mom."

Charlene got out, her hands at her sides, her fingers chilled without gloves. "Pamela?" She walked to the rear of their vehicles as Pamela slammed the hatch shut and turned to Charlene, something bulging from her down coat pocket. Despite the cold weather, Pamela had a sheen of perspiration across her forehead.

"Merry Christmas," Charlene said. *Just talk, convince her to turn herself in.*

Pamela's smile was of the grimace variety as she skipped the pleasantries. "I saw you following me."

Charlene stepped backward.

"Why?" Pamela took a step toward her.

"I know about what happened at Felicity House this morning."

"You're a snoop, Charlene Morris."

The tone was singsong, Pamela's eyes frazzled. Charlene's neck tingled with apprehension. She eyed the black SUV. Freddy had told her that it had seemed like a black shadow had come toward him from Bella's parking lot.

Pamela's jaw clenched. "You should leave and mind your own business."

Pamela had been packing the unclaimed prizes into the SUV. Alice had suggested Avery help, but Avery had been too distraught over being fired to do it. Pamela *could* have been in the parking lot, angry at David for not giving her the check to cover her theft, and acted in a moment of rage to run him over.

And not given a hint of her crime away in the last week?

Charlene rubbed her hands together to warm them. "Don't you want to know if Alice is okay?"

"Of course she's okay—I used packing tape, not handcuffs. What do you want?" Pamela snapped. Lank black hair clung to her forehead, and her face was pale.

"I have a message from Alice—she wants you to give the money back and turn yourself in. She's thinking of your family." Charlene was acutely aware of being the only two vehicles in the rear lot of Salem Federal.

"Not gonna happen," Pamela chortled. "I can fix this. I have to fix this, and then everything will be okay again. Alice will understand, and things will go back to the way they were."

Charlene wasn't certain of that. Needing proof, if possible, she walked to the front of Pamela's SUV. The chrome was shiny silver, as if brand new. Not a speck of dirt or sign of wear. Had Pamela gotten it replaced to hide evidence of the hit-and-run? She put her hand on her stomach—she'd wasted so much time thinking it was Vincent who was guilty, but she'd been wrong.

Sam was searching in the wrong place for David's killer.

"What are you doing?" Pamela had followed her, trapping Charlene between the snowbank behind her, Pamela in front, the Lexus to her right, and the Pilot to her left.

She dared a glance at her mother inside the Pilot—

who wasn't there. She risked another quick look. The passenger door wasn't closed all the way. Where was her mom?

"Well, now that I've delivered my message, I'll get going. Should I tell Alice you'll return the money?" Charlene reached for the driver's side door of her Pilot.

"I can't return the money. I don't have the money." A sad laugh escaped her painted lips, the lipstick too bright, too perfect. "My son needed a new car."

"A car? You stole from Alice because your son wanted a car?" Charlene regretted her sharp words immediately.

Pamela pulled a dull black handgun from her coat pocket, her aim unfortunately steady as she pointed it a foot away from Charlene's chest. Charlene scrambled backward to the snowbank.

"Shut up. You have no idea what my life is like."

"You don't have to do this," Charlene said. "Alice doesn't want for you to be arrested."

Pamela pulled the hammer of the gun back with a click.

"I never intended for people to get hurt," she said in a conversational tone. "Do as I say and I won't kill you." Her voice slipped at that and she giggled nervously. "Kill. I couldn't even hurt a spider last week and now look at me."

Charlene faced Pamela, dragging her gaze from the weapon. "Just let me go. I won't tell anyone."

"Of course you will! You think I was born yesterday?" She leveled the gun. "You saw the new grille."

Charlene had to stall for time. If she could roll to the right of the Lexus in front of the brand-new bumper, then she could get Pamela away from the Pilot, and her mom.

"Why did you kill David? Where is Tori?"

Pamela lifted the gun, her fingers trembling as she

shared the poisonous truth. "It was an accident. God help me, I didn't mean to hurt him, but when he didn't give us that hundred thousand?" Her shoulders bowed, but she quickly straightened. "I needed that money to return everything I'd had to *borrow*." She gulped and searched the parking lot. Charlene dared a glance, too, but there was nobody else around—including her mother.

"I always managed to put the money I needed back before Alice noticed. But this time," she cried frustrated tears, "my son needed a car, my husband needed treatment—he can't work anymore."

"Is that an excuse to *kill* someone?"

Pamela's skin lost all color, leaving her makeup garish. "When I saw that check, only ten thousand, I was sure I had to be wrong. He wouldn't do that, would he? I couldn't see straight. I think I actually blacked out." Her eyes filled. "It wasn't my fault! David promised us that money. Spouting off like some big shot after winning the lottery."

"It was in bad taste," Charlene agreed, hoping to keep her talking long enough to escape. She shuffled toward the Lexus.

"I overheard Tori telling David by the kitchen that there would be no more donations." Her grip on the gun firmed and Charlene froze, terrified to move an inch. "What was I supposed to do? I couldn't tell Alice that I'd borrowed against Felicity House for my husband's treatments. I'd always been able to pay it back—David screwed me over!"

"Does your husband know how you've raised the money?" Charlene pointed at Pamela's earrings. "Why don't you sell those, or maybe not buy your kid a car?"

She laughed off-kilter and tossed an earring to the

pavement, crushing it beneath her boot. "I'm surprised this didn't turn my skin green. And I needed something to drive while my Lexus was being fixed."

Charlene quaked at the disconnect from reality in Pamela's tone and feared for her life. "Maybe, if you drop the gun, you won't have another charge against you."

"Oh, Charlene, we both know it is too late for that." Her white teeth gleamed in her horror clown's smile. "I need that money now, and that stupid bitch"—she glanced backward at the SUV—"needs to write me a check. Then she can go—everybody can go—but she won't wake up." A single tear fell from her eye.

Charlene, sick, realized that Tori must be in the Santa bag—for how long? "What did you do to her?"

"It was an accident," Pamela stressed, tears now falling. "I didn't mean to hurt her, but she wouldn't cooperate. I had *no* choice."

Pamela's fingers trembled on the trigger. How to get out of this alive? Pamela's vision was clouded by tears. If the gun went off, Charlene was a sitting duck. Charlene said a prayer, hunched her shoulders, and tackled Pamela at the waist—they slid backward, the fabric of Pamela's coat snagging on the salted asphalt. The gun slid beneath the Lexus.

Her mom raced around the snowbank she'd been hiding behind, Charlene's cell phone in hand. "I called nine-one-one."

Charlene sat on Pamela, who was on her back beneath her, still crying—her sobs held a hopeless sound. "Don't move, Pamela. Good job, Mom!" Her heart hammered crazily in her chest, and she felt nauseous but swallowed it down.

Sirens blared as an ambulance screeched into the parking lot and a single patrol car arrived, followed by Sam's SUV. She would never admit to her relief that he'd shown up. He jumped out and rushed toward her, in jeans and a bulky jacket. "Sam! Tori's in the back—I think she's hurt."

An officer reached for her to help her up. "We can take it from here, ma'am."

Sam was at her elbow immediately, his hair tousled as if he'd just gotten out of bed. "Are you okay, Charlene?"

"Yes." Her body shook, but she figured that was normal, considering she'd just faced down a crazy woman.

Her mom was at Charlene's other side, her eyes wide behind her glasses.

"I got your mom's text," Sam said with concern. "Tried to call back, but there was no answer—I've never driven so fast, Charlene."

"Thanks, Sam." She would show her appreciation later, over prime rib, but for now she pointed at the Lexus, worried about a woman she didn't even like. "Tori?"

Sam opened the hatch. The wheel panel was loose, which must have been where Pamela had hidden the gun she'd pulled on Charlene. Presents stacked high had been knocked over. A giant red Santa's bag, bulkily shaped, listed right.

The detective reached into his jeans pocket for a pocketknife and sliced at the jumble of knots at its top. A spill of blond hair was striking against the red of the bag, the young woman's eyes closed in her drawn face. Sam felt for a pulse on Tori's neck. "She's alive."

Charlene, relieved, stepped back with her mother as the paramedics sprang into action. The last half hour caught up with her and her knees shook. She didn't know what to feel as she watched the officer handcuff Pamela and load her into the back of a patrol car. Pity, as well as justice for David.

Sam joined her, his warm brown eyes golden with worry. "I leave town for a day, Charlene . . ."

Her mom huffed protectively. "None of this was Charlene's fault."

"I'm going to have to rethink my policy about not communicating with you during a case," he drawled. "If we're talking, then I know what's going on."

Charlene allowed a reluctant smile.

Sam, always mindful of his job, smoothed his mustache with strong fingers. "I'll see you later? We can discuss it then."

Her heart lifted—Sam, for Christmas. "Can we go, then? I'd like to get home."

But his attention was already drawn to the ambulance driver, who needed to speak with Sam before leaving for the hospital. She and her mom watched him stride away.

"Ready, Mom?"

They got into the Pilot and she turned the car on. "You were really great, Mom, to find the phone and call the police."

"I was terrified, honey, I don't mind saying." Her mom buckled up. "And I want you to tell me exactly what he was talking about on the drive home. What other cases, Charlene?"

Chapter Twenty-six

It was Christmas Eve, holiday carols played, and Sam was on his way. The logs in the fireplace crackled and burned brightly, giving the living room a woodsy scent. Candles glowed on the hearth and in the kitchen and dining room. Crystal goblets and white and gold china gleamed merrily on the dining table. Long, slim red candles were set amongst pine cones and greenery, the table festively set for four.

Charlene had a shaker ready in the fridge with their Christmas martinis, and a feast prepared for them all to enjoy. Earlier today, her mother had made a Béarnaise sauce and prepared the oven-roasted potatoes before changing into black slacks and a green silk blouse. Christmas tree earrings dangled from her lobes. Her father was not quite as festive in jeans and a tailored red plaid shirt.

Charlene and her mom had prepared a crab dip to serve with crackers, and a smoked salmon with capers. Dinner would be a prime rib roast with crisp roasted potatoes, asparagus, and mushrooms.

She glanced at her Cartier watch, wanting to be sure the timing for the prime rib would be correct. In a few minutes it would go in the oven. But where was Sam? He was twenty minutes late.

"That's the third time you've looked at your watch. It's just five forty, he'll be here before long." Her father put a hand on her shoulder. "Now that the case has been solved, he can take the night off."

"I wish I could be so sure. David's case is closed, Pamela arrested, but Sam always has more than one case going on at any given time. And you know how it is around the holidays. People's emotions are running high." She glanced out the window. "I hope nothing has come up."

"He'd call if it did." Her mom removed the martini glasses from the freezer, perfectly chilled. She lifted one and wiped a spot on the rim.

Her father took out the crab dip and put it on a poinsettia-shaped platter, surrounding it with an assortment of crackers. He dunked a cracker into the dip and handed it to his wife. "Here. Try this."

She ate it in two bites and looked at Charlene. "That's good. Should we have our drink now, or do you want to wait a little longer?"

"There he is," her father said. "Didn't you hear the knock?"

Charlene's head snapped up. "No, the music's too loud."

She smoothed her red wool dress over her hips and rushed to the door, eager to see Sam. "Hey!" She grinned.

"The party's started without you." She took his arm. "Come on in. I was getting worried."

"Sorry, thought I'd make it in time. I had paperwork to do." They were in the foyer and he pulled her into his arms, put his hands around her waist, and gave her a kiss. Then he pointed overhead at the mistletoe.

She laughed. "I wondered if you'd notice."

"I did, and other things." He gazed at her with admiration. "You're beautiful tonight, Charlene. I love that dress on you—red's your color." Jared had always loved this red dress on her as well, but she'd worn it tonight for Sam.

"You don't look so bad yourself, Detective." Ruggedly handsome, he'd changed into a tailored dark gray suit with a red shirt, his muscled shoulders stretching the suit beautifully.

Her mother poked her head around the corner. "Hi, Sam. Can I pour you a drink?"

"I'm off duty tonight. Go ahead." He rested his hand on Charlene's back and they ambled toward the kitchen.

She peeped at the kitchen table and there was Jack—seated in his favorite chair, wearing a dinner jacket and tie. His piercing blue eyes glared daggers at her. Had he seen the kiss? She turned her back to him, refusing to feel guilty by a ghost.

"We made Christmas martinis," she told Sam, a little too brightly.

"Sounds good." He shook her father's hand. "Hello, Michael. Hope I didn't keep you all waiting."

"Nope, we were snacking on the crab dip. Just my girl, getting antsy."

"That a fact?" Sam's deep, melodious voice zinged right through her, and she sucked in a breath.

Brenda handed Sam and Charlene a white chocolate martini. Chocolate sauce lined the glass, and the martini contained vodka, white chocolate Godiva liqueur, and white crème de cacao.

"What's this?" Sam drawled. "Looks too pretty to drink."

Charlene smiled guiltily. "While you were delayed at the airport, we were sampling holiday martinis. This is Mom's favorite, but Dad preferred the candy cane one."

"I would rather have been here, believe me." Sam took a sip and licked his lips. "Wow. That's some drink. Charlene, you don't have to get me drunk. You had me at hello." His gaze traveled from her sexy black heels to her face in slow approval.

Charlene's eyes widened and she felt like a million bucks. "Cheers." She lifted her glass to his and tried not to notice Jack standing right behind Sam, his jaw tightly set with jealousy.

What was Charlene supposed to do? She was entertaining her parents and one special friend, and as much as she wished Jack was a flesh and blood man, he was not. He couldn't eat or drink with them, or converse with anyone other than herself. She couldn't hug him or give him a Christmas kiss.

She hurt for him, but right now this evening was about sharing a wonderful family dinner with her parents and Sam.

They brought their drinks and appetizers into the living room and sat facing the fire. Her dad took his favorite chair, and Silva lay curled up on the ottoman in front of him. Her mom sat in the ornate gilded chair, like a lady on her throne. That left the sofa for her and Sam.

Deliberately, perhaps?

If so, she didn't mind. The music was turned down low so they could talk, and Sam asked her mother and Charlene how they were faring after the earlier ordeal.

Her mother was quite animated as she eagerly discussed the trauma—how Charlene had tackled Pamela, who had dropped her gun, while she had escaped to call 911. It had been terrifying, she told him with a gleam in her eye.

Charlene reached out to touch her hand. "You were so incredibly brave, Mom, and smart to think of the cell phone." She shivered. "I almost feel sorry for Pamela. I mean, she helped the kids out for years. Her heart was in the right place, and then her life began to unravel."

"Doesn't mean she can hurt people, does it?" her mother said, jaw set.

"No, of course not. But I'm sure that deep down she was a very nice woman who ended up doing a very bad thing. It escalated and she couldn't get out from under it. Clearly, she's not well."

Sam leaned forward and put his drink at his feet, rubbing his hands together. "Pamela had been stealing for some time. It started shortly after her husband was diagnosed with MS. He lost his job, and she couldn't make ends meet. She started 'borrowing,' where she'd take out a little for grocery money and replaced it the following week. But the bills got bigger, and her kids' expenses grew too. She had to take more and more, and the weight of that made her desperate enough to forge banking information, putting Felicity House at risk."

"Desperate." Poor Alice was still in shock, but Charlene had promised to be there to help in the upcoming year.

Sam took her hands and studied her for a long, heart-stopping moment. "If things hadn't worked out as they did, I'd never have forgiven myself. You tackled a woman with a gun."

Her heart warmed at his sultry expression. She hadn't forgotten that he'd promised to discuss relaxing his policy on speaking about cases with her.

"Not as crazy as it sounds," she said. "I learned that in a self-defense class. Minus the gun."

Jack moved around the room, clearly agitated. She hadn't told him about the attack on her and her mother so she veered away from the subject. "What will happen with Pamela now?"

"She's under a doctor's care—she had a complete mental breakdown," Sam said. "Not sure if she'll be able to stand trial, but she'll get the help she needs." He stroked her arm. "I feel really badly for her children. Her husband can't take care of them. Hopefully, she'll have relatives to step in."

"Those poor kids! What an awful thing." She could imagine their shock and pain. "Unfortunately, this will be a Christmas they will never forget."

"She'd hoped the money from David would be the gift to save the place, add on a new addition, and bail her out. She kept saying how she loved the children and Felicity House—it was her life's work helping children in need. Now her own children will need it more than anything."

"And I was wrong about Vincent?" She'd been so sure he was lying.

"Not completely—he'd been siphoning money from Bella's, but technically, the place was his. What he does with it is up to him. Now, how about some of that crab dip?"

She was glad to change the subject. They each took a small plate and enjoyed the food and drink. Silva danced near the decorated Christmas tree, her paws in the air as she tried to catch Jack, who teased her mercilessly.

"What's up with the cat?" Sam said, popping a caper-loaded piece of salmon into his mouth.

"That cat is pure crazy," her dad said fondly. "Amuses me all day."

For fun, Jack zapped the fire and had it shoot sparks in the air.

"Do you have a window cracked open, Charlene?" her mother asked, glaring at the curtain-covered glass. "That fire is getting a draft from somewhere. I found the name of someone who can check the seals on all the doors and windows. Your dad and I are doing that as our housewarming gift to you."

Charlene grinned at Jack, who winked back. "Thanks."

Her mother nibbled on a cracker, then wiped her mouth. "Sam, is there any good news coming out of this?"

"Matter of fact, there is." His mustache twitched as he shared, "Kyle Baldwin, David's son, is about to inherit fifty percent of his father's estate. His father willed it to him before his death. The call from David's lawyer had been why Kyle had wanted to talk with David that night."

Charlene clapped. "That is wonderful!"

Her mom cackled. "Tori must be spitting mad."

"Got that right." Sam put his plate down at his feet. "She's furious, threatening to sue—but the will is legit."

"Oh, I'm so glad." Her eyes met Jack's—she knew they would talk about what had happened with Pamela in detail later—but what amazing news.

"Know what he wants to do?" Sam stretched his arm

along the couch behind her back. "Kyle wants to honor his father's checks, especially the one to Felicity House for Children."

"No way!" Charlene's mouth fell open. "That is the best news yet, Sam."

"Yes, his father would be proud."

Charlene stood up. "Well, let's take our seats at the table and celebrate with dinner."

"Smells great," Sam said, following her to the kitchen. "Prime rib?"

She took the foil off the dishes to show him. "Hope you like your roast beef rare . . . want to carve?"

"My pleasure." Sam held her gaze for a super-charged moment.

Charlene fanned her face and handed him an electric carving knife. She put the crispy potatoes onto a serving platter, and her mom took it to the dining room. Her father had poured wine into four goblets. This was home.

When everything was on the table the four of them held hands and gave thanks.

Jack stood behind her, and although he couldn't touch her, she knew he was with her, sharing this family moment, the joy of Christmas present—the past at rest.

Charlene's heart filled with healing light as she sat with Jack behind her and Sam on her right.

"Merry Christmas, everyone. I am so fortunate to have you all with me tonight."